A Novella Collection
COWBOY
COUSINS

MOLLY NOBLE BULL

KATHI MACIAS

KATHLEEN L. MAHER

Scrivenings
PRESS
Quench your thirst for story.
www.ScriveningsPress.com

©2022 Molly Noble Bull, Kathleen L. Maher, and Kathi Macias

Published by Scrivenings Press LLC
15 Lucky Lane
Morrilton, Arkansas 72110
https://ScriveningsPress.com

Printed in the United States of America

Paperback ISBN 978-1-64917-193-1

eBook ISBN 978-1-64917-194-8

Editors: Elena Hill and Linda Fulkerson

Cover by Linda Fulkerson, www.bookmarketinggraphics.com.

All scriptures are taken from the KING JAMES VERSION (KJV): KING JAMES VERSION, public domain.

LUCY
AND THE
LAWMAN

MOLLY NOBLE BULL

Scrivenings
PRESS
Quench your thirst for story.
www.ScriveningsPress.com

Molly Noble Bull has crafted a good, light romantic western, with a solid faith content. It pulled me in and kept me turning pages until the end. I recommend it to lovers of Christian westerns.

This is the first novella I've read written by Molly Noble Bull, and I loved it. The storyline is unique and the characters well-developed for a novella. There were enough plot twists and surprises to keep me turning pages. You won't want to miss this story.

Charlie, Bret. Burt, Bren, Jana, Linda, Angela, Bethanny, Hailey, Dillard, Bryson. Grant, Grace, Kameron, Jared, Jeanette, Kathi, Kathleen, Kathrine, Teresa, Mary Kaye, Joyce, Marie, Dee, Alice, Dana.

But to God give the glory.

THEME SCRIPTURE

If you forgive others the wrongs they have done to you, your
Father in heaven will also forgive you.
But if you do not forgive others, then your Father will not
forgive the wrongs you have done.

Matthew 6:14-16
(Good News Bible Version)

1

Juniper, Texas
Spring 1890

A man staying at a hotel said he saw Daisy. Maybe it *was* Daisy. Maybe not.

Caleb Caldwell had to find out, and not because he was the county sheriff. It was personal. He left his office at the county jail and crossed the street. Shorty, one of his deputies, could handle whatever came up. Caleb headed for the hotel.

He intended to really talk to this man—dig for details. His search would continue until he found Daisy—no matter how long it took.

A sign in the barbershop window caught his attention.

Fielding Grimes for Governor

That crook? Caleb shook his head in disbelief. A man like Grimes should be running for the Mexican border, not for the highest office in the state of Texas.

Caleb entered the hotel, glancing through the archway into the dining room. A skinny little man with white hair and a white mustache sat hunched at a table, reading a small book. In a starched shirt, black tie, and dark suit, he looked as if he belonged back East somewhere, not Juniper, Texas.

Caleb hoped the small man was the witness he'd been searching for. He would have prayed, if he still did things like that.

The stranger looked up from his reading. Their gazes connected. The man put down the book and reached for his cup. Caleb moved closer to the table, and the scent of coffee reached out to him. The man didn't smile.

Caleb forced one. "Are you Stanley Kipple?"

The man nodded over his coffee.

"I'm Sheriff Caldwell." Caleb offered him his hand. The man shook it. "Glad to know you, Mr. Kipple. May I sit down, sir?"

"Of course."

Caleb slid into a chair. "My deputy said you stopped by the office and wanted to talk to me about Daisy. Reckon it means you saw her somewhere."

"I *might* have seen her," Mr. Kipple corrected.

"Where?"

"San Antonio. I live there, but I travel a lot with my business. I sell books and Bibles to churches."

"San Antonio?" Caleb repeated.

Caleb's cousins, Jake and Boyd, mentioned before they moved away that maybe Daisy was living in San Antonio now. She had raved about how much she loved that town. He'd wondered if maybe his cousins were right. Now the book salesman confirmed it. *Maybe.*

The man held up the small book he was reading when he came in. Caleb studied the book's title, *New Testament.*

"Interesting title, Mr. Kipple. What's the book about?"

The man sent him a look that said Caleb might be a little slow in the head. "Are you saying you never heard of the New Testament?"

Caleb grinned. "Of course I have. I was fooling you a little."

"Fools could be headed for the bad place. So here, consider this book as my gift to you. Be *sure* to read it," he warned, "all of it." Mr. Kipple handed the small book to Caleb.

Though he had no intentions in reading it, Caleb took the New Testament, tacking on another fake smile. Then he tucked the small book inside his vest pocket.

Enough small talk. Caleb needed to get back to the reason he was sitting there. "Thanks, sir. But I need you to tell me all you know about Daisy."

The stranger hesitated. "I saw a young woman the last time I was home," he said. "She might be the one you're looking for."

"How long ago did you see her?" Caleb asked.

Mr. Kipple shrugged. "Two weeks, maybe three."

"How did you know I was looking for a young woman?"

"Sheriff Brown told me. He's the sheriff over in Kasperton County. I visited with him some when I made a trip to his part of Texas. He bought a copy of one of the books I'm selling." Mr. Kipple was looking down, but he turned, glancing over at Caleb. "Did you know he was saved?"

Caleb shook his head because he didn't know what else to do. What he did know was he had to get Mr. Kipple back on the right track. "I know Sheriff Brown. What did you tell him?"

"About a woman I saw there in San Antonio. Beat up. Face bruised. All black around one eye. He said I should tell you all this. Since I'm here in town anyway, I stopped by your office."

"Besides the bruises, what did she look like?" Caleb asked.

Kipple cocked his head to one side. "Short but thin. Brown

eyes. Long golden hair. I bet she'd be pretty if she wasn't all bruised up. Sheriff Brown told me you sent him a letter—that you were on the lookout for a pretty woman with long blond hair."

"I sent out a lot of letters," Caleb said. "Go on."

"Sheriff Brown said the woman I saw fit the description you sent in your letter. I have a layover here in Juniper anyway. So I stopped by the jailhouse. You weren't there." Kipple looked around the all-but-empty room as if he feared someone might be listening. "I don't want any trouble." He peered down at his coffee cup. "I'm a law-abiding citizen. I've already visited all the churches here in town and have a stagecoach to catch in less than an hour. If I miss it, the man at the depot said another one might not come by again for days."

"Juniper is off the main stage route," Caleb said. "And I won't detain you. But I do have a few more questions." Caleb pulled a small photograph from the inside pocket of his leather vest. The little New Testament came out with it. He handed Kipple the photo, putting the New Testament back. "Is this her?" Caleb asked. "The woman you saw?"

Kipple studied the photograph for a moment. "Well, I don't rightly know, sheriff." He handed the picture back to Caleb and shook his head. "It looks like her. But it would be hard to say for sure."

Caleb leaned forward in his chair. "Do you remember where you saw her? Where in San Antonio?"

Kipple shrugged. "Sorry, Sheriff. I can't remember anything more for sure. If I remember anything else, I'll let you know."

"I'd appreciate it."

———

Instead of going right back to his office, Caleb headed for the general store for a cup of coffee. He didn't care for the hard stuff, but there was a time when he did.

The bell over the doorway chimed when Caleb entered the store. He paid his respects to Mr. Gregg, the storeowner, drinking his coffee he looked out the window. He kept thinking about what Mr. Kipple had said. Did the salesman really see Daisy in San Antonio? Regardless of his preachy talk, Kipple was a nice fellow, giving him the New Testament and all.

Back in the days when Caleb read the Bible, he also prayed. Now he knew the truth. God answered prayers—just not his.

Maybe he should send the New Testament to one of his cousins, Jake or Boyd. He hadn't seen either of them since they moved away. At least, *they* wrote to him. Caleb was slow answering. He owed both of them letters, but with all the business he had to attend to as the county sheriff, he had little time for letter writing—especially to family members.

Still, good memories came when he thought about Boyd and Jake. They grew up together right here in Juniper County. *We played together all the time when we* were *kids.* Now, Jake and Boyd lived hundreds of miles away.

He thought of Daisy again. The book and Bible salesman hadn't given him much to go on. What encouraged him the most was the fact that Kipple thought he saw Daisy in San Antonio.

Mr. Kipple mentioned selling books in Colorado. He'd heard a Mrs. Gordan and her daughter lived in Searten, a small town about fifty miles from Denver. Caleb was obligated to go to Colorado next week to identify an outlaw in the Denver jail, and he had a desire to help the women, especially after he learned Mrs. Gordan was blind. He'd promised to go to Colorado as a favor to the local sheriff there, and the trip would take several weeks. Ordinarily, he'd never stay away from Juniper County so long, but the trip seemed like the perfect opportunity to give his deputies the chance to be the boss for a while, learn the ropes, before he left for good. He planned to quit sheriffing after his return and run cattle full time.

Maybe I'll stop by Searten on my way to Denver—tell Mrs. Gordan and her daughter the news. He could tell them about the recent death in Juniper of the elderly Mrs. Gordan, about the property they now owned, and about the danger they might be in. Fielding Grimes, *the scoundrel*, and his brothers were after their land. Somebody had to tell them. They might already know about the death and the land they now own, but they couldn't know what Grimes might be up to. But for a slip of the tongue, Caleb wouldn't know either.

As he headed back to his office at the county jail, he glanced off beyond the greening pasture to the Texas hills, but his thoughts focused on San Antonio. He'd be there for a day or two before taking the train to Denver, and if Daisy was in San Antonio, he'd find her.

————

Searten, Colorado
One Week Later

Lucy noticed the tall, young-looking cowboy as soon as he turned the corner. He was easy to describe—thin, strong, dark hair, and straight as a toy soldier. The stranger strolled down the stone walk in front of her house beyond the picket fence, wearing a wide-brimmed, tan hat, a blue shirt, light-brown jacket and tan trousers tucked in his boots.

"I'm looking for a Mrs. Annette Gordan or a Miss Lucy Gordan," he said. "Could Miss Lucy be you?"

She'd moved to the yard gate but didn't try to open it. She didn't respond, yet she was drawn to the stranger with the sapphire-blue eyes.

At last she said, "I'm Miss Gordan." She leaned toward the gate. "Can I help you, sir?"

"I'm Sheriff Caleb Caldwell—from Texas."

His deep baritone voice sounded smooth—warm.

"Reckon you're wondering why I'm here," he went on.

She nodded.

"I have an important message for you and your mother."

"I see," she said. But she didn't.

Lucy wanted to believe the sheriff was exactly who he appeared to be—a warm and friendly person. But she was hesitant.

She finally opened the yard gate, motioning for him to come inside. As he walked through, the gate slammed shut behind them. The heavy weights and bells jingled and clanged for several moments, a tinkling echo of their first meeting.

"I like that gate chain of yours." His grin deepened. "Very musical. But in Texas, we don't use bells on our gates. Just weights."

"Most folks don't use bells here either," she explained. "Just me."

He kept looking at her—especially her face. "As I said, I'm here with important news to deliver to your mother. But if this is a bad time for y'all, I'll be glad to come back later." He paused as if he expected her to make a reply. "On the other hand, if you'll invite me inside to meet your mother, I promise to explain everything."

She smiled. "Won't you come in, sir?"

Despite an inner warning, Lucy led the way to the porch, up the steps and into the house. She settled the sheriff onto an overstuffed blue chair in the parlor.

———

Caleb couldn't keep his eyes off Miss Lucy Gordan. Those spies Fielding Grimes had working for him were right. She was a fine-looking lady, no doubt about it. A bit of white lace edged the ruffle around the collar of her dress. Lucy reached up, straightening her collar as if she sensed his interest in her.

A mental image of Daisy in a pink blouse with ruffles around the collar paraded across his brain. He blinked but was unable to remove the memory from his mind. *Daisy.* Like Daisy, Miss Gordan's blonde curls and brown eyes set off a slender and petite form. There, the similarity ended.

Lucy sat on the blue velvet settee near his chair and sent him a slow smile.

Caleb straightened his shoulders. The two young women were nothing alike. Miss Gordan was a lady and probably a churchgoer. Daisy was—

Laughter and high-pitched, female voices came from elsewhere in the house, interrupting his musings. One of the women let out a girlish giggle. Amused, he glanced toward the sound, holding in a smile.

Lucy blushed. "My mother is entertaining some of her lady friends in another part of the house. I'll give her a minute. Then I'll go and tell her you're here."

"It must be hard for you and your mother—living here without a man in the house."

"Of course we miss my father, but we've managed since he died." She pushed back a golden curl that had escaped the comb, holding her long hair in place. "How did you know there wasn't a man living here?"

"A man I know told me. He has friends who live here in Searten."

Her forehead wrinkled. "I see."

14

Regardless of the frown on her face, she looked lovely in the blue dress she wore. Its blue-violet color reminded him of the mountain laurels often found on the spring hills in his part of Texas, and her golden hair and brown eyes made him think of—of Daisy. *No!* He bit his lower lip. *I won't think about Daisy now.*

"Sheriff, you haven't told me why you came here today."

"I came to Colorado because I have business in Denver. I'm on my way there now. I stopped by Searten on my way to talk to you and your mother about land you own near Juniper, Texas—where I live."

"Land?"

"Yes. I hope to convince you to come to Texas as soon as possible to look it over. It's mighty important. I also want to discuss the other reasons I came here today."

"Do we really own land?" she asked.

He nodded. "I would have thought you knew."

"I know nothing about any land in Texas or anywhere else. And I doubt my mother does either. We live here in Searten with my young cousin, Bethy Loring. With Bethy in school and Mama in poor health, it would be impossible for us to travel to Texas. But I would love to hear more about the land you claim we own."

"I hope you'll change your mind about Texas, ma'am. I plan to buy a team of mules and a covered wagon in San Antonio on my way home. If you, your mother, and the little girl could see your way clear to meet me there, we could travel the rest of the way together. Otherwise, you would have to go by stage. And Juniper is off the main stage routes. Stagecoach connections are not good and often delayed."

"I'll keep it in mind if we decide to go."

Thumping noises came from the hallway. Caleb turned toward the sound.

A petite, middle-aged woman stood in the foyer, gripping a wooden cane for support. She looked like an older version of Miss Lucy, but in place of Lucy's golden curls, her dark hair was streaked with silver and braided in a coil on the top of her head.

"Oh, there you are, Mama," Lucy said. "Where are your guests?"

Mrs. Gordan turned cloudy eyes toward her daughter. "My friends and I heard a man's voice in here. What is going on?" Regardless of her blindness, her penetrating gaze appeared to be aimed at Lucy. "And since they intended to leave anyway, Ada and Nora went out the side door." Mrs. Gordan paused. "Now, who are you, sir? And why are you here?"

"Forgive me for not introducing you to our guest, Mama. This is Sheriff Caleb Caldwell from Texas. He came with important information." She turned to Caleb. "Sheriff Caldwell, may I present my mother, Mrs. Annette Gordan?"

"I'm honored to meet you, ma'am."

"Same here—I hope." Mrs. Gordan selected the rocker near the door and sat. After hooking her cane over the arm of her chair, she turned her blind eyes in Caleb's direction. "So, Sheriff Caldwell. What information have you brought us today?"

He cleared his throat. "I'm afraid I have some bad news to report."

Mrs. Gordan gasped. "Bad news did you say? Oh no!"

2

"Sorry to be the one to tell ya, ma'am," Caleb said after a long silence, "but your mother-in-law died in Juniper, Texas, several weeks ago."

"Bless her soul." The older woman shook her head.

"I'm sorry for your loss, ma'am." Caleb paused before continuing, "The late Mrs. Gordan owned land near the town where I live," he explained. "It's on a river and fairly near an abandoned silver mine. I reckon the land is yours now."

Mrs. Gordan's mouth gaped open. "Silver mine did you say?"

"Yes." He glanced at Lucy. Her sudden gasp indicated her astonishment as well.

"I never knew silver was mined in Texas," Lucy's mother said.

"It's not well known. The mine was built a long time ago."

"Was silver found there?"

He grinned. "Not much, ma'am, if any. Some think they were digging in the wrong place. Folks only mined in Juniper County for a little while. Then they gave up. Frankly, I think they gave up too soon." He shifted around in his chair to avoid the temptation of staring at Lucy. "The digging came to nothing. All mining stopped. However, some think there might still be plenty of silver in those hills. If I'm right, some, if not most of it, could be on your land."

"This is incredible." Mrs. Gordan thumped her cane on the floor as if to confirm her statement. "Now what was the name of the town near our land again?"

"Juniper," he said, "Juniper, Texas."

"I wonder why Oliver, my late husband, never told me about any of this when he was alive." Mrs. Gordan sent a smile in Caleb's direction.

"Could it be he didn't know about the silver mine, ma'am? As I said, the mine was around there a long time ago. If your husband moved away when he was fairly young, he might not have known."

"Yes," Mrs. Gordan said, "that's possible, I suppose. I lost my sight in a buggy accident some years ago. Then my husband had bad pains in his chest. One day they got really bad, and it killed him. That's when we moved into town. I never met my mother-in-law. And we never visited Texas even when my husband was alive."

Caleb steepled his hands, elbows on the arms of his chair. "I would never want to give you ladies false hope, but it's possible you might be rich one day."

"Or worse off than we are now," Mrs. Gordan said under her breath.

He laughed. "Yes, ma'am. Or worse off than you are now." He gazed at the tasteful furniture and colorful decor. "You have a nice place here, if you don't mind me saying so. Reminds me of my mother's home in Juniper."

"Your mother lives in Juniper?" Mrs. Gordan said.

He nodded. "My mother and stepfather have a home at the edge of town."

"So, your real father is dead?" Mrs. Gordan asked.

"Yes."

"And do you have other members of your immediate family?"

Caleb smiled because her questions amused him. Like Mrs. Gordan, his mother might be called a friendly interrogator. But when he glanced at Lucy, frown-lines creased her forehead, indicating something displeased her.

"My father died when I was six," he went on. "My sister was eight."

"Does your sister live in Juniper too?"

"Mama, please," Lucy protested. "No more questions. This poor man must be exhausted from his trip."

"I don't mind answering questions, Miss," Caleb said.

"See, Lucy," her mother said. "Sheriff Caldwell likes answering my questions."

"But I have something else important to say, ma'am. I must warn you of Fielding Grimes, his brothers, and their uncle."

"Who's Fielding Grimes?" Lucy asked.

"A man from Juniper, Texas. He wants your property. I don't want to scare you, but who can say what he might do to get your land? I think you should come to Juniper as soon as possible and claim what's yours."

"Are you saying Mr. Grimes is a dishonest man, Sheriff?" the older woman asked.

Caleb nodded, glancing down at his cowboy boots. "Nobody really knows what Mr. Grimes is willing to do or where his money comes from. He lost his bid for county judge. Now, he's running for governor of Texas."

Mrs. Gordan cocked her head to one side. "He must be very rich."

"Oh yes, ma'am. Fielding Grimes and his younger brothers are rich, powerful men. When Fielding Grimes sets his mind on something, there's no stopping him or his brothers. They could pressure y'all into selling." Caleb looked away. "The law is on your side, though, and the Grimes brothers must know it."

"Is there anything else we can do other than travel to Texas?" Lucy asked.

He hesitated. "You might want to get a lawyer to go over your deed with you."

Lucy shrugged. "What deed? I know of no deed to land—in Texas or anywhere else."

Her mother shook her head. "Neither do I."

"You must have a deed somewhere," Caleb insisted. "Take a look around, see if you can find it, and as soon as possible. I never had much schooling, but I'll do all I can to help you. I know your rights, ma'am, and if you ever need any help, I'll defend those rights the best I know how."

Nobody spoke for a moment.

Caleb forced another smile. "I'll be heading back to my hotel in a little while, and I'm leaving for Denver on the morning train. Somehow, I must convince both of you to leave for Juniper, Texas, and as soon as possible.

"I plan to buy a wagon while I'm in San Antonio," he continued, "and you are welcome to travel to your land with me. Think about it. I won't be stopping by your home again on my way back to San Antonio, but if you need to contact me, I'll be staying at the Old Tree Hotel in Denver." He hesitated. "You ladies are in danger."

As unlikely as it seemed, Caleb was able to talk Lucy's mother into saying, openly, that a trip to Texas was vital. He assumed Lucy disagreed with her mother.

Before leaving their home, Caleb reached, unconsciously, into the inner pocket of his vest for the picture of Daisy. His hand touched the thin New Testament. *Well, I'll be jiggered.* He'd forgotten it was there.

Caleb didn't want it. At the same time, he couldn't throw away the word of God. It wouldn't be right. Maybe Lucy would like a copy of the New Testament.

———

"I like that young man," Lucy's mother said after Caleb left. "I think we should do everything he said to do."

Lucy sat shaking her head. She couldn't disagree with her mother's decision more.

"Go up in the attic and look for the deed," her mother said with excitement. "In fact, why don't you go right now?"

Lucy knew the attic would be dark. She remembered only one small window providing sunlight. She took a lamp and climbed the narrow stairs. Her mother waited in the parlor for her return.

Stale air filled her nostrils as soon as she opened the attic door. She coughed from all the dust. Then she sneezed.

Lucy made her way across the wooden floor, set down the lamp, and opened the trunk. Cautious of scorpions and spiders, she rummaged through the trunk's contents.

Old clothes, toys, family portraits, papers, letters, and other objects filled the trunk. She gathered all the papers and letters to read downstairs in a better light. Several wooden crates loaded with items they didn't need and would probably never use were stacked around as well. She would explore them at another time. For now, she wanted to read the papers and see if one of them might be a deed.

She noticed a book behind the trunk. Lucy picked up the yellowed volume, blew the dust from its brown cover and sneezed—again. She pulled a handkerchief from the pocket of her white apron, wiping her nose. She stacked the book with the papers to read later and hurried downstairs.

After a moment, her mother said. "Well, what did you find?"

"I found some papers. One could be the deed. I'll let you know as soon as I finish reading."

Her mother thumped a rhythmic beat on the pine floor the way she often did when she felt anxious. "Maybe the deed was never here in the first place," her mother replied.

"I won't believe that. The deed has to be in the house somewhere."

There was a knock at the door.

"Someone's at the door, Lucy."

Lucy went to the door and opened it. A big man with broad shoulders and a barrel chest stood on her front porch—one huge hand propped against the doorframe. He had a balding head and looked to be over six feet tall. She stepped back at the mere size of the man.

"My name is Hutch Fletcher," he said in a monotone, "and I work for Mr. Fielding Grimes. I'm here in town to deliver this here letter in person. It's from him." He reached out and handed Lucy a white envelope. "I'll be staying at the hotel in town. Mr. Grimes hopes you'll have signed them papers *very* soon. It's all in the letter." He tipped his hat. "Well, good day to ya, ma'am." He turned and walked away.

Lucy remained in the doorway a moment longer, digesting what had taken place. Mr. Fletcher's abrupt behavior seemed more than strange. The way he spoke almost sounded like he'd been coached, regardless of the folksy grammar. Was he merely repeating a speech he'd learned by heart?

She glanced down, studying the envelope. To *Mrs. Annette Gordan and Miss Lucy Gordan.*

The sheriff from Texas warned them about Mr. Grimes, and

this Mr. Fletcher worked for him. A warning light turned on inside her head. Sheriff Caldwell might be right about a lot of things.

———

After the supper dishes were done and Bethy and her mother were tucked in for the night, Lucy noticed a thin little book by the chair the sheriff sat in. A quick glance at the cover resulted in a smile. *So, the sheriff is a Bible believer. How nice.*

She would need to return the New Testament to the sheriff the next time she saw him. *If I see him.* She reminded herself that he wouldn't be stopping on his way back to Texas.

That night, Lucy took the New Testament, all the letters, and the book she found in the attic to her upstairs bedroom, opening the letter from Fielding Grimes first. He offered to buy the land in Texas, and in a separate document, he gave the amount of money he was willing to pay for her land. She'd read both papers umpteen times and knew she would read them again and again, but for now, she would read the book. She opened to page one.

This is the diary of Judith Harken Gordan, she read.

Lucy clasped the book to her chest. *This was written by my grandmother. Grandma Gordan.*

She had a vague memory of her father reading letters aloud from Grandma Gordan when she was a small child—long before Lucy learned to read. Lucy swallowed. Living on a remote farm in the high country with a blind mother and an illiterate house maid made moving to town vital. Otherwise, Lucy would never have had the opportunity to attend school. Lucy's schooling was one of the main reasons her mother sold the farm and moved into town—that and her mother's health.

She thumbed through the pages of the diary. Suddenly, her

father's name, Oliver Gordan, jumped out at her. Lucy began to read.

Though my son, Oliver, doesn't care one fig about it, I'm leaving the home place in Texas to him. He doesn't think the land will ever be worth anything. I know better. Sometimes, tales told by old timers come true. When Oliver needs money badly enough, he'll be glad I left him my land.

Lucy closed the diary, placing it on the table by her bed. The deed had to be here. She had to go into town in the morning, but she'd start looking in the attic again as soon as she got back.

———

Three cowboys trotted their horses down the main street of Searten.

Lucy stood near the entry door of the local bank, peering out a big window at a sudden rain. She hoped the rain would stop. She wanted to go home. She glanced down at her purse. Her mother had insisted she withdraw all the money from their savings account.

"Sooner or later," her mother had said, "we are traveling to Texas—whether you like it or not, dear. We'll need extra money for the trip in case we decide to stay a while. I don't want to leave our money in Colorado if we settle in Texas."

"Settle there!" Lucy had said.

"Don't let the idea upset you. It's just a thought."

Lucy recalled more about that conversation as she made the bank withdrawal her mother had requested, and she still didn't think Texas was a good idea.

As she continued to look out, she wondered about the three riders. Strangers seldom stopped in a little town like Searten unless they had relatives living here. She wondered who their kinfolks might be.

To pass the time, she counted the wad of cash the teller gave her. The greenbacks smelled fresh—like new money. Smiling, she put the cash back in her purse, pulling the drawstring. It hadn't been easy to close their account after all these years. Mama insisted, but they didn't need two hundred dollars to pay for a trip to Texas.

Lucy gazed out at her surroundings again. She never tired of glimpsing the magnificent mountains, dominating the landscape in the distance, or the little town of Searten with its cozy houses and friendly people.

Dark clouds banked in the northern sky. When strangers came through town, especially on a rainy day like this, they stopped at the hotel. But the horsemen aimed for the local bank.

Merely drizzling now, Lucy opened one of the double doors. A wave of cooling air moistened her face. She noticed the three strangers had dismounted and were tying their horses to the hitching post directly in front of the building. One looked younger than the others and had a black mustache.

It started raining again—harder than ever. Lucy shut the door and stood back from it, waiting for the rain to stop.

The doors opened. The three cowboys burst inside, pistols flashing. Their clothes were drenched. Bandanas covered their noses and mouths.

Lucy's jaw dropped. *The cowboys are outlaws! This is a holdup!*

3

The bandits stormed past Lucy, nearly knocking her down, and rushed right up to the teller's window.

Lucy froze. She glanced at Mr. Pike, the teller. His eyes looked enormous. She thought he was scared. She *knew* she was.

Her purse with the money in it dangled from a string attached to her wrist. She pushed her purse down into the wide side pocket of her blue muslin dress and covered it the best she could with the folds of her skirt.

If she hoped to escape, she would have to act. Now.

The gray-haired cowboy pointed his gun at the teller, motioning toward Lucy with his left hand. "Keep that girl quiet, Slim?"

The young-looking cowboy nodded. "Sure, Boss."

"Take care of her if you have to," the gray-haired man added.

Take care of her? Lucy's pulse raced. *Would he shoot me?*

Slim pointed his pistol at her. Lucy's heart jumped in her chest.

His mustache peaked out from under his bandana.

She saw a flash of his dark hair, and, of course, his gun. The older man still aimed his pistol at the teller.

"Bones," he shouted. "Go see who's behind that there door and bring 'um in here. I want to keep my eye on everybody."

Bones left the room. The older outlaw peered at the teller.

"Now," he said, glaring. "Give me all the money you got. And make it quick."

The color drained from Mr. Pike's long slender face. He hadn't moved or said a word.

"Are you deaf?" The one they called Boss cocked his gun. "I said get me the money." Obviously shaken, Mr. Pike handed the outlaw a few dollars through the opening at the bottom of the barred window.

The older outlaw frowned. "This ain't enough. Where's the rest?"

"In—in the va—vault." The teller glanced toward the door Bones was coming out of. "It's all kept back there."

"There ain't nobody else here, Boss," Bones interrupted. "Least, none I can see."

"Back the teller into the bank vault, Bones." The boss nodded toward the door. "Shoot him if he looks at ya funny. Slim and I will stand guard out here. And hurry up."

Mr. Pike raised both his hands. Bones was behind him with a gun to the teller's back. They entered the other room.

Lucy stood with Slim's pistol pointed at her head. Minutes seemed like hours. Lucy prayed the bandits would leave without killing anybody.

If only she was outdoors. A stick or a rock would be handy there, but she didn't see one thing within her reach to use as a weapon.

She heard a click. Slim must have cocked his gun. His

clothes looked soiled as well as wet. Oily strands of his jet-black hair hung down from under the edges of his brown hat.

Mr. Pike came back into the main part of the bank carrying a burlap sack. Bones was still right behind him. Like a long finger, the gun pointed to the teller's back.

"Bring the money out here so we can all see it," the older outlaw demanded.

"Right away, Boss."

The one they called Boss nodded to the teller. "Put the bag on the floor there."

Mr. Pike dropped the sack.

"Now open it," the gray-haired robber ordered.

The teller bent over, untied the leather strap wound around the sack and stuck his hand in. He pulled out a pistol, aiming it at the gray-haired gang leader. "D-drop it," Pike exclaimed.

The older cowboy kicked the gun out of Mr. Pike's hand and fired. Mr. Pike fell back, moaning and holding his shoulder.

Lucy moved forward to see if she could help him.

"I wouldn't do that if I was you, Buttercup," Slim said. "And give me that there purse you got!"

"No, I can't!"

Lucy hadn't realized she'd pulled the purse from her pocket and that it now dangled at her side. She tried to push it back in her pocket in a weak attempt to save its contents.

"I said give it here." He grabbed her purse with his left hand and yanked, breaking the drawstring.

"Hey," she exclaimed. "That hurt my wrist!"

His laugh held a mocking sting. "Now ain't that a shame?"

The teller had stopped groaning and appeared to be dead or unconscious. Slim had his finger on the trigger. The boss grabbed the sack filled with money. He and the other outlaw hurried toward the double doors.

"Finish up here, Slim," the boss said. "Then meet us outside. Make it fast. We need to ride."

The two outlaws left. Slim turned his full attention on Lucy.

"You sure are pretty," he said. "I hate to do this, but you might be able to identify us."

"Wait," she exclaimed, "you can't just shoot me!"

"Sorry, Buttercup, you're in my way. But I sure do like your yeller hair."

He's gonna kill me! Lucy trembled, and a Bible scripture came to mind—*no weapon formed against you will prosper.* If only she could believe that. "Please don't."

He pointed the gun at her head. Lucy shut her eyes, waiting. She heard a click, but nothing happened. She was still alive. *Why?*

"My pistol won't fire! Guess this is your lucky day, little lady. But if I ever see you again, we'll settle up." He hurried outside to join his waiting gang.

Lucy stood, frozen in place. Then she remembered the teller was shot. She needed to help but was too scared to move. At last, she hurried to the big window by the front door, gazing out. No sign of the outlaws.

A shot rang out. There at the end of the lane, the bandits headed out of town. Lucy ran outside and down the muddy street.

"Help!" she exclaimed. "Somebody! Help us!"

The sheriff and two riders rode past her. Guns at the ready, they charged down the street toward the fleeing outlaws. Hands grabbed Lucy from behind.

She twisted around, squirming and kicking. "Let go of me!"

"Stop that, Miss Gordan." Mr. Baker held her tight. "Can't

you see I'm trying to get you in off the street? Some of the robbers might still be out there. You could be killed." The middle-aged shop owner pulled her inside the general store.

"The bank teller was shot," Lucy exclaimed. "I think he might be dead."

"I'll send someone over there right away." Mr. Baker motioned toward his wife at the back of the store as if he expected Lucy to join her there.

She went over and stood next to his wife. Mrs. Baker looked dazed. Lucy heard what sounded like teeth ratting. She glanced at Mrs. Baker. Could it be her own teeth that she heard?

"Get down!" Mr. Baker shouted from the front of the store. "There might be more." Lucy dropped to the floor, pulling Mrs. Baker with her.

———

An hour later, when the coast was confirmed clear, Lucy hurried out of the store, running home. She didn't slow down until she reached the white picket fence in front of their two-story cottage.

Dark clouds still hovered overhead. Lucy smelled rain. A line of steppingstones led to the front porch. In her haste to reach the porch, she stepped too far to the right—missed one of the stones. Off balance, she stumbled but managed to keep from falling to the ground. She climbed the wooden steps, gasping for breath.

"Why are you in such a hurry?" her mother asked from the doorway. "I can hear you huffing and puffing from here."

"It's—." Lucy breathed in and out deeply, one hand pressed against her chest. "It's about to start raining."

And I was almost killed today. The thought swirled in her mind, but she didn't *say* anything.

"Well, come inside then." Her mother thumped her cane on the pine floor like she often did when things weren't happening fast enough to suit her. "I was worried."

Mama opened the door all the way and moved to one side to let her pass. Lucy went into the parlor, with her mother a few steps behind.

A mental picture of the bank robber's black mustache flashed before her. She winced and sat down. Mama settled into her chair—the high-backed maple rocker.

Lucy barely listened while her mother told about her morning visit with two widows from the local boardinghouse. She had witnessed a bank robbery, lost all their money, could identify the outlaws, and could have been killed, but she had no idea how to explain it all to Mama. Due to her mother's delicate physical condition, maybe she shouldn't say anything right now.

She had read in the newspaper about outlaws who came back to the towns where they committed crimes, killing their witnesses. Lucy made her living sewing for others. If somebody killed her, who would provide for Mama and Bethy?

Lucy closed her eyes. *If I ever needed God, this is the time.* She glanced at her mother. Mama sat quietly in her chair. She'd stopped hitting the floor with her cane.

"Mama, I have something to tell you."

"About Texas, I bet," her mother said. "I know. You're wondering how we can go to Texas when we can't find the deed?"

Finding the deed was the least of Lucy's worries now.

"We must have faith we'll find the deed, Mama. Now ..." Lucy cleared her throat. "Mama, there was a robbery at the bank this morning."

"Well, I'll say. How terrible. Do you know if anyone was hurt?"

"One of the bandits shot Mr. Pike in the shoulder. He pretended to be dead. I think he's going to be all right though. All the other bank employees happened to be celebrating Marge Ryan's birthday in the cellar, so the robbery only involved us."

"What do you mean, *us*?"

"I'd closed our account at the bank, and the robbers took all our money."

"Every single penny?"

"Yes. They grabbed my purse. But they would have taken it all anyway since the bank was robbed. We have nothing now. No money for a trip Texas, even if we find the deed. Nothing."

Her mother's face turned pale. Lucy sprang from her chair.

"Mama, are you all right? I should have waited 'til Dr. Smith came for a visit to tell you all this."

"Nonsense."

"What about your heart?"

Mrs. Gordan took a deep and labored breath. "My heart is still ticking."

"Then you aren't upset about losing the money?"

"Of course, I am. Anybody would be." Her mother looked exhausted, struggling for every breath, yet she managed to smile. "I know Sheriff Steen will get our money back for us, somehow. And if he doesn't, the nice sheriff from Texas will." She hesitated, "I know you don't want to go to Texas, but I want you to go for all of us. Will you please find that deed, dear?"

"I'll try. But you could never make a long trip like that, Mama, and I'll never go without you. Besides, we'd have to take Bethy out of school. And with our account at the bank flat empty, I don't know where we'd find the money for the trip."

"I want to sell the house."

"Sell our home, Mama?"

"I've wanted to sell it for a long time. I want to move to the boardinghouse with Luella Drake and my other friends. Frankly, I don't know why I ever bought a two-story house in the first place, but with Dr. Smith living there at the boardinghouse, too, I should be in safe hands."

"You can't be serious."

"Oh, I'm very serious," her mother insisted. "We should make enough from the sale of the house to pay for a trip to Texas for you and Bethy and enough left over to pay for my room at the boardinghouse for a long time to come. And when you return, we'll have money from the sale of the land in Texas the sheriff was telling us about. That should fill in the money gap."

"I don't think selling the house is a good idea, Mama."

"Well, we could sell the land in Texas to Mr. Grimes, now, and be done with it."

Lucy shook her head. "I don't think that's such a good idea either. The sheriff from Texas said not to sell to Mr. Grimes. Remember? He must have a good reason for saying it."

Eight-year-old Bethy bolted through the front door and into the parlor, panting as if she ran a long way. Her long auburn pigtails fell around her shoulders, and her cheeks look as pink as her muslin dress.

Lucy leaned forward in her chair, preparing to rise. "Where has the morning gone? I haven't had time to start our noon meal yet."

"Did you hear about the bank robbery in town this morning?" Bethy's chocolate-brown eyes twinkled with excitement. "We heard gun shots all the way to the schoolhouse. Everybody went to the windows and looked out. We didn't get to see much though because Miss Clinton made us go back to our desks and sit down. But we heard what happened later when Pastor Higgins and his wife came to the school and talked to our teacher. Miss Clinton thought we were reading our lessons, but we were listening. At least, I was."

"Miss Clinton was right to make you sit back down," Mama said. "Children have no business listening to adult conversations or standing at windows when outlaws are around. You could have been shot in the crossfire."

"Go upstairs now, Bethy, and wash up," Lucy put in. "And don't start reading your book of fairy tales again. You can do that later. I'll call you when dinner is ready."

"Yes, Cousin Lucy."

———

Lucy spent the afternoon in the attic, looking for the deed. She searched every box and every nook and corner she could think of—throwing away odds and ends as she went along—and sneezing her head off in the process.

Exhausted, Lucy set the lamp down. She'd inspected everything. She decided to go back to the trunk—the place where she started. Maybe she'd missed something.

She opened the lid, shined her lamp inside and stared in frustration. The edge of the blue-velvet lining of the trunk's lid was torn. About an inch of the wooden frame showed through. Lucy yanked off as much of the rotting material as she could.

Sticking her hand deeper into the torn lining, she felt something. Slowly, she inched a paper into the light, put the paper close to the lamp and read.

The deed! I found it. Finally.

Lucy dropped the document in the big pocket of her white apron and grabbed the lamp, hurrying downstairs. "Mama," she shouted. "I found the deed!"

4

Lucy heard Mama's high-pitched laughter as she entered the parlor.

"Well." Her mother thumped her cane on the floor by her chair and smiled. "Aren't you going to read it to me?"

"Of course."

Lucy opened the document and began reading. Though she didn't understand all she read, the deed confirmed that she and her mother owned a large piece of land in Texas including a big two-story house. She assumed the house was her ancestral home mentioned in the diary.

She didn't know if the amount Mr. Grimes offered for the property was a fair price, but since she had nothing, it sounded good. Still, the land and improvements might be worth more to another buyer. Apparently, Sheriff Caleb Caldwell thought so.

———

Caleb Caldwell pointed out the criminal he came to Denver to identify and would be leaving on the train the next morning. He thought of the New Testament he left at the Gordan home, wondering if Lucy found it. Why did he keep thinking about Lucy? He had to stop. To continue was insane. He was *never* going to find Daisy. Many knew he was searching for her—few knew why. He planned to keep it that way.

Caleb glanced at the desk across the hotel room, and the word *Letters* came to his mind. He liked action, he liked to read, especially books on the law, but he hated writing letters. Still, he should reply to all letters related to his job as county sheriff and write to the Texas Rangers again—see what else they had found about Fielding Grimes.

The telegram he received from Lucy was on the desk, too, stating that she, the little girl, and a chaperon, would be meeting him in San Antonio. He went over and sat down at the desk, avoiding the urge to think about Lucy again.

He wrote to the Rangers and responded to five messages pertaining to his job as sheriff. After a moment, he wrote a quick note to his mother and stepfather.

His ma had been urging him to write to his cousins, Jake and Boyd, since they moved away. He had time, and there was plenty of free stationary left in the box on the desk. But writing personal letters was always hard for Caleb—especially to people he cared about like family members. He decided to put off writing to his cousins for now.

———

"Mama, I'm a grown woman now," Lucy explained. "I don't need a chaperone."

"Yes, you do," her mother insisted. "You know it wouldn't be proper for a single young woman like you to take a trip like that without a chaperone. And with a child? Really, dear." Mama sent her a look that would stop a ticking clock. "Mrs. Brant is a widow woman as well as a respectable Christian lady, and she is a former schoolteacher. She will tutor Bethy during the trip and maybe afterward. I know you've always liked her. Everybody does. Besides, I think Mrs. Brant could use the money."

They would travel by train—first to San Antonio and then on to Juniper County in the Texas hill country. Despite all she would be leaving behind, thoughts of the trip were exciting— maybe profitable as well. Yet, she kept wondering. Was the attraction adventure and the state of Texas or a sheriff by the name of Caleb Caldwell?

Lucy packed hers and Bethy's belongings and replied to the letter from Mr. Fielding Grimes, stating that she and her mother had no wish to accept his offer. She ran into Hutch Fletcher, the man who worked for Mr. Grimes, several times in town. He seemed to be watching her—perhaps following her. Maybe he hoped she would change her mind about the land. He could be harmless. But seeing his bulky frame at every turn made her feel uncomfortable. She gazed up at blue mountains in the distance. Their melting white peaks seemed to call out to her. *Don't leave. Stay a while longer.*

Lucy had heard that there were hills in Texas, numerous rivers and streams filled with clear rushing waters. Yet, the beauty of her current surroundings had always inspired her.

The next morning, she hitched up the borrowed wagon, and with the help of a neighbor, she loaded her mother's trunks and suitcases in the back. As soon as Bethy left for school, she drove her mother to the boardinghouse. She stayed all morning, helping her mother settle in.

Sheriff Caleb Caldwell sat next to the window. The train rumbled down the tracks, and, looking out, all he saw was midnight blackness. He'd left Denver three days ago, traveling day and night. Thanks goodness for the law books he brought to read along the way.

He wished he'd stopped at the Gordan home, and then continued on. He'd looked forward to seeing them again. *Them?* It was Lucy he was eager to see. But in an hour or so, he would arrive in San Antonio—none too soon.

Wheel noises together with the back-and-forth motion of the train made him sleepy, but he found it difficult to get comfortable in the narrow seats. The backs weren't high enough for Caleb to rest his head. He needed more padding, and there wasn't enough room between the seats to spread out his legs.

He'd scrunched them up for so long, now he questioned if he'd be able to walk when the train stopped. He could be thankful the space next to his was vacant. If he'd shared a seat with a stranger, he would feel more cramped.

He thought of Lucy again and then Daisy. Daisy had been spotted in San Antonio. Though he hadn't found her on his way to Colorado, he planned to continue searching. Thoughts of Daisy mingled with more memories of Lucy.

Lucy Gordan. He shook his head and sighed deeply. She played on his mind a lot now. Remembering her face—her lips—the winsome sound of her voice.

He had to stop thinking about her. If Lucy knew the truth, she would have nothing to do with him. Caleb must become more reserved around Miss Gordan—indifferent to her charming ways. *But I'll need God's help to do that.* He blinked. When had he started thinking about God again? He shook his head as if to wake his brain.

Work would keep his mind off Miss Gordan and thus save

his integrity and perhaps his sanity as well. Then he would turn in his badge.

The rhythmic motion must have lulled Caleb to sleep. He awoke with a jerk. The train had slowed. Smoke from the engine poured into the open window nearby. He coughed and shut the window, looking out again. The dim lights of a city came steadily closer.

The conductor walked briskly down the aisle. "Next stop, San Antonio. San Antonio, next stop."

Caleb yawned and reached for his suitcase. It was going to feel good to stretch out in a bed at the hotel. As he started down the aisle, he heard a man say, "Fielding Grimes."

Caleb tensed and slowed his pace.

"Then do you think Fielding Grimes and his brothers are dishonest?" the first man whispered. "And what about that uncle of theirs, Boss Grimes? Now there's a strange one."

"They are all strange, if you ask me," a second man said.

The two men were having a conversation somewhere behind him. Caleb wanted to turn around to see their faces but figured it might not be wise to let them know he was listening. He needed a distraction—a reason to stop and see what he could learn.

He let his brown jacket drop from his arm. Then he stopped to pick it up.

"The way I hear it," the first man added, "Grimes has friends in high places. I understand he's running for governor."

"That scoundrel?"

"Yep, I heard he took money under the table when he ran for county judge, making promises he never intended to keep. What do you think he'd do if he was governor of the state?"

Their conversation could be based on hearsay. Still, Caleb wanted to talk to the two men—find out what else they knew. He waited on the platform outside until they left the train. But when he moved toward them, they disappeared into the night.

All Caleb's suspicions related to Fielding Grimes and his brothers appeared to be true, but he would need proof. If only someone was able to prove their misdeeds in a court of law.

———

Lucy sat in a chair in Mr. Joel Mason's office at the bank, waiting as he studied her deed. She'd been sitting there a long time, hoping he would hurry and finish.

He was an attorney as well as an old friend of her late father, and Lucy liked and respected him; she coveted his advice. As Mama had always said, "Mr. Mason is an expert on deeds and other legal papers."

She opened her purse, pulled out the recent message from Mr. Grimes and read it again.

Dear Miss Gordan,

I'll be waiting for you when you get to Texas. I will buy your land—one way or the other.

Fielding Grimes

Lucy wanted Sheriff Caldwell to know about the letters. She would need to tell Caleb everything, if she expected him to keep her and her companions safe. What she wouldn't tell was what happened at the bank. It wasn't related to Fielding Grimes in any way, and Sheriff Caleb Caldwell was a busy man. No need to bother him with personal matters. She'd keep what happened at the bank in Colorado locked in her heart. Besides, she seriously doubted she would ever see Slim again.

As the elderly gentleman continued reading the deed, his eyes narrowed. A look of surprise creased his already wrinkled forehead.

"Mr. Mason," Lucy said quietly, "have you learned anything important that I should know about?"

"I might have. Give me a minute more."

Lucy thumped a rhythmic beat with her fingertips on the arms of her chair. Then she stopped, remembering that some would say it was unladylike to reveal herself that way.

Why, I'm just like Mama—only I tap my fingertips instead of a cane.

Mr. Mason had spread out the document on his desk. He peered at her over his spectacles. "This deed seems sound, I'm glad to say. I wouldn't think you'll have any trouble proving your rights to the land. However, you'll need complete control of the property legally before you negotiate a sale, and you'll need a second copy. We can make a second copy for you right here, if you would like."

"Yes, please do that," she said.

"I would also suggest you have everything put in your name, Miss Gordan, before you leave town. I will be glad to do the legal work."

"I'm sure we'll do as you suggest," Lucy said. "But until I've talked all this over with Mama, I can't say for sure." She swallowed before going on. "I'll get back to you regarding the matter as soon as I can."

"Good enough." Mr. Mason glanced down at the deed again. "I know we had a second copy of this document back when your father was alive. Second copies of deeds were kept in a special file here at the bank. I remember seeing yours. But I haven't seen yours since George Lawrence left. It might have been misplaced when the bank was remodeled three years ago —that was back when Mr. Lawrence still worked here."

"I remember Mr. Lawrence," Lucy said. "Whatever happened to him?"

"Who knows?" Mr. Mason shrugged. "He moved away. A lot of things were misplaced then. But we will certainly keep looking for your deed. With luck, we'll find it. Nevertheless, I want to work up a second copy."

Lucy nodded. "Yes." She hesitated. "I wonder why my mother never knew about this deed or our land in Texas."

"Miss Gordan, your father adored your mother. He protected her as if she were a delicate flower. Perhaps he didn't want to bother her with matters he could handle."

"Maybe he shouldn't have been so protective."

"You could be right. It's always easier to avoid potholes when the buggy has already passed safely onto solid ground." He gazed at her over his spectacles again. "Please leave your forwarding address. I may need to contact you while you are away in Texas, and don't forget to have everything put in your name. We can do it here, if you like."

"My mother is living over at the boardinghouse now. But as soon as I leave here, I'll walk right over and tell her what you said. If she agrees, and I think she will, we'll be here in the morning and sign everything. I'll put it all in my name, as you said."

"I'm looking forward to seeing both of you again."

As she left the building, she remembered how his eyes had narrowed when he read the deed and when he mentioned Mr. Lawrence. Her father hid things from her mother for her own good. Was Mr. Mason doing the same thing? Or was he merely surprised to be reading a deed he'd read for the first time some years ago? However, that didn't explain how Fielding Grimes got a copy of the deed, if, in fact, he did. He couldn't merely go out and buy a copy.

Or could he?

5

"All aboard!" The porter set wooden steps painted black on the platform in front of one of the train's entry doors. "All aboard!"

"Oh, it's time!" Lucy hugged her mother.

"Yes, it is." Mrs. Melinda Brant's girlish giggle rang out. "I can hardly wait." She glanced toward the passenger car. "Shouldn't we go if we want to get a good seat?"

"Why don't you go on, Mrs. Brant, and save us seats together? Bethy and I will be along in a minute."

When her chaperone had gone, Lucy hugged all the women in the farewell party and shook hands with the men for the last time. A line of passengers formed in front of the steps. Lucy pulled Bethy in, single file, behind them. They climbed the steps and boarded the train.

Ladies in fine store-bought hats and expensive-looking dresses sat beside men in dark-colored suits with vests. Lucy glanced down at her brown dress with its white collar, feeling fortunate. She not only made her own clothes, but she was a dressmaker—sewing for other women and their children.

Mrs. Brant waved and motioned toward their seats. Lucy remembered that Bethy requested to sit by a window so she could look out.

"Is this where we are going to sit?" Lucy asked Mrs. Brant.

"Yes." She put her hand on the crown of her wide-brimmed, black hat as if she thought it might fall off her head. "Been saving these seats for you."

"Good thing you did. From the looks of the crowd on this train, we might not have found one otherwise." Lucy motioned to Bethy. "Go on, sit down."

"You mean I get to be by the window?"

"Isn't that what I promised?"

Normally, Bethy would have sent Lucy a childlike grin of gratitude, but there was nothing normal about today. Bethy hadn't smiled since they arrived at the train station—probably because none of the children from her school came to see them off.

From the train's windows, they waved to those standing on the platform. Then the whistle blew long and loud. Despite all that had happened previously, excitement filled every part of her when Lucy heard the powerful engine come to life. If only Bethy felt what she was feeling.

The train moved with a jerk. Bethy's small body yanked forward—then back.

"You all right," Lucy asked.

"Oh, yes, ma'am. I'm fine."

Was she really? How could Lucy cheer Bethy up on a train? She thought of the book of fairy tales Bethy was holding. Mama never read to Lucy as a child, but she told her stories. Maybe Lucy would do the same.

She looked down at Bethy's storybook. "That book of yours sure has a nice cover. Mind if I look at it for a moment?"

"Sure. Take it." Bethy handed the book to Lucy, and she

studied the cover. "I really like this cover. The colors are beautiful. I like the stories inside too." She gave the book back to Bethy, waiting a moment before speaking again. "Would you like for me to tell you a story, Bethy?"

She looked away, and then she said, "Yes."

Lucy cleared her throat. "Once upon a time that was a beautiful girl by the name of Cinderella."

The corners of Bethy's mouth turned upward but only slightly.

Lucy smiled internally. *It's already working.*

When the story ended a few minutes later, Lucy remembered her mother always asked questions at the end of each story. "Bethy," she said, "one day we will both marry, and each of us will think of our husbands as Prince Charming. But did I ever tell you that Jesus is my real Prince Charming?"

"Prince Charming? Like in the story of Cinderella?"

"Yes." Lucy paused. "Jesus rescues those He loves, and then He marries them, exactly like the prince married Cinderella. Then he took Cinderella to his castle where they lived happily ever after, and Jesus has a bride too."

Bethy inched closer to Lucy. "You must be joking. Who is His bride?"

"The church."

"You mean all of us?"

Lucy's nod became a smile. "All who truly turn to God the Father will marry His only begotten Son—Jesus. In the Bible Jesus is called the Bridegroom, and the true church is called the Bride of Christ."

"Like in the story of Cinderella?"

"Oh yes, Bethy, only a million times better. And the Bridegroom will take His bride to His Kingdom in heaven."

Bethy didn't say much after that, but she smiled a lot and opened her storybook. Slowly, she turned the pages, looking down at the pictures—one after the other. Lucy had no way of knowing what Bethy was thinking, but she did wonder. Was Bethy thinking about the future prince in her life, and had Lucy planted a seed? She could only hope that Bethy would search for King Jesus now.

———

Lucy could almost feel the heat of the engine—hear its *chug-chug* as the locomotive clanged and clattered down the tracks. The train's wheels clicked and clacked as they rolled along, drowning out most other sounds.

So, this is what it feels like to be aboard a genuine railroad train.

The conductor in a dark suit and a different kind of hat checked their tickets. Lucy and Mrs. Brant settled back in their seats. Lucy hoped to get some sleep. Bethy had never seemed more alert and ready for an adventure.

Three children raced down the aisle and out the door at the end of the passenger car, giggling as they went. A few minutes later, they ran back through and out the door at the other end of the car.

"May I do what they're doing?" Bethy asked. "It sure looks like fun."

"Maybe so." Lucy was reading the sheriff's New Testament —the one he left behind. But she put it down. "I always want you to have fun. But we'll have to wait and see."

"I don't like 'wait and see' or 'maybe so,'" Beth said. "That always means no." The young girl crossed her arms and huffed a sigh.

Lucy grinned. "Not *always*."

She was about to say *yes* to Bethy's request to take a walk, when Hutch Fletcher, in a brown suit, walked toward them down the aisle. Her grin disappeared. When Hutch got even with their seats, he stopped, glaring at Lucy, a taunting reminder that he *was* following her. Could Fielding Grimes, his brothers, and their uncle be far behind?

Lucy lifted her head, hoping to convince Hutch that his presence didn't bother her. "Why are you following us, sir?" she demanded.

"Following you? Who says I am?" he shot back. "I'm a passenger on this here train. Same as you."

Lucy pressed out imaginary wrinkles from the skirt of her brown linen dress to keep from looking at him. She would have said more if Bethy wasn't seated beside her, and she hated to make a stir in front of so many strangers. When she finally looked up again, Hutch was storming down the aisle. She wanted him to leave her sight entirely, but he took a seat at the other end of the passenger car.

"Who is that big man?" Bethy asked.

"Nobody." Briefly, Lucy clenched her jaws. "He's nobody."

"Then why are you shaking?" Bethy asked.

"I'm not."

"You are too."

"I—I could be coming down with a fever." Lucy glanced out a window to keep from meeting the child's gaze. "That always makes me seem a little nervous."

"So can I go and do what other children are doing now?" Bethy asked.

"No. You cannot walk around the train without me."

"Why?"

"We'll talk about that later."

Bethy sent Lucy a sour look but didn't say anything.

Then Hutch walked up and down the aisle again, finally sitting back down in his seat.

Lucy didn't want Bethy to know how threatened she felt,

but the uneasy feeling in the pit of her stomach grew worse. Hutch had probably been watching them since they boarded the train. It was time to do something.

"Come now, Bethy." Lucy grabbed Bethy's hand. "It's time to take that walk you've been wanting." Lucy took Bethy's hand and led her to the exit door at the other end of the passenger car from Hutch Fletcher.

!# # #

That night, Lucy heard Mrs. Brant snoring in the seat in front of them. She needed to wake her and tell her that Hutch Fletcher was following them. She'd wanted to tell her sooner, but she hadn't wanted to say anything in front of Bethy. However, the child was sound asleep now, finally, in the seat beside her.

Lucy leaned forward. "Mrs. Brant," she whispered.

The woman jerked around.

Lucy shushed her with a gesture before saying more. "Don't make a sound."

The older woman was in the ladies' room when Hutch Fletcher had arrived. Mrs. Brant might not have noticed him. She might not have known he was the big man on the train. Now she would know. Lucy planned to explain everything, and as soon as possible.

When she'd said all that needed saying, Lucy looked down at Mrs. Brant, patting the woman on the shoulder. At first Mrs. Brant had appeared slightly frightened, on hearing about Hutch, but after a moment, the woman smiled back at her. Then Lucy gazed down at the sleeping child beside her, realizing she must warn Bethy too. With three more days and nights on the train, she would have more than enough time.

Such a journey would be difficult for most adults. To

someone Bethy's age, it was almost more than a child could stand. At least Bethy had her book of fairy tales to read, and Lucy had the sheriff's New Testament. Her Bible was in one of the trunks.

But boredom was not all they had to contend with. Hutch Fletcher was seated by the passenger car's exit door. He appeared up to no good, and Lucy had no idea what he might do.

———

At first, Bethy appeared to enjoy the train ride. However, by the next afternoon, her excitement had all but died.

Besides asking if they were in San Antonio yet, the child squirmed in her seat. She fidgeted constantly—talking—asking questions—counting barns aloud, and begging to get off the train so she could play outdoors.

She'd tried to prepare Bethy for what the long journey would be like. Obviously, she hadn't been clear enough. She knew if her young cousin didn't stop counting barns and houses along the way, she would go mad.

Much later, Lucy glanced out a window but saw only darkness. All three of them were tired—drained of energy. They needed sleep. But how could Lucy close her eyes with Hutch Fletcher lurking at the other end of the passenger car?

———

Three days later, they arrived in San Antonio.

Lucy grabbed the carpetbags. Bethy had been sleeping with her head on Mrs. Brant's lap.

"You carry the bags," Melinda Brant said. "I'll take care of this sweet little girl."

"All right." Lucy leaned forward in the dim overhead light and saw a streetlight through the trains' windows. She noticed when Melinda gently shook the child's shoulder.

"Wake up, Bethy." Melinda helped Bethy to a standing position. "We're in San Antonio."

The little girl muttered under her breath, leaning against the chaperon as if she was still half asleep.

"I'd like to carry you, honey, but you're too big." Mrs. Brant smiled down at the child. "You're gonna have to walk. Can you do that?"

"Yes ma'am."

"Good."

Lacy saw Sheriff Caldwell through one of the trains many windows as they walked down the narrow aisle to the exit. He stood under what some called a streetlamp with a buggy parked nearby. But when she stepped down from the train, he was standing right in front of her, his hand outstretched as if to help if she needed it.

"Welcome to God's country." The sheriff motioned toward a black two-seater carriage. I've ordered a wagon. Until it gets here, I rented this."

"Thank you." Lucy felt too exhausted to say more.

He reached for Bethy, helping her down from the train. Then he took Melinda's hand, easing her to the rocky ground. "That little girl looks too sleepy to walk," he said. "Let me put her in the carriage for you."

"I would appreciate it."

Lucy and Mrs. Brant joined Bethy in the buggy while Caleb Caldwell loaded their baggage. When he'd untied the reins, they started off.

Lucy heard the *clop-clop* of the horses' hooves and little else, and the street looked well-traveled. Strange, unfamiliar smells mingled with the odor of horse manure as they rode along.

Caleb motioned toward the remains of a large, stone building, "That's the old Alamo mission just ahead."

Lucy heard the clamp of horses' hooves. She glanced back. Another carriage had pulled right behind them, but she was unable to see who was in it. Was Hutch Fletcher in the buggy behind them? A chill like cold fingers ran down her spine.

The carriage rolled under a streetlight, making it possible to see those inside. A large man in a dark suit sat behind the driver. Lucy gasped. It was Hutch Fletcher!

6

Lucy opened her eyes. Blinked. The morning sun beamed through the east window of their hotel room.

Bethy, in the big bed beside her, turned over, pulling the cover with her, and Mrs. Brant snored loudly. Lucy jerked back her half of the covers and shut her eyes. Sleeping late was a luxury. It was time to get up before she fell asleep again.

I'm in Texas. A place Sheriff Caldwell calls God's Country.

Lucy crawled out of bed, opened her trunk, and pulled out her dusty pink muslin dress and matching jacket. Lifting out her parasol in a darker shade of pink, she propped it against the chest of drawers. Her mother had always said a proper lady should carry an umbrella on a warm and sunny day like this to prevent freckling.

She spread the clothes on her bed, pressing out a few wrinkles with the palm of her hand. To her surprise, her clothes looked decent considering the long train ride. Maybe she wouldn't have to set a hot iron to them after all.

Lucy dressed for breakfast in minutes while Bethy and Melissa Brant slept. When she finally woke them, they groaned and dawdled getting ready. If Sheriff Caldwell had waited until they came down before eating his breakfast, he must be famished.

As they started down to breakfast, Lucy saw Sheriff Caldwell seated in a chair near the entry door of the hotel. He must have seen them because he rose from his chair and stood at the foot of the stairs, smiling up at them.

"The food here at the hotel is excellent," he said. "But I also know of another good place to eat. It's across the street and has more of a San Antonio flavor. Would y'all like to try it first? Or eat here?"

Lucy looked at her chaperone. "Where would you like to eat, Mrs. Brant?"

"The place the sheriff suggested sounds nice. We can eat at the hotel at another time."

The sun felt hot on Lucy's fair skin. Hotter than Searten, Colorado, on the warmest day in summer. If she was going to freckle, now would be the time. The weather also seemed dry and breezeless.

Lucy opened her parasol and started to reach for Sheriff Caldwell's arm. But he already had Bethy and Mrs. Brant, one on each arm. She fell in behind them.

The café was decorated in shades of red, white, and green, and the air inside the restaurant felt as hot as the cook stove. Fanning herself with a paper fan, she gazed at a plate of food on one of the tables. She saw what appeared be scrambled eggs amidst a mixture of cheeses, peppers, onions, and garlic. The food looked hot and spicy—but strangely tempting. Still, she couldn't imagine preparing eggs and bacon with all that seasoning.

They sat down at a large table in front of a line of windows, waiting for the waiter to take their breakfast orders. Lucy glanced up from her menu as a large man strolled down the walkway outside. Her breath caught. *Fletcher*.

She looked again. It wasn't him after all. Lucy released a big breath of air. *What's the matter with me? Is my imagination playing games with my mind?*

"What's wrong, Miss Lucy?" Caleb asked. "You look like you've seen a ghost."

"I'm fine, really." When she glanced out the window again, the man had disappeared from her line of vision. The memory of Hutch Fletcher hadn't.

During the meal, Caleb told them about the Alamo and that the old mission was in ruins. At first, Lucy barely listened. But as he continued to talk, she paid attention, learning many things including the locations of other old missions. Until that moment, she hadn't known that other missions surrounded the city of San Antonio.

Soon the conversation changed to the agenda for the day. Plans were made for the trip to Juniper County. Lucy thought about the New Testament that Caleb left at their home. At last, she mentioned it.

"You must have thought I left the little Bible by accident, Miss Lucy, but I didn't. I want you to have it." He paused. "I don't have much time to read, especially books on religion. I thought it might be something you'd like. Read it yet?"

"Yes. Thank you so much. I really like it, and it was kind of you to leave it for me. I read the Bible daily, have for years, and the little New Testament fits in my purse perfectly. I read it on the train getting here. You read the Bible, too, don't you?"

"I once did, but cannot say that I do now, ma'am. My parents are church-goers, though. I went with them to church some when I was young."

He's not a believer after all. How sad. Lucy put on the best manufactured smile she could manage.

"Can we go shopping?" Bethy asked, interrupting their conversation. "I saw a store next door to this restaurant that sells toys."

"I thought we would walk over and visit what is left of the old Alamo mission first, Bethy." Lucy tried not to think about the real possibility that Caleb wasn't a believer. "We can stop at the toy store on our way back to the hotel."

Bethy looked disappointed.

"I have to check on the wagon and the team of mules I ordered," Caleb put in. "By the time you get back from your tour of the Alamo, I reckon I'll have finished with what I have to do, and we can all get in the buggy and visit some of the other places of interest in San Antonio."

They finished eating and left the café, gathering on the walkway out front before going on. As the adults engaged in more conversation, Bethy went over and looked in a store window. "You've been awfully quiet, young lady," Lucy finally said. "Are you all right?"

"Oh, yes, ma'am." The child's attention returned to the window of the toyshop. "I like to look at things is all."

"Like the dolls in that store window?" Lucy suggested.

The child nodded, pointing to one special doll. "Yes, ma'am, especially *that* one."

Bethy would be celebrating her ninth birthday in two weeks. If Lucy kept her spending to a minimum while in San Antonio, maybe she could buy Bethy the doll before they left.

A man turned a corner at the other end of the block, a big man. A shiver shot down Lucy's spine at the look of his powerful body in dark clothing against the blinding morning sun. All happy thoughts were overshadowed. Darker ones hammered her mind. Was Hutch the man at the other end of the street?

———

Three days later, Lucy stood near the street in front of the hotel waiting for Sheriff Caleb Caldwell to pick them up. Bethy hugged her new doll close to her heart. With the child's birthday still days away, she went on and gave Bethy the gift. It was a long drive in a covered wagon from San Antonio to Juniper County. The new doll would give the child comfort.

Today, they would leave for the land Caleb claimed she owned. The trip would take days with nights spent camped along the way, cooking over an open fire, and living in cramped quarters. Lucy, Mrs. Brant, and Bethy would be sleeping close together in the covered wagon. She hadn't asked where the sheriff would be sleeping but supposed he would bed down near the fire or under the wagon.

Lucy turned her head to swat a gnat flying about her nose and noticed the young man from the hotel, standing a few feet away and watching her. He had positioned their baggage in a line at the edge of the street and would help load their belongings into the covered wagon when the sheriff arrived.

The covered wagon appeared at the corner. Caleb's team of brown mules stirred up a small cloud of dust as he made the turn. Bethy had inched too close to the road. Lucy grabbed her hand, yanking her back. When she looked again, Caleb had jumped out of the wagon, and was heading toward them.

In brown cowboy boots, a light tan, western-styled hat, and a cream-colored canvas jacket, he looked taller and slimmer than Lucy remembered, and downright handsome.

"Is that the man you've been waiting for, ma'am?" the hotel attendant asked.

"Yes. Yes, I think maybe he is." Lucy blushed when she realized what she'd said. "I meant he's the man who will be driving the wagon. Please go on and load our things into the back of the wagon."

"Yes, ma'am."

Caleb pushed his hat back from his face, wiping his brow. "Are you ladies ready to go?"

Mrs. Brant and Bethy responded enthusiastically. Lucy merely nodded. For some reason, Caleb seemed standoffish. He hadn't smiled once since he got out of the wagon. She didn't intend to make matters worse by appearing overly eager.

With Bethy under foot all the time, she still hadn't found an opportunity to tell Sheriff Caldwell about her pursuer. Today she would tell him—even if it meant mentioning it in front of Bethy.

Caleb loaded Bethy into the back of the covered wagon first. Then he offered Lucy his arm to help her up, leaving Mrs. Brant waiting with the baggage.

"Sit in the back there, ma'am," Caleb said to Lucy, "with the little girl."

After studying him for an instant, she slowly nodded. "Very well." Without another word, Lucy did as she was told.

She'd hoped to sit up front with Caleb so they could talk. They had a lot of things they needed to discuss. Apparently, he intended for Mrs. Brant to sit beside him on the long journey. But then, Mrs. Brant was an older woman and worthy of respect and special attention.

A large man on a big gray horse crossed the road in front of them.

"Well, I'll say." Caleb gestured toward the man on the horse. "I know that man. He's from Juniper. Wonder what he's doing in San Antonio?"

Hutch Fletcher. Lucy tried to swallow a mouthful of irritation.

Off to one side and some distance away, she saw another man on a chestnut horse. Though she couldn't see his face, his narrow shoulders and skinny body reminded her of someone. The two men stopped their horses and engaged in what looked like a conversation. If only she could hear what they were saying.

Caleb turned and looked at her. "Is something wrong?"

"Those men, riding off together," Lucy said. "One looks like ..."

An unwelcomed thought entered Lucy's mind. Was the other man Slim, the outlaw who tried to kill her at the bank that day? *He sort of looked like Slim.* Lucy hadn't mentioned what happened at the bank to anyone, including her mother. Mama's heart didn't like conflict.

The second rider could be the outlaw she met that day in the bank. *Maybe not.* Lucy couldn't be sure because she'd seen him at a distance. Nevertheless, she knew the matter would continue to trouble her. To clear her mind, she focused on the journey.

The covered wagon rolled south and west toward Juniper. Lucy studied the dusty road ahead. The soil on the ground had turned a rusty red, she noticed, and the trees were different from those found in Colorado.

She'd expected to feel cramped with her trunk and their suitcases piled in the covered wagon but hadn't envisioned Caleb's belongings stacked there as well. Lucy ran the tips of her fingers across a rough, wooden barrel and read the word *Beans*. The other barrel said *Nails* in black letters.

There was barely room enough for Lucy and Bethy to sit, much less stretch out. The barrels looked heavy too. She tried to move one of them and couldn't budge it. Had Caleb planned for them to unload all these items each night before falling asleep? If not, Lucy and her two female companions might be forced to sleep under the wagon. In that case, Caleb would need to make other arrangements.

The wagon's wheels had creaked as they rolled down the rocky streets of San Antonio on their way out of town. Now the wheels made other sounds when they sounded at all.

Briefly, Caleb turned away from the road ahead, looking back at Lucy as if he knew what she was thinking. "Don't let those noisy wagon wheels bother you, ma'am. They need oiling. I'll get to it—first chance I get.'

Lucy nodded. Then she gazed through the arch at the back of the wagon as they moved along. She saw more trees, a river not far from the road and hills in the distance. The wheels squeaked on rhythmically.

Later, the road melted into ruts filled with rocks, big and small. Then, even the ruts disappeared into a vast isolated area of open, hilly land. Sheep and goats grazed on the hillsides, and Lucy also saw a few farms. She felt every jerk when the wagon's wheels hit one of the big rocks, and time after time, bigger bumps threw her and Bethy against the barrels and boxes. Lucy wondered if oiling the wheels would make a different in the quality of the ride, assuming it probably wouldn't.

"Sheriff Caldwell," Lucy said. "Would you please stop the wagon again? I need to take Bethy on another walk in the woods." This would be their second nature walk before noon.

Caleb kind of grinned, pulling back on the reins.

"You took Bethy on her last walk." Mrs. Brant started to climb down from the wagon. "I'll take her this time." She held out her hands. "Come on, Bethy, and let me help you down."

Bethy and Mrs. Brant moved behind a clump of spiny bushes and out of sight. Lucy sat on the wooden seat beside Caleb. Had she imagined it? Or did he inch to the other end of the bench and as far front Lucy as possible? She didn't have the pox, after all. He tied up the reins.

"I'm glad for the chance to finally talk to you alone," she said. "There are a few things I need to say."

"I'm listening." Caleb kept his distance but turned toward her. Their gazes connected, and a wave of tenderness swept across his face. However, it quickly vanished. A wary expression replaced it. "I'll be happy to hear whatever you have to say."

Lucy cleared her throat. "Sheriff, I—" She finally had the opportunity to say what was on her mind but didn't know how to say it. "I—I think someone is following me—following us."

Lucy nodded, confirming her decision to finally say what was on her mind.

"Following us?" Caleb's eyes narrowed. "Who?"

"Hutch Fletcher. He works for Mr. Fielding Grimes."

"I know. How long has this been going on, ma'am?"

"Since before we left Searten. He—he gave me a letter from Mr. Grimes."

"What?" If facial expressions contorted to anger. "Let me see that letter!"

"It's in my trunk. I need to tell Mrs. Brant more about all this. So far, I haven't found a time to tell her much with Bethy around all the time."

"Can you tell me a little more? And I want to read that letter you talked about."

Lucy told him everything she could remember—except what happened at the bank. Then Bethy and Mrs. Brant appeared from behind a group of trees.

"We'll continue this conversation later," he said. "And as I told you, I need to see that letter. You and Mrs. Brant meet me tonight down by the river after Bethy goes to sleep."

"All right. But guess I better go now."

Lucy moved to her spot at the back of the wagon. Caleb climbed down from the wagon and went around to help Bethy and Mrs. Brant up onto it.

"We'll be stopping for our noon meal in an hour or so," he said loud enough for Lucy to hear in the back of the wagon. "I hope we won't have to stop for another nature walk until then."

Lucy smiled because she knew exactly what he was talking about.

7

After supper, Lucy sat in the seat of the wagon with Melinda Brant. Bethy played under a tree with her dolls.

Lucy wanted to tell Melinda what she told Caleb earlier. With Bethy so absorbed in playing with her dolls, this might be the perfect time.

"Mrs. Brant," Lucy said in hushed tones. "There are some private things I've been meaning to tell you."

"All right." Mrs. Brant moved closer, turning her back to Bethy. "I'm open to anything you want to say, honey. Let it all roll off your tongue."

As quickly as possible, Lucy whispered what she had told Caleb, and what he said to her.

"Then do you think we're in danger?" Melinda Brant asked.

"I'm not sure. But Hutch Fletcher, the man we saw on the train, has been pressuring me to sell my land to Fielding Grimes. Common sense tells me he wouldn't want to hurt us. But if he is trying to scare us, he's doing a good job."

"I wish you'd told me all this sooner, but I understand why you didn't," the older woman said in a kind-sounding voice.

"Had all this happened to me, I wouldn't have been able to hold it all in. Must have been awful, bearing this burden alone."

"I managed," Lucy said, thinking of the outlaw at the bank in Searten and all the other things she never mentioned to anyone. "Now both you and the sheriff know," she added. "That's why he wants to meet us later—down by the river. To talk about what we should do next."

"Since he's a sheriff," Melinda pointed out, "I guess he'd know."

Bethy moved toward them. With her back turned, Mrs. Brant wouldn't notice.

"Hi, Bethy." Lucy waved at the child. "How do your dolls like being out in the sunshine again?"

"They liked it fine," Bethy said. "And what does the sheriff know that we don't?"

Bethy heard what Mrs. Brant said. Lucy sent up a silent prayer. "Gather your dolls, Bethy." Lucy ignored the child's recent comment. "And come inside the wagon. It's time for you to go to bed."

———

"My," Mrs. Brant said with a chuckle later that evening. "Going fishing tonight?"

"Fishing? What are you talking about?"

"I was a young woman once, you know. Got married too. I know when I see a young woman fixing up pretty for a man."

"Fixing up pretty? I am not!" Lucy shook her head, regardless of the fact she just finished her nightly one hundred stroke hair brushing. Her cheeks felt warm; was she blushing? "Besides, it's almost bedtime. I always clean up a little before turning in for the night."

"Then why didn't you wait until we returned from our meeting with that handsome sheriff?" Mrs. Brant laughed again. "Hmm?"

Lucy shook her forefinger at the older woman. "Shame on you, Mrs. Brant," she said in a teasing tone. She put her hands on her hips. "I always heard, back in Searten, that you were a matchmaker. I'm starting to believe it."

"Me?" Mrs. Brant giggled, pressing her hand to her heart. "A matchmaker? I'm not really what you would call a matchmaker. But I see nothing wrong with pushing two young people who seem so right for each other closer together."

"I barely know Sheriff Caldwell," Lucy protested. "Besides, I don't think he likes me very much. He's always stepping back from me as if he thinks I have the pox or something."

"Oh, he likes you all right, Miss Lucy. Anybody with eyes in their heads can see that. I think he steps back because he's afraid of you."

"Afraid?"

"Yes. Now all we have to do is find out why."

Lucy wondered what Mrs. Brant could possibly have meant but decided not to ask. She'd said enough about Sheriff Caldwell for now. They would be talking to him shortly—down by the river.

———

Bethy didn't fall asleep as soon as Lucy had hoped. It was late by the time Mrs. Brant and Lucy walked through the tall grass to the river. Their oil lamps lit up the ancient Cypress trees lining the river's edge, their long roots like gigantic fingers dipped into the cold, rushing water.

Caleb sat on one of the roots. He rose to his feet when they joined him.

"Welcome, ladies," he said, "and be careful where you step. The ground is wet, rocky, and slippery."

He reached out and took Mrs. Brant's hand, guiding her to a nest of roots that reminded Lucy of a chair. When he came back to help her, she'd already found a comfortable place to sit.

"By now, I reckon you've told Mrs. Brant what you told me this morning, Miss Gordan," he said. "Am I right?"

Lucy nodded. "She knows everything you do now."

"And did you remember to bring the letter?" he asked.

"Yes, I brought it. There were other letters, but this is the only one I didn't tear up."

Lucy pulled out the letter and handed it to him. When their fingers touched, a sweet and tender connection surprised her. From the look of astonishment on Caleb's face, she knew he felt it too. Yet he pulled back his hand before she did.

Caleb moved closer to his lamp. His eyes narrowed as soon as he began reading. He cleared his throat. "Dear Miss Gordan," he read aloud. "I'll be waiting for you when you get to Texas. I plan to buy your land—one way or another. Fielding Grimes."

Lucy hadn't expected him to read the letter aloud but was glad he did. Now, Mrs. Brant knew the content of the letter as well.

He folded up the letter. "I don't like this," he said. "Sounds like a threat."

Caleb handed back the letter. Currents crossed between them again at least on Lucy's part. She couldn't explain her reaction, but she knew she'd never known anything like it, even with the young man she once thought she loved back in Colorado.

"Threats are dangerous," he went on.

She nodded. "I know."

"I've been thinking about what you told me, ma'am, when

you sat beside me in the wagon. But until now, I hadn't read this here letter. Now I have, and I want you to tell me every important thing that happened since the day I visited you at your home in Colorado."

It took a while, but Lucy told him all she knew. She'd almost finished when thoughts of what happened at the bank came to her. She wondered if she should tell that too. Ordinarily, she wouldn't bother others with personal matters, but the man with Hutch did sort of look like the man who tried to kill her at the bank. She reluctantly added that part of her story.

"Do you know the names of any of the outlaws?" Caleb asked when she finished.

"I know what they called each other."

"That's good enough."

"They called the head outlaw, Boss," Lucy said, "and the one with high cheekbones, Bones. They called the skinny man that wanted to kill me, Slim."

"If I'd known all this while we were still in San Antonio, I would have sent out a couple of telegrams," he said. "But don't worry, ma'am." He smiled before speaking again. "Yes, Fielding Grimes, his brothers and their uncle are bad with a capital B, but I'll be protecting you every step of the way. My deputies are working on all this right now. I thought Hutch Fletcher was Fielding Grimes' bodyguard. Now, I'm wondering. Maybe his duties go way beyond that. How far beyond? Who knows?" He shrugged. "Fielding Grimes is running for governor of Texas. But if I have my way, he'll soon be running for the Mexican border."

He must have noticed how frightened Mrs. Brant looked and how scared Lucy felt, because his lips turned up at the edges a bit. It was only a hint of a smile. However, it lifted Lucy's spirits.

At last, Caleb said, "Miss Lucy, I think Hutch Fletcher wants to scare you—scare you so you'll sell your land to his boss." He cocked his head. "Still, let's all keep our eyes open. Let me know if you see anything out of the barn—as they say."

"What about Bethy?" Lucy asked. "Should we tell her about Hutch Fletcher now?"

He nodded. "I think you should. The sooner the better. That way, Bethy can be on the lookout for strangers. I'm sure you ladies will tell what must be told in the right way."

Lucy thought of Bethy curled up in a quilt, sleeping in the wagon. "I should never have left her alone," Lucy said. "I need to go now."

"There's no need for you to do that," Mrs. Brant put in. "I'll go and stay with Bethy. You stay here, Miss Lucy, and finish your talk with the sheriff. There could be other things the sheriff needs to tell you."

Lucy couldn't think of a reply. She kept sitting there, on the root of the tree, watching as Melinda Brant trudged back to the campsite.

It was apparent Mrs. Brant was scheming to make sure she and Caleb were alone together, while Caleb's actions suggested he wanted nothing of the sort. Lucy wondered what a properly reared young lady should do when her chaperone vanished and she found herself alone with a handsome young sheriff who appeared to want to be anywhere but here.

Caleb moved closer to the river and sat down on the biggest root out there. "While I was in San Antonio, I heard a lot of things about Fielding Grimes."

"What kind of things?" Lucy asked.

"Some of the talk is just plain gossip. I won't talk about any of that." He put his hands behind his head, resting against the trunk of the tree. "As I said, Mr. Grimes is running for governor. He'll need a powerful lot of money to do it. According to what I read in the newspaper, he lost a fortune last year in bad investments." Caleb leaned forward. "And if you're wondering where all his money comes from, I don't have an answer." He shrugged. "I was unable to find the name of a single financial backer."

Lucy's glanced at the path up the hill, wondering if she should get up and hurry back to the campsite. Instead, she turned, gazing at Caleb. "But what does any of this have to do with me?"

"I think Fielding Grimes needs money for his campaign," Caleb said. "Bad. But he must have some money, or he wouldn't be trying to buy your place. My guess is he thinks there's silver on your land. Maybe he hopes by buying you out for not much money, he'll be left with enough silver to cover all his debts and then some. Still, that doesn't explain where he is getting all this money in the first place." He hesitated for a moment. "Grimes is a desperate man right now, ma'am, and he wants what you have." He shook his head. "I should never have encouraged you to come to Texas. I don't know what he might do. But I would urge you to watch your back."

He was still seated on one of the tree's roots. Lucy went over to join him there. She sat down beside him. "I won't bite. I don't have the pox either. The root you're sitting on looks like the most comfortable-looking place to sit out here, and I have more questions."

All at once he whirled around in order to face her. "What kind of—" He was studying her lips. "What kind of questions do you?" His face moved closer to hers. "Do you want to ask?"

His face was mere inches from hers. She thought—no *knew* he was going to kiss her. He took her in his arms. Now she knew for sure. But he suddenly pulled away without a word, turning his back he walked back to the wagon.

Did I do something wrong? Lucy sat stunned for a moment before also returning to camp.

————

Caleb remained quiet and aloof the remainder of the journey. Four days later, they arrived in Juniper County. Caleb drove the wagon down the town's main street so they could see Juniper, Texas, and Lucy discovered it was about the size of Searten, except a river ran through it. She also saw a hotel, a general store, the sheriff's office, several other structures, a livery, and a blacksmith shop.

Two buildings, one at each end of the main street, stood like bookends—holding the town together. A small white church with a steeple was perched on a hill. Lucy saw a little red schoolhouse in the middle of the block.

Bethy hadn't shown much of an interest in the town, yet when she saw the school, she stopped and looked. "Will I be going to that school?"

"Not now," Lucy said. "I don't know how long we will be staying here. Until I do, Mrs. Brant will be teaching you at the hotel, or I will."

Bethy's shoulders slumped. "Who will I play with?"

"Maybe the sheriff knows of children your age. I'll try to remember to ask him.

Bethy hugged her new doll close to her heart, leaving Lucy wondering if she'd made the right decision. "But if we decide to stay, Bethy, you'll be going to school."

Bethy didn't make any kind of reply, but at least she didn't look as lost as she had earlier.

Caleb stopped the covered wagon in front of the Riverside, the only hotel in town, and helped carry their bags up to their rooms on the second floor, promising to meet them later for supper downstairs in the hotel dining room.

After he departed and they had unpacked, Lucy suggested that they take a walking tour of Juniper. She'd noticed a poster when they arrived nailed to an oak tree in front of the hotel that read *Vote for Fielding Grimes for governor in the upcoming primary election.* She wanted to take a closer look at it. But they finally decided to take an afternoon nap instead. It had been a long journey.

————

That night, Caleb was sitting at a table near the stairway, waiting for the women, when the little girl came into the restaurant followed by Lucy and Mrs. Brant. His breath caught at the sight of Lucy in a rust-colored dress and gold ribbons in her hair. She looked beautiful, and the reddish-brown material of her dress looked soft, like velvet—like Lucy. He planned not to look at Lucy at all. He sure didn't intend to talk to her. He would eat his supper. Then he would get up from the table and go.

He pulled out Mrs. Brant's chair. If he kept his attention on the older woman, he wouldn't have to look at Lucy. Still gazing at Mrs. Brant, he asked, "So how are you ladies doing this evening?"

"Very well." Melinda Brant smiled. "And thank you so much for inviting us to share a meal with you. It can get lonesome when night comes in a new town."

"I was glad to do it," Caleb said.

The child plopped down on a chair and started fiddling with the arrangement of yellow roses in the center of the table.

"Leave the flowers alone, Bethy," Lucy said.

"Yes, Cousin Lucy."

He'd thought Miss Lucy would sit down, too, but she stood behind her chair, perhaps waiting for him to pull it out for her.

"Good evening, Sheriff," Lucy said.

Caleb looked away to keep from meeting her gaze. "Evenin', ma'am." He pulled out her chair but still didn't glance in Lucy's direction.

"Thank you, sir."

As they waited for their orders, Caleb told them a little more about Lucy's land. There wasn't much left to tell until they saw it for themselves and started asking questions but explaining was better than complete silence. Apparently, neither of the ladies felt like talking, but he noticed them frowning at each other several times, and whispering back and forth. Once, the older woman poked Lucy in the ribs so hard he was afraid she might fall out of her chair. What was going on here?

They were halfway through the meal. The entry doors at the front of the hotel flew open. Fielding Grimes and Hutch Fletcher stormed inside. They stood in the entry, staring at them through the archway leading to the restaurant. Caleb glanced at Lucy—noticed when she bit her lower lip.

"Hutch Fletcher," Lucy whispered.

He nodded. "I know."

She's plenty scared, that's for sure. Anger boiled inside him, waiting to spill out. He wouldn't leave early now.

The two men came right up to their table as if they thought they belonged there.

"So, here you are," Fielding Grimes said in a loud voice, "a little bird told me y'all would be here in the hotel tonight, eating." His laugh was seasoned with sarcasm. "Of course, I know Sheriff Caldwell—have for years. But I've not met the ladies before, formally at least. I'm Fielding Grimes, and of course you know my assistant, Hutch Fletcher."

Caleb gritted his teeth. He glanced at Lucy. She did not look pleased. "As you can see, sir, we're having our supper. Is there something I can do for you?" He started to get up—show them to the door.

"Keep your seat, Sheriff." Fielding Grimes tipped his hat. "Ladies."

Neither of the women said a word.

"I stopped by," Grimes went on, "to welcome Miss Gordan and her friends to Juniper County."

"I'm sure they appreciate your interest," Caleb put in. "But if you will excuse us, I would like to finish my steak."

"Don't let us stop ya. Keep right on eating," Grimes insisted. "Have you heard, I'm running for governor?"

Caleb frowned and looked down at his plate. "I saw one of your posters."

"Yeah, they're might fancy, ain't they?" Grimes pulled a chair from a nearby table and dragged it to theirs. "Miss Gordan, I still want to buy your land."

Hutch pressed his back against the wall, glaring at the women at the table. If that wasn't bad enough, Fielding Grimes chuckled after Lucy frowned.

Caleb glared at Fielding Grimes. He'd had enough. He was ready to fight, if it became necessary. At the same time, he didn't want to make a scene in front of the women and the little girl.

Grimes placed his chair beside Lucy's and sat down. Lucy inched her chair away from his. Fielding Grimes laughed.

The muscles in Caleb's body tensed. His hands became fists.

Lucy stood—back straight—head held high. "If you will excuse us, Bethy and I will be leaving now." She turned to Mrs. Brant. "You stay and finish eating if you want to. We will be in our rooms." He glanced at Caleb. "Thank you, Sheriff, for an excellent meal."

Caleb nodded. But what he wanted to do was hit Fielding Grimes in the jaw.

"I'm leaving too," Mrs. Brant said.

Fielding Grimes giggled as the women and the child climbed the stairs in the entry hall beyond the arch. "Looks like the ladies deserted us, and I never got around to telling Miss Gordan all I came to say."

Caleb stood, dropping three coins on the table. "I reckon you've said plenty for one night." His jaw tightened. "If both of you don't leave this hotel right now, I'm going to knock your lights out." He didn't touch his gun, but he pulled back his jacket. Anyone standing nearby could easily see his pistol, gleaming in the leather scabbard.

Without a word, Fielding Grimes, followed by Hutch Fletcher, left the eating area with Caleb following them. At the door of the hotel, Fielding and Hutch went out. Caleb slammed the door behind them.

It rained during the night, but the sky was clear by the time Lucy awoke the next morning. Yet none of her problems had vanished. Nevertheless, a feeling of exhilaration filled her heart at the thought of seeing her land for the first time.

Caleb waited for them in front of the hotel after breakfast. He had removed the wagon's cover and nailed a wide board across the back so Lucy and Bethy would have something to sit on. Mrs. Brant was to sit up front. The oak plank was rough and splintery, but should the bumpy ride become dangerous, at least they would have something to grab onto.

"The ride will be plenty rugged," Caleb warned from the front of the wagon. He turned away from the reins to meet Lucy's gaze. "The ground is hard and mighty stony from here on, not much soil to speak of, and I don't want one of you to fall out and hurt yourself. So, hold on to the sides of the wagon. Hear?"

"Yes." Lucy turned to Bethy. "You heard what the sheriff said. Now, grab hold of the sides of the wagon and hold on tight."

"Yes, ma'am, I will."

The hilly land was as rocky as Caleb predicted. The mules strained to keep the carriage moving, and the wagon's wheels still squeaked. Then the sheriff explained that the wheels would be oiled as soon as he got to his ranch.

Further on, he chose a route along the river where the ground was damp, fairly level and the rocks weren't as large. Ancient cypress trees with their towering trunks lined the river —their branches shading the river's edges. The magnificent beauty of the Lord and His world always amazed her.

About a half an hour later, Caleb turned his mules away from the river. They entered a large valley surrounded by hills.

"We're getting close to your land now, Miss Lucy," Caleb said.

Lucy saw goats and sheep on some of the hills but no cattle or horses at all. "I thought this was Texas."

Caleb laughed. "It is. Where else would we be?"

Lucy crawled to the front of the wagon so she could better see what lay ahead. When Bethy sidled up beside her, she stroked the child's head lovingly. "I expected to see cowboys and horses and cattle here in Texas."

"We have all those things here."

"About all I've seen, so far, are sheep and goats. You're about the only cowboy I've seen, and you're the sheriff."

Caleb looked away for a moment. Then he motioned toward the hills. "This whole pasture, such as it is, belongs to me, and I have a small herd of white-faced cattle closer to my cabin."

"You own this valley?" She couldn't have been more surprised. "I didn't know your land was close to mine."

"The only thing that separates my land from yours is a fence. But that will soon change."

"Change?" She shrugged. "How?"

"I plan to sell my place. I wanted to sell to my parents. They want more land. But they insisted I sell to whoever offers me the most money. Once the land is sold, I'll turn in my sheriff's badge and buy land way south of here."

"Why?" she asked.

"It's beautiful here in the Texas hill country, but the land is too rocky for cattle ranching. Goats and sheep like to climb these rocky hills. But horses and cows prefer level ground."

"So, south?"

"Yes. I have my eye on a piece of land I want to buy southwest of Corpus Christi. That's where the big ranches are. Until then, I'll wait and see." He gazed at the landscape ahead before speaking again. "Your land starts around the bend there," he said loud enough to be heard above the whoosh of a sudden breeze. "By the way, I won't be able to show you the silver mine today. The bridge over the creek is out."

"Oh ... that's all right." Lucy tried to hide her disappointment.

———

A rickety, wooden gate connected to a wire fence appeared before them.

"Well," Caleb said, glancing back at Lucy. "Here we are. Your land starts at that gate."

Her surroundings were lovely. Still, Lucy hoped to see something new beyond the gate. Though the ground looked softer, probably from recent rains, all she saw were rocks, bushes, a few trees, hills, and more rocks.

Caleb tied up the reins and started to climb down from the wagon.

"The house is about half a mile farther on," he said. "But

you won't be able to see much until we're practically there. It's around that hill on a sort of rise."

"Will I be able to see the river from the house?" Lucy asked.

"Yes. It's some distance away, but there's a smaller house down by the river."

"Everything is so beautiful around here," Lucy said, "but I was hoping the house would be close to the river."

"Up here in these hills, folks learn fairly young to build their homes as far from rivers as possible." He looked away as if his thoughts were elsewhere. "When the river's on the rise, water comes rushing though these canyons fast. Sometimes houses are lost during one of our floods."

Lucy noticed Bethy was frowning as if the child didn't like what she was hearing, and after Lucy was given a tour of the two-story house, she didn't like what she was seeing. The main house needed repairs. The cabin by the river was too small for the three of them. They would continue living at the hotel until other arrangements could be made.

———

It was mid-afternoon by the time they got back to Juniper. Caleb dropped the women and the little girl off at the hotel. He would make a brief appearance at his office at the county jail, check with his deputies, then he would drive to the edge of town where his mother and stepfather lived. By now, his parents would have heard he was back in town and would expect him to visit them as soon as possible.

An hour later, Caleb parked the wagon in front of the big two-story colonial-style white house with its columns and wide front porch—the home his stepfather had built after he married Caleb's mother.

He never really got to know Jim Caldwell, his real father as he had died when Caleb was a child. Then, his mother married Raymond Montemayor, an immigrant from Mexico who traced his family line all the back to Spain. Caleb loved his stepfather as if they were flesh and blood, but his sister, Polly, never really accepted him.

"I fear it would dishonor our real father to call Mr. Montemayor 'Papa,'" she'd said to Caleb many times. "To me, he'll always just be Mama's new husband."

The double doors opened, and his mother rushed out to meet him, arms outstretched, chuckling loudly. His stepfather was right behind her, smiling from ear to ear.

Caleb jumped down from the wagon. Moving forward, he embraced his mother warmly. When he'd released her, he shook his stepfather's hand.

They went inside, and with a flourish, his mother led the way into the parlor off the entryway. The large room, adorned in shades of deep purple, violet and blue, reminded Caleb of Lucy.

"How did your trip go?" his stepfather asked.

"Very well."

"And how is my sweet Polly?" his mother put in.

Caleb glanced at his stepfather to measure the expression on his face at the mention of his sister's name. "I haven't seen Polly in over a year. She and her husband were away from San Antonio when I stopped by to see them. But I'm sure they are fine, Mama."

"We can thank the Good Lord for that." She paused. "You're staying for supper, aren't you? We're having roast and potatoes."

"Yes, Mama, I'll be happy to stay and eat."

"Were you able to learn more about what happened to Daisy?" his stepfather put in.

"No." Caleb looked down at his cowboy boots and shook

his head. "No, I wasn't."

His mother leaned forward in her chair. "Now tell us about the folks you brought with you from Colorado."

"So, you heard about them, did ya?"

"Of course. Sally Jones at the hotel told me. You know how close we have always been."

"We heard you traveled from San Antonio with two women and a child," his stepfather said.

Caleb spent the next few minutes catching them up on all that had happened since he met Lucy and her family. He left out that he had fallen in love with Lucy Gordan.

"I'm worried for their safety," he said at last. "Fielding Grimes and his brothers are evil men. So is their uncle. They want the land Miss Lucy inherited from her grandmother."

"Caleb," his mother said. "The Bible says, 'Don't bear false witness against thy neighbor.'"

"What neighbor?"

"Fielding Grimes, his brothers, and his uncle."

"According to what I hear, the Rangers and others have plenty more than two witnesses."

"Good," she said. "But don't forget what I just said."

"Yes, ma'am. I won't." He sent his mother a big grin before going on. "Miss Lucy Gordan wants to sell her land, but not to Fielding Grimes. I'm hoping to find someone who might be interested in buying the old Gordan place."

"I might be interested," his stepfather said. "Let me think about it. I'll let you know what I decide."

———

Shorty, one of Caleb's deputies, was slumped over the sheriff's desk snoring when Caleb arrived back at his office at the county jail. "Hey, Shorty," Caleb said loudly. "I'm back!"

The deputy jumped and opened his eyes.

"Anything interesting happen while I was gone—other than you taking a nap?"

Shorty blushed. "Sorry, sheriff. But with no prisoners in the cells, I sort of drifted off."

"Don't let it happen again. You know when I turn in my badge, this job will go to one of my deputies."

"Yes, sir. Oh, you got a letter from one of your sheriff friends while you were gone." Shorty pulled a letter from the stack of mail on Caleb's desk and handed it to him. "Here, sir."

"Thanks." Caleb opened the letter and began reading.

Dear Sheriff Caldwell,

I think you should stop looking for Daisy. Nobody here in her hometown has seen her since she moved away. Her parents are dead. I talked to her former boss at the saloon like you wanted me to, and Mr. French didn't know a thing.

Well, that's all I know. I'll keep looking like you want, but I doubt it will do any good. Daisy is gone. Maybe she is dead. If you don't mind me saying so, it's time you start over.

Yours truly,
Dexter Olson, Sheriff of Gulf County, Texas

Start over? If only he could. It was exactly what he wanted to do. Caleb put the letter back in the envelope. *Daisy—where are you?*

Caleb met Daisy when he and her father both worked on a ranch way down in hot and flat south Texas–several years before he became sheriff. Caleb was a church-going man then. When Daisy took a job as a barmaid in a nearby town, he married her to pull her away from that lifestyle. How could he have known she would pull him away from his?

———

At breakfast the next morning, Lucy finally met Mrs. Sally Jones, the head cook at the hotel. Mrs. Jones was also over the hotel's cleaning staff and was in charge of bringing meals to the prisoners at the county jail. Lucy liked her immediately. The woman's warm smile was hard to miss. She also learned that Mrs. Jones and Mrs. Martha Montemayor, Caleb's mother, had been best friends since childhood.

"Now if any of you ladies need anything," Mrs. Jones said, "anything at all, just let me know. I live here at the hotel now that my dear husband died. One pull of the golden rope in your rooms will bring help from the front desk. Two will bring a maid, and three pulls will have me at the door of your hotel room."

Lucy returned her smile. "Thank you, Mrs. Jones. You've been a big help."

After breakfast Lucy, Mrs. Brant, and Bethy went on a walking tour of Juniper. They were on their way back to the hotel when a flash of pale blue in a store window caught Lucy's eye. She stopped in front of a milliner shop to admire a display of spring hats.

"My," Lucy said, "aren't these lovely?"

"Yes, they're pretty, all right." Mrs. Brant stood a short distance away. "Well." Mrs. Brant put her hands on her ample hips. "Are you coming or not?"

"You and Bethy go on. I'll join you at the hotel later."

"All right, then. Guess I'll see you later." Mrs. Brant and Bethy went on down the street. Lucy looked back at the window display.

A shadow fell on the store window. Lucy whirled around, then shrank back. Fielding Grimes stood beside her on the covered walkway, grinning from ear to ear. "So, we meet again,"

He tipped his hat. A tremble birthed inside her.

"Mighty glad I ran into you again, ma'am," he said, "cause there's something I've been meaning to ask ya."

"Sorry." She lifted her head. "I'm in a hurry." Lucy tried to go around him, but he blocked her way. "I would appreciate it if you would move out of way, sir. My friends are waiting for me."

He stared at her for a moment as if testing her in a war of wills. "Go then," he snapped and stepped to one side. "But sooner or later, we'll have our little talk, and you're gonna sell me your land—one way or another."

"Are you threatening me, sir?"

"Take it any way you like." His eyes narrowed. "But remember this. I'm not likely to change my mind—about anything." He turned then, heading down the walkway in the other direction.

Lucy peered at Fielding Grimes until he disappeared from view. *I should have talked to him at the hotel with the sheriff there to protect us. Now, I'll be forced to talk to him when I'm alone or maybe with Bethy.*

———

Caleb sat at his desk in the county jail. He could see all the cells from there, and he was glad there were no prisoners inside. Then he glanced over at the mail basket.

The stack of letters he saw earlier still stared at him. He hated correspondence and would not miss that stack when he turned in his badge. He never did reply to recent letters from two of his cousins, Jake and Boyd. He should at least answer the nice letter he got from the sheriff of Gulf County, the sheriff who mentioned Daisy. But all the letters about Daisy were the same. She was nowhere to be found. Who but Caleb had a wife nobody had seen in years?

Caleb grabbed a sheet of paper and a pen, hesitating before dipping his pen in the bottle of ink. All right, he would write to his cousins, but he wouldn't tell them or anyone about Lucy. No point in burdening relatives and friends with the fact he hated one woman and loved another who he could never marry.

Dear Jake,

How are you doing, cousin? I miss you and Boyd. I still haven't heard from Daisy. Nothing new here since we talked before you moved away. If I learn anything new, I'll let you know, and thanks for the letters. By the way, I'll be turning in my sheriff's badge soon. Gonna ranch full time. More later.

Yours truly,
Caleb

He addressed the envelope, put the letter inside, and picked up another sheet of paper. *Why is letter writing so hard?* Caleb took a deep breath and began writing.

Dear Boyd,

I sure am glad some of my kinfolks stayed right here in Juniper instead of moving so far away—like you and Jake did. It's such a comfort to Mama, having family still living right here in town. She has all the family for supper a couple of nights each month, and she and my stepfather are doing fine.

Mama also said she was lucky to have your mother and Jake's as her sweet sisters. But with me in and out of town so much, I hardly ever see my kinfolks. If I could wish for anything besides finding Daisy, it would be to see you two once in a while.

One more thing! I'm tired of sheriffing. I want to get into ranching full time.

Yours truly,
Caleb

He put down his pen, glaring at the basket of letters. He'd need to read and answer all of them. It was his job. But for some strange reason, he wanted to read the letter from the sheriff of Gulf County again—as if merely reading it would change things—as if reading it would make a future with Lucy possible.

9

Lucy received two letters. They must have been mailed right after she got on the train—one from her mother, the other from Joel Mason—the attorney from Colorado.

Records showed that the deed was once kept at the bank. The original version of the document had vanished. Long-time employee, George Lawrence, might know what happened to the deed, but he no longer worked for the bank.

Lucy's mother never liked Mr. Lawrence. *Did Fielding Grimes somehow manage to get a copy of the deed, and did it come from Lawrence?*

Early the next morning Lucy, Bethy, and Mrs. Brant sat at a table in the hotel dining room, waiting for their orders to arrive. Mrs. Sally Jones stood at the entry of the hotel, talking with a middle-aged couple of about her age.

When Mrs. Jones glanced Lucy's way, she waved and smiled. Mrs. Jones returned her smile with one of her own. Then, all three of them headed straight for their table. Mrs. Jones introduced Lucy and the others to Caleb's parents, Mr. and Mrs. Raymond Montemayor.

"We've wanted to meet all of you since you arrived in town," Caleb's mother said. "Our son, Caleb, and now my friend, Mrs. Jones, have nothing but good things to say about all of you. We want you to know you are welcome at our house at any time." She paused before speaking again. "In fact, we are hosting a church social at our home on Wednesday night. We would be delighted if all you came as our guests. You could meet members of our church, and they could get to know you."

"I'll be happy to have someone from the church drive all of you to the social," Mrs. Jones put in, "if you might be interested."

"Can we go, Cousin Lucy?" Bethy begged. "Please don't say 'maybe so' or 'we'll see.'"

"I do use those terms a lot, don't I?"

"You sure do."

Lucy giggled.

Then everybody did.

"About the social," Lucy said. "I'd like to go. But I have a lot to do and think about right now. I could forget." She glanced at Sally Jones. "Mrs. Jones, would you be so kind as to remind us to get ready for the social on Wednesday? We don't want to miss."

"I would be glad to."

"Miss Lucy," Mr. Montemayor said with a charming Spanish accent. "Caleb mentioned you might be selling the land you own here. No?"

Lucy grinned internally. "Yes."

"Well, we are interested in buying land around here," he went on. "If you decide to sell, please let us be the first to know."

"Of course. If I decide to sell, you and Mrs. Montemayor will be the first to know."

Lucy had planned to sell her land and return to Colorado as

soon as she found a buyer she could trust. Now she had. Yet what she really wanted was to stay until her problems with Caleb were resolved—one way or another.

———

After breakfast Wednesday, Mrs. Brant took Bethy by the hand, leading her to their rooms on the second floor. It was time for the child's schooling. Lucy took another walking tour of the town.

She found herself once again in front of the hat shop's display window, gazing at a rust- colored hat with a wide brim. It would be burdensome to carry around while shopping, so she went inside and bought the sun bonnet, promising to pick it up later that day.

Lucy continued her window-shopping tour of the small town, knowing full well she was moving in the direction of the county jail. Caleb would be there. She wanted to see him. At last, she stood at the jailhouse door, peering inside through a much smaller window.

The sheriff sat behind his desk, talking to another cowboy. He glanced her way, nodded, and then he continued his conversation.

A wave of embarrassment heated her face. She turned away and hurried down the wooden walkway. At the corner, she went down a side street she'd never noticed before. All at once, Lucy realized she was on a street filled with empty buildings.

She was about to turn around and go back in the direction from which she came when Fielding Grimes blocked her way. Then two other men stepped out from one of the buildings. Lucy gasped. She didn't know the man wearing spectacles, but she knew George Lawrence, the banker from Searten.

A fourth man joined the others. Lucy's heart pulled into a hard knot. Slim, the outlaw, was dressed in a suit and tie like the others. Every muscle in her body tensed. His mere presence shattered her. Lucy took a step backward, pressing her back against the rough brick siding of the building behind her.

"I believe you know my lawyer, George Lawrence," Fielding Grimes said. "And may I present my brothers." He motioned toward the one in spectacles. "This is Granger Grimes, and this is my youngest brother, Hunter—Hunter Grimes."

Lucy was surrounded. Slim stared at her—or should she call him Hunter now? Trembling, she prayed for divine protection. Was Slim planning to kill her since he failed to do it the first time?

"Miss Gordan," Fielding Grimes went on, "I will buy your land. But first—."

All at once, Sheriff Caleb Caldwell stood beside her. *Where did he come from?* Did he know the danger she was in? Then Caleb took her hand in his, and she felt safe.

"Come with me," he demanded. Caleb escorted her away from the Grimes brothers and their lawyer—away and on down the street.

"That land will be mine, Miss Gordan," Fielding shouted after them. "Don't you forget it!"

"Don't listen to them!" Caleb squeezed her hand. "Keep walking!"

Further on down the street, he said, "I was having an important conversation with a Texas Ranger when you walked by earlier. Otherwise, I would have invited you inside. When I saw you looked distressed, I excused myself, followed you, and heard enough to get you out of there as soon as I could."

He paused as if he expected Lucy to make a reply. So far, she'd managed to keep up with his fast retreat, yet was too overwhelmed to speak.

"You all right?"

She nodded.

"Good." He smiled. "And according to the Texas Ranger I talked to, Fielding Grimes and his brothers are about to be arrested."

The edges of her mouth turned upward, glad that they would pay for their crimes. She hadn't wanted to talk about Slim, but Lucy finally told Caleb that Hunter and Slim were one and the same.

"Lucy," his voice was tender, "I've known the Grimes brothers all my life. They have always been one step ahead of the law. I know Hunter best. We are the same age. I know who they are and what they can do. I want to stay at the hotel with you and protect you, Mrs. Brant, and the child for as long as you need me, but as sheriff, I must round up a posse. The Ranger I was telling you about said to be on the lookout. A bunch of outlaws could be headed this way. So ..." He didn't speak for a moment. "Stay in your hotel rooms, Lucy. Lock all the doors. Promise?"

"I—I promise," she managed.

———

"Are you all right, Cousin Lucy?"

Mrs. Brant came over and gave Lucy a motherly hug. "Don't try to talk now, dear," she urged. "We're here when you're ready."

Lucy's sobs slowly faded turning to whimpers. Finally, she was able to tell them what happened. Afterward, she felt better. Later, they discussed the hat, waiting at the hat shop.

"We are safe behind locked doors," Lucy pointed out.

Mrs. Brant nodded. "I agree."

"So, I think I'll contact the hotel's main desk. I'll request that one of their staff pick up the bonnet and bring it to me."

"Are you *sure* you're all right?"

Lucy turned to Mrs. Brant. "I'm fine now. Why don't you and Bethy go back to your rooms? It's time for Bethy's lessons. The hat should be here soon. After it gets here, I think I will lie down—maybe take a nap. It's been quite a day."

Mrs. Brant shook her head, and from the expression on her face, Lucy thought the woman disagreed with her decision. "I'm going to be better than fine, Mrs. Brant. See you both later."

They left the room, closing the connecting door behind them. Lucy pulled the cord, hanging from the ceiling of her hotel room. Then she sat down in a chair facing the door.

A few minutes later she heard a knock at her door.

"Room service," a man said from the other side of her door. "What do you need, ma'am?"

Lucy explained about the bonnet at the hat shop as best she could without opening the door. He agreed to go and pick up the hat for her.

Half an hour later, Lucy heard another knock at her bedroom door. Assuming it was the man with her bonnet, she opened immediately.

Hutch Fletcher stood in the hall outside Lucy's hotel room, holding a sheet of white paper. She tried to slam the door, but he grabbed her with one powerful hand and the door with the other. He threw her onto a chair.

Lucy wanted to cry out for help but couldn't. Bethy and Mrs. Brant were in the room next to hers. If she screamed or called out, they would rush through the connecting door, and they, too, would be trapped.

Then Hutch said, "Did you know your sweetheart Sheriff Caldwell is married?"

Married? Lucy's heart sank. She attempted to mask her despair.

"Oh," he said. "I see you didn't know." His hurtful laugh taunted her. "He married Daisy Swenson, a girl he met when he was working down in South Texas." He laughed again. "Fielding Grimes will have someone get back to you about the sale of your land by sundown. And if you haven't agreed to sell by then, you will—and soon." He sent her a hard look.

"By the way." He held up the sheet of paper he was holding. "Slim sent you a message. I'll read it." Hutch cleared his throat. "Nice to see you again, Buttercup. I'll be seeing you soon, maybe sooner than you think." He dropped Hunter's letter on a lamp table by her bed. "I'll leave this love letter here so you can read it again and again." As quickly as he entered, Hutch left, slamming the door behind him.

Lucy wanted to sit down and cry. Moisture already gathered at the edges of her eyes, but she managed to get up and lock the door. Bethy and Mrs. Brant came in through the connecting door, looking as shattered as Lucy felt.

"Now what are we going to do?" Lucy asked to nobody in particular.

"Pray?" Mrs. Brant suggested.

"Yes. Let's pray."

They prayed. Afterward, they all came to the same conclusion. Regardless of the emotional state they were all in, they needed to leave town immediately. But how? Where would they go? Apparently, the man from the main desk was connected to the outlaws.

Lucy heard another knock at the door. But this time, she would not reply.

"Miss Lucy," Mrs. Jones voice filtered in from the other side of the door. "Let me in! It's important!"

She didn't stop to consider who truly stood in the hall

outside. Lucy opened the door. Mrs. Jones raced inside, carrying a bundle of some kind, and locked the door behind her.

Lucy grabbed Mrs. Jones, hugging her as if her life depended on it. She buried her head on Mrs. Jones's shoulder, sobbing.

"I'm here to help," Mrs. Jones said.

Lucy sniffed, wiping her eyes with the back of her hand. "You are an answer to prayer."

"Amen," Mrs. Brant put in.

"I know the trouble all of you are in," Mrs. Jones said. "The Montemayor's gathering is tonight, remember? I was on my way to see you when Mr. Fletcher started banging on your door. I saw the whole thing."

"Thank you so much for coming. But we're trapped. There is no way out for us. You should leave at once or you'll be trapped here too."

"No, Miss Lucy. I won't be trapped here—neither will any of you. I have a plan. But you must do exactly what I tell you to do as quickly as possible." She held up the bundle she was holding. "There are three maid uniforms in this bag. Bethy's might be a little long." She tossed the sack to Lucy. "Now, put on these uniforms. I have a carriage waiting behind the hotel."

"But how did you know we—?"

"I'll explain everything after we get out of here," Mrs. Jones ordered. "Hurry and dress—all of you."

Ten minutes later, Lucy found herself in a buggy pulled by two horses and on her way to the home of Raymond and Martha Montemayor. Like Bethy and Mrs. Brant, she wore a white apron over a navy-blue dress and a white maid's cap.

"Now that we are out of danger," Mrs. Jones explained, "I'll tell you my plan." She smiled. "I was hired to cater the

Montemayor's party. I was on my way to remind you to come when Hutch Fletcher showed up.

"You must pretend to be the maids I hired to serve the refreshments during the event tonight at the Montemayor home," she continued. "And the Montemayors will be in on the plan as soon as I explain it to them. Then all of you will hide in one of the upstairs bedrooms. The real maids I hired will do the actual serving. They will arrive later. Any questions?"

Lucy raised her hand as if she were a child in school. "I have one."

Everybody laughed, including Lucy, and she truly relaxed for the first time that day. They had prayed. God answered. What a blessing.

"All right, Miss Lucy," Mrs. Jones said. "Let's hear your question."

"What happens after the church social is over? What do we do then?"

"I've been thinking about that, and I have a second plan. As soon as the guests leave, all of you will be driven east of here. My mother lives in the little town in Mountain View. I'll have all of your things packed and sent to you there, including Bethy's dolls. Mother has plenty of room. You'll stay there. Later, you'll leave on the stage for San Antonio and on to Colorado. Is this plan satisfactory?"

"Yes," Lucy said, "and I never did get to see the silver mine. But before we leave Juniper, I want to sell my land to Mr. Montemayor. He's been wanting to buy it, now I'm ready to sell. But I'll keep the mineral rights. Who knows? They might find silver there someday."

10

Once back at the county jail, Caleb relayed Lucy's encounter with the Grimes men to Hopkins, the Texas Ranger he'd been working with. Her words stuck in his head. *Hunter Grimes is Slim—the outlaw who tried to kill me.*

He'd always wondered where all the Grimes money came from. Now he thought he knew. Robbing banks was certainly one way to make a lot of money.

"I'm not surprised," Ranger Hopkins replied. "We've been watching that bunch of crooks for a long time. Very soon the Texas Rangers will be arresting Fielding Grimes, the lawyer, the uncle they call Boss, and the rest of the Grimes family."

Caleb nodded. "And don't forget to add Hutch Fletcher to your list. He's almost as bad as Hunter Grimes—better known at Slim."

"The outlaws call him Slim, all right," the Ranger said. "We know because we've already captured a couple of them, and I'll be sure to add Hutch Fletcher's name to our list."

"Thanks." Caleb cleared his throat. "By the way, a mess of tough-looking cowboys are holed up in a shack south of town.

I learned about it just before you came in. Could be Slim's bunch. Shorty is rounding up volunteers for a posse. They will meet me in front of the hotel here in town as soon as possible. We'll check the shack first—just in case. The outlaws have a head start. But we'll find 'um—one way or another."

"Good luck," the Ranger said, and then he left.

Caleb buckled his gun. He'd intended to tell Lucy about Daisy before someone else did. He hated keeping the truth from anyone—especially Lucy. But after what happened on the street earlier with those four men, she'd had enough trauma for one day. He would tell all later, when Lucy was feeling better.

The front door opened. A young woman with long golden hair stood in the doorway. Lucy? No. Then he knew. Coldness surrounded her, a kind of hardness, and he saw dark circles under her eyes.

"Daisy! What in the cat-hair are you doing here?"

"You've been searching for me, haven't you? I think that's very touching."

"Touching? I've been hoping to find you, all right, so I can put you out of my life."

"I've been out of your life since I left you for Hunter."

"True. You picked him and his lifestyle, and I need to end this charade of a marriage legally. But right now, you're blocking the door. We will discuss this later. Now, move."

She stared at him for a long moment, then lifted her chin in defiance, turned, and walked away.

Caleb frowned. He didn't have time for this. He headed to the meeting area. The posse consisted of himself, two special deputies, and fifteen local volunteers. The men were lined up in front of the hotel, horseback and ready to ride. Caleb left Shorty behind to protect the citizens of Juniper.

He wanted to hear from the men before starting out —

know their thoughts, feelings, hunches, and gripes. They could be tracking outlaws for days, weeks, and if there was discord, Caleb wanted to take care of it now—before riding off.

"We'll be heading southeast. Any suggestions or objections? If so, now's the time to speak up!"

Nobody made a sound.

Then Caleb said, "Let's ride!"

———

Caleb and his posse rode six days straight. Later, at a watering hole in South Texas, a snake bit one of the horses throwing the rider. Juan was pitched off, breaking his leg.

Caleb doctored him as best he could, but it wasn't enough. Juan needed a doctor, meaning they needed to find a rancher or a farmer willing to take Juan in and nurse him back to health before they could move on. The delay caused a knot in Caleb's plan to capture the outlaws. At last, they found a farmer willing to help, and they rode out.

The next day Caleb ran into Willis, a sheriff he knew.

"A gang of outlaws robbed a bank in Creek City," Sheriff Willis explained. "The rotten bunch ran right through town here followed by a posse from Creek City." He shook his head. "I don't know who they are, but I saw the outlaws and the Creek City posse turned south toward Mexico." He pointed to a well-traveled road nearby. "That road takes you straight to Gulf County on the Mexican border."

Caleb swallowed. *Gulf County? That's near the ranch where Daisy lived.*

———

Caleb heard gunshots on the outskirts of a town in Gulf County —a lot of them. He reined his bay mare to a slow stop just inside the city limit. The other riders did the same.

The town looked deserted. He didn't see a soul. The town-folk were likely inside behind locked doors. Riderless horses with saddles wondered outside a wooden building. A poster marked Gulf County Bank caught his attention. Bullet holes marred its windows as well as the windows of some of the shops nearby.

The posse moved closer. Caleb squinted at the main street of town. He saw cowboys, lawmen with pistols, in the shadows between the buildings. Someone was perched on the roof of the hotel across the street from the bank, rifle in hand and ready to fire. Caleb didn't think they needed his cowboys to finish the job. But he couldn't ride away until he knew for sure. From the looks of things, if any outlaws remained inside that bank, they were probably wounded or dead.

All at once a tall man in boots and a white hat came out of the bank holding a girl in his arms—a girl that looked like— Daisy. Her limp body hung down like she was—dead. Her golden hair nearly brushed the ground. Caleb dismounted and walked toward her. He had to know. He had to see the girl.

Somehow, the tall man must have known Caleb was harmless. He didn't try to stop him. Caleb went right up them, but he tensed when he saw the girl up close because blood covered the front of Daisy's blue dress.

"She was caught in the crossfire. All the outlaws are dead," the tall man said. "Do you know her?"

"Yes. Yes I do. She is—was an old friend. Where are you taking her?"

"To that church down the street there."

"That's probably best. I'll follow you. I want to pay for her burial before I leave." *It's the least I can do.*

Caleb tried to swallow but something must have been lodged in his throat as well as his heart. He didn't love Daisy anymore, hadn't in years. He'd wanted her out of his life. But he hadn't wanted her to die. She made her choice, and she died alongside Hunter Grimes, in the shootout.

His quest was over. He could return to Juniper now and resign as sheriff.

———

Caleb returned to his office in Juniper.

"I'm sure glad you and the posse are back, Sheriff. We missed you. Sorry you weren't able to catch them outlaws in time. But I'm glad we are done with them," Shorty said. "Oh, and I have some bad news to tell ya."

"Let's hear it."

"Miss Lucy, Mrs. Brant, and the little girl disappeared, the same day your posse rode out."

Caleb tensed. "Disappeared?"

Shorty nodded. "Well yeah, but later, we learned they left on the stage—caught a train back to Colorado."

"Thanks for telling me, Shorty."

Caleb tossed his hat on the rack by the door. Then he slumped down onto the chair behind his desk. *I didn't even get to tell Lucy good-bye.* He tried to ignore the pain of disappointment, now hammering inside his heart. He also wanted to ignore the stack of letters on his desk. *I'll have to make another trip to Colorado now—as soon as possible.*

He'd been away from his job a lot. Even if he planned to quit, he had things to do. As the sheriff, Caleb was obligated to do what he was hired to do—including correspondence. Now that the Grimes gang was gone, he could wrap up loose ends and resign to become a full-time rancher.

"Heading for the café for some lunch now," Shorty called from the front door of the jailhouse. "Be back soon as I can."

"Take all the time you need." Caleb glanced back to the letters, studying the stack again.

A small package lay at the bottom of the stack. *Who would be sending me a package? It's not my birthday or anything.* He removed the stack of letters and slide out the package.

There was no return address. Yet he felt it was important. He ripped into the package. Strange, there was a small book inside. A New Testament. He couldn't be sure, but it looked like the little book he'd left for Lucy when he first arrived in Colorado. A letter flutter out as he lifted the book. He opened the letter and began reading.

Dear Sheriff Caldwell,

I am sure you heard by now that Bethy, Mrs. Brant, and I are back in Colorado. Thanks for all your help. I really appreciate it. But I will always wonder why you never told me you were married.

I hope you finally find your wife. Hutch Fletcher told me her name was Daisy. I'm returning your New Testament. I think you might need it more than I do.

I pray the Scriptures found in the Bible will help you. They sure helped me, and don't forget to forgive. In Matthew chapter 6, verses 14-15, the Bible says, "For if you forgive men their trespasses, your Father in Heaven will also forgive you. But if ye forgive not their trespasses, neither will your Father forgive your trespasses."

Sincerely,

Miss Lucy Gordan

Lucy! Caleb was shattered. *Am I too late?*

Daisy had left Caleb for another man, causing him to lose his faith. But, since he'd met Lucy ... now what?

He reached for the *New Testament. Maybe it isn't too late to forgive—forgive Daisy.* Maybe it was time to read the Word of God—find out what the Bible actually said.

11

One month later.

L ucy sat on the front lawn of the boardinghouse where her mother lived now.

Bethy was jumping rope in the grass beside her. A white envelope and a folded sheet of paper lay on Lucy's lap. She gazed down at the letter one more time. It was from Mrs. Martha Montemayor, Sheriff Caldwell's mother. Lucy had it memorized but intended to read it again.

Dear Miss Lucy Gordan,

My husband and I thank you for allowing us to purchase your land. A copy of the deed has already been sent to you. We send this letter to you with love and news.

Caleb is no longer sheriff of Juniper County. He turned in his badge, so we bought his land here too. Caleb regrets not declaring his feelings for you sooner, but he couldn't because he was married. But his wife, Daisy, was killed recently in the crossfire during a bank robbery. The shootout killed Hunter Grimes and all the other outlaws.

Caleb told me to tell you he is on his way to Colorado, whether you want to see him or not.

"Does God answer prayer?" Bethy asked, interrupting her reading.

"Yes. Yes He does." Bethy had stopped jumping rope, and Lucy hadn't even noticed. She put the letter back in the envelope. "Bethy, why did you ask me that question?"

"I learned in church school this week that God answers prayer. Is that really, *really* true?"

"Yes, it's true! It's in the Bible. You can read it for yourself."

"Guess it means I need to repent, Cousin Lucy, because I hate somebody. I hate Sheriff Caldwell for being married and making you cry like he did."

"We're not supposed to hate, Bethy. We must repent of our sins, bless our enemies, and forgive those who have harmed us, if we want God to forgive us of our sins."

"Did you forgive Sheriff Caldwell?" Bethy asked.

Lucy smiled. "Yes, Bethy, yes I did. But I want you to go inside now to my mother's room and do your homework. Mrs. Brant should be arriving soon to help with your arithmetic assignment."

"All right, Cousin Lucy, I'll go. See you later."

"Yes," she said as Bethy walked away. "See you later."

Lucy caught sight of a rider on a bay horse galloping toward her. She couldn't see the man from that distance. Nevertheless, she prayed he was Caleb. Could it be him?

It *was* Caleb. She got to her feet. Was she dreaming, or was

God answering another of her prayers? Lucy started running—racing toward Caleb.

He rode right up to her. Instead of getting off his horse and greeting her as she would have expected, he reached down and grabbed her, sweeping her up onto the saddle—like those fairy tales Bethy was always reading.

"There isn't time for long speeches, Lucy." He turned her around in the saddle facing him and smiled. "Explanations can come later. I just want you to know I love you and want to marry you." Then he kissed her.

She was so surprised and downright thrilled, she almost fell off the horse. But he grabbed her—just in time.

"Are you all right?" he asked.

"I'm fine. Now!"

"Good. So, where were we?"

"You just said you loved me and ... and wanted to marry me."

"I'm doing this all wrong." He scratched his head. "I should have apologized, first, for not telling you about Daisy as soon as we met. I have a lot of explaining to do." He glanced over at the boardinghouse. "Let's find us a private spot when we can talk. The folks in that boardinghouse could be watching us." He loped his horse around to the back of the two-story building, through the thick brush behind it, and onto the pasture beyond. "Let's walk the horse for a while. I explain better when my boots are on solid ground."

He dismounted. Then he helped her down from his horse. "Now—."

"You don't have to explain anything. Your mother told me everything I need to know in a letter she sent after you left Juniper."

"Did she tell you I'm reading the New Testament now, and that I forgave Daisy?"

"Yes! It's an answer to prayer."

"It is? And did she tell you I love you?"

"She did. And Caleb, I love you too."

"You do?" He looked surprised.

"Of course, I do."

"Then you'll marry me?"

"Yes—a thousand times yes."

His tender grin warmed her heart. "Let me tie up my horse, and we'll sit down under the shade of that there tree." He pointed to the biggest tree in the clearing. "Then I'm going to kiss the daylights out of you."

She giggled. "And then what?"

"We're going to find a preacher. Do you know of one who lives around here?"

"As a matter of fact, I do." She pointed in the direction of the boardinghouse.

Later, they would go inside the boardinghouse and talk with the preacher. But now was the time for kisses, joy, and a love that would last a lifetime—and then some.

The End

ABOUT THE AUTHOR

I am a wife, a mother of three sons, a grandmother, and the daughter and granddaughter of ranch managers, real Texas cowboys. I spent part of my growing up years on a 60,000-acre cattle ranch in South Texas where *When the Cowboy Rides Away* is set. I know cowboys, and many of my ranch scenes were written from first-hand experience. A popular country song warns mamas not to let their babies grow up to be cowboys, but all three of our sons did just that.

THE
MEDDLESOME
MAVERICK

KATHLEEN L. MAHER

Scrivenings
PRESS
Quench your thirst for story.
www.ScriveningsPress.com

With delightful characters, clever dialogue, and a fun ranch setting, award-winning author Kathleen L. Maher delivers a satisfying story that will keep readers turning the pages to find out what happens with headstrong tomboy Sadie and the new cowboy who brings with him a Stetson full of secrets.

— CARRIE FANCETT PAGELS, MAGGIE AWARD WINNING ECPA BESTSELLING AUTHOR OF *MY HEART BELONGS ON MACKINAC ISLAND*

1

Jefferson County Nebraska
Spring 1891

"**T**sk. *Tsk*. Your Da will be bellowing, for sure and for certain."

Sadie leaned forward on one of the kitchen's long benches and tied the leather chaps over her pantlegs. One leg done, she paused to throw a scowl over her shoulder at Widow Garrity. The ranch's beloved cook would be a candidate for sainthood if she weren't such a fussbudget.

"Pa hollers at his mules now and then. So what?"

"No, Miss Sassafras," the widow said. "He'll be throwing fits about you! You know good and well, no *lady* wears pants."

Sadie would chuckle at the woman's genuine shock at her riding apparel, but irritation clipped the impulse. She'd worn the same outfit every workday since she was eight, yet ten years later, the woman imposed the same conversation on her.

"Pa doesn't trifle over my riding gear. It's *you* who doesn't like it." A huff of laughter seeped out once she'd spoken her mind.

"So, you mean to gallivant about the ranch like a boy when a young lady should be catching a husband."

It wasn't a question, the way Cookie Garrity said it. It was an Irish lament, almost wailed the way the widow had *keened* at Mr. Garrity's wake. Sadie had never forgotten the sound, though it had been years ago, and because the widow resurrected the tone whenever she wished to employ extra drama to her lecture.

Sadie clenched her teeth. A twinge at her temple reminded her that if she didn't loosen her jaw, she'd get a headache. Those hushpuppies the cook had fried up sure looked good. She whisked a few off the platter and popped one in her mouth, chewing as she spoke. "Womenfolk ought to know how to take care of their own selves instead a puttin' all their hopes in a man. You of all people know that."

Widow Garrity's bluebonnet eyes grew wide, and her ample mouth grew small. She looked stricken.

"I'm sorry, Cookie. But you know I'm bound to speak my mind."

"That's another thing, Miss Sadie," the widow began with gusto, proving that her hurt was only feigned. "A young lady should refrain from expressing opinion ..."

Sadie took her leave as the widow's lecture waxed in both volume and pitch. She swung her brown braids behind her, sending them bouncing against the suede of her jacket as she marched from the grub hall. The morning air stirred with more than the scents of cinnamon and bacon. A tangerine sun stretched warm waves over the prairie's dips and slopes, and it looked to be a beautiful spring day ahead of her.

She relished the slanting rays on her face, not caring if it made her skin as bronzed as the hired men from south of the border, or the native folk who traded with her daddy over a chaw of tobacco. Her sun-kissed blush only made fodder for Widow Garrity, who never missed an opportunity to lecture her, even if it was only about her complexion.

Bounding around the end of the building, she nearly collided with a slim cowboy swinging a big black case. If she hadn't had the reflexes of a sidewinder, the man would have clobbered her with the thing. That would have left a nice bruise to add to Cookie's worries.

"Hey, pardner. Why don't you watch where you're going?"

The young man made a full stop and pulled up his big black murder weapon to his broad chest. "I beg your pardon, miss." He tipped his hat and flashed a grin, showing a brighter stretch of white than a full moon over the Platte River. Sadie's legs did a strange little wobble, and she broadened her stance.

"I'm Sadie Mitchell. Who might you be?"

He removed his hat and took a bow. "Pleased to meet you, Miss Sadie. I'm Boyd Hastings." He straightened and his gray eyes met hers. Something in them danced, almost as mesmerizing as the glint off a polished steel pistol. They sure were purty eyes, for a man.

She blinked, then remembered herself. "What ya got in that-there contraption? You aimin' to kill someone?" She gave him a crooked grin. Some folk needed assurance that she was teasing. She'd been told—by Widow Garrity—that she had a rough humor. *Too rough for a lady.*

He chuckled and plunked the case down with a thump, then set about unhinging a couple metal clasps. Presently he produced a stringed instrument and held it up as though it was the finest thing since Colt made his handy revolver.

"Nothin' like music by a campfire under the stars. A banjo can sure break the ice for a new buckaroo." He set the thing back in its case with a wink and then, giving a deferential nod, he punctuated his friendly explanation.

The spark of Sadie's curiosity had been kindled. "You must be our new bronc buster."

"That's me." He spun his hat in midair and caught it in a quick draw. With another dazzling grin he clapped it back on his sandy-haired head.

That grin and twin dimples on his smooth-shaven cheeks brought a twitter to her tummy. She rubbed the leather belt at her waist to make sure she'd cinched the buckle properly. Land sakes, why was she getting all soft and squishy around this cowboy? Just because he had a baby face and cut an image like some sculpted figure ...

"Well, it's been a pleasure to meet you, Babyface." She said with a teasing lilt to her tone. "Maybe I'll see ya 'round the campfire later. Right now, I got some steers to rustle."

"Babyface, eh?" Boyd gave her a sideways look and shook his head. "Well, I'm no greenhorn, in case you're wond'rin', Miss Sadie. Stick around for the show, and you'll see for yourself." A tug of humor lifted one side of his mouth into a lopsided grin.

"That sounds like a date." She shoved her Stetson down over her brow, hoping it hid any schoolgirl, starry-eyed look, and headed her way to the other side of the yard to the horse barn, his chuckles carrying back to her on the easterly breeze.

Ack! She wasn't the type of girl to flirt—she despised those who did. A girl ought to be more than a fancy face and practiced charm. Shoot, a cornstalk might be slid into a dress and posed to look fetching, but it was still a scarecrow with a head full of cornsilk and stuffing.

Roping a man won't help nothin'. Some of her friends had found out what catching a husband had cost them. Sadie shuddered. No, she'd rather catch cowpox than have her dreams scrubbed away in wash water with every dirty supper dish and diaper. No siree, marriage was not for her. No man, not even Baby-faced Boyd Hastings, would claim her hard-won independence.

"Hey, Miss Sadie. Which way to the bunkhouse?"

She hadn't gotten far. His voice stopped her, and she turned to look back at him.

He held up his banjo case with a sheepish shrug. "I'll need to set this somewhere safe before I start."

She laughed. "This way, Greenhorn." She swung her arm in a wide arc to compel him to follow.

The cowboys would have fun with this kid. Might as well show him what awaited if he didn't get his bearings straight, and right-quick. But she wouldn't exactly throw him to the wolves—just to Widow Garrity.

―――――

Boyd surveyed the building the girl had led him to with a squinting appraisal. "Hey, this doesn't look like the bunkhouse." He rested his banjo case on the top of his boot to avoid dirtying it in the dust.

"You're right, clever fox. It's where we eat. Come in and I'll introduce you to our cook."

The girl disappeared through the door and left him standing there. Grunting, he hefted his instrument and reluctantly followed. First impressions mattered. *Hope they don't think I'm the type of fellow who lingers around the waterhole all day.*

"Oh, you're back." The matron wiped her hands on her apron and set her face in a deep scowl.

He removed his hat, tempted to wave it at his face. He'd suddenly grown flushed, and it wasn't the heat from the kitchen. "I'm sorry, ma'am, I got turned around looking for the bunkhouse."

"Not you, sonny." The cook folded plump forearms over her bosom, and she shook her head in disapproval at the girl who stood between them. "Sadie and I were just conversing. I was telling her—"

"Watch this cowboy's banjo while he works today, Mrs. Garrity. If I know Teddy and Sven, they'll be pulling pranks on the new kid."

"What do I look like, a nanny? Saints alive, Sadie. Why should I do this for you when you won't listen to a word I say?"

"It's all right, ma'am," Boyd fiddled with his hat, really wanting to clap it back on his head and skedaddle from these women and their argument. "I best get to work."

"But Boyd, the *vaqueros* here have no common respect. They might destroy your nice ... whatchamadoodle."

"Banjo."

Mrs. Garrity heaved a sigh that filled her ample, though squat, frame. "Very well, I'll set it behind the flour bin. But you owe me, Sadie Mitchell. And don't go thinking I'll be forgetting."

"No, ma'am." Sadie shook her head in resignation. "Not with your memory." She murmured the last part so quietly that Boyd barely heard it.

If he wasn't mistaken, a twinkle of dread lit in those light brown eyes of hers. Whatever the matron expected for this favor, he would pay it, not Sadie. Would the cook force the girl to shuck bushels of corn? Or pluck a half-dozen chickens for dinner?

"I thank you kindly, ma'am. You be sure and let me know if you need wood for the fire, or water buckets carried from the well." He flashed his best grin at her, and the woman's face burst with color.

"Miss Sadie, if you want to keep this nice young man out of trouble, you show him around, you hear? Make sure the others know he's a friend of your father and that he's a *special friend* of yours."

Boyd's pride prickled. *As if I'd hide from the bunkhouse toughs behind a little tomboy.* He knew how to handle himself.

"Now here's an extra nibble for you to be on your way. I must see to my chores."

The woman shoved an apple into one of his hands while whisking the banjo case from his other.

Before he could thank Widow Garrity, Sadie took his arm and spun him toward the door. He tucked the apple into his shirt pocket and bit back the impulse to protest. Sure, they were only trying to be nice, but if he didn't put a halt to this, he'd be henpecked.

"Whoa there, little lady. I got it from here. Thank you kindly, but—"

"Don't look now but here comes Sven, Teddy and Miguel. Three prickly pears you don't want to step on. Follow my lead."

"I reckon I can handle—"

Sadie raised her voice over his, cutting him off. "I was just saying to my father how nice it would be to have real music around the campfire. And who knows? maybe a social. You're mighty generous with your talent, Mr. Hastings. Why, I'll bet these cowboys would be glad for a concert at the end of a hard work-week."

A swaggering *vaquero* broke from the trio and spit a stream of tobacco juice off to the side. "Who's your new friend, Sadie?"

"His name is Boyd," she replied. "Boyd, this is Miguel."

Miguel's dark brown eyes shone with a bit of mischief. Boyd clasped the man's hand in a firm greeting. *"Buenos Dias."*

A tall man with platinum blond hair poking out from

under his hat approached next, inhaling through a long nose. "Smells green, *ja?* Fresh off the turnip vagon." He gave the other cowboy a sidelong look and snickered.

Sadie put a hand on her hip. "Better than the rotten fish you rolled in, Sven."

The others hooted in laughter and clapped the Swede's back. Boyd stood back to take the man's measure.

The three cowboys took up positions around to his sides and behind him, but Boyd kept his stance loose like the time he'd been surrounded by coyotes out on the range. Neither afraid nor aggressive, he stood his ground.

The last man, a blunt-looking figure with a shape not unlike a big toe, swaggered closer, swiveling his no-necked head to the side. "You git hired on for your good looks, or are you gonna get to some real work, *Boyd?*"

Done sizing him up, the others fell back behind the *big toe* Sadie had called Teddy.

"You Ted McAllister? The foreman?" Boyd neither reached out a hand nor shifted his direct gaze.

"That's me. Boss man says you break horses. Let's see what you got."

Boyd reached out then with a sturdy grip and shook McAllister's hand with a pump he intended would not soon be forgotten. "Lead the way."

"I reckon I'll stick around for the show." Sadie almost skipped along, matching the long strides of the men with a double-quick step on her sprightly legs. She had the enthusiasm of a tag-along kid, and he wondered exactly how old she really was. Hers were not the legs of any child.

He blinked away the stray thought. Observations like that had gotten him tangled up with the wrong sort of young lady. Thank the Lord he had escaped, but the singe of fiery indignation still kindled upon every recollection of her.

"Hastings, we'll have you pick out a horse from the corral. We'll send him through the chute, and you'll have the round pen all to yourself."

"Just you and the horse, *ja*." The Swede hung his mouth in a grin that did not improve his long face any.

Boyd wiped his palms down his trouser seams and approached the pen of skittish horses. Some of them broke from the herd and pushed to the other side of the corral at his approach. Most hung back, except one large paint with a blue eye. The animal stood his ground and snorted, pawing the ground.

Boyd grinned. "Looks like you'll do right nicely, Ol' Blue Light."

Ted's toe-head bobbed in a nod and Miguel pulled the cord, lifting the lever to open the chute. The skewbald stallion charged through the opening and thundered into the round pen, claiming it with powerful strides, blowing and neighing with his head in the air.

Boyd's blood stirred. He climbed the five-foot barrier, and with one leap, landed square inside the enclosure. Arms loose at his sides, he faced the big stallion whose articulated muscles quivered with the tension of a cat about to pounce.

2

Sadie gulped a lungful of air as the half-wild creature faced off against the new buckaroo. She wasn't sure if she should feel excited or horrified. If this bronco buster didn't know what he was doing, he'd be the one busted in the exchange.

The stallion was blowing and snorting, and Sadie's stomach got a sour feeling. "Ted, you ought to put a stop to this."

Boyd made a sudden dart at the same time the stallion charged him, and with a pivot and a leap, he landed on the white-and-bay-spotted back. The rider had the agile reflexes of a winged creature. A thrill rose inside her, admiring his skill.

He stayed on the animal's back, his long legs wrapping around the horse's barrel, his fingers clutching white-and-red-streaked strands of mane. His form moved as one with the stallion's frantic leaps and twists, as though his connection through legs and hands made them of the same mind. He had skill, just like he'd promised.

After a succession of bucks with mid-air direction changes failed to unseat the bareback rider, the animal charged headlong toward the fence.

Sadie gasped. If Boyd thought to stay on, the animal would crush him like an empty tin can against the thick wooden beams. With one stride to spare, Boyd slid from the horse's back and landed on his feet. The stallion's momentum ended with a crash against the fence. The impact shook the perimeter. Sadie stepped back at the same time as the animal released an outraged trumpeting call.

"*Primera ronda*, Boyd Hastings." Miguel's tenor voice carried the announcement, lively with laughter.

Who would Miguel call as the winner of round two? Sadie clutched her hands together as if saying a prayer in anticipation.

The animal's dark eye grew wider, showing the whites surrounding the pupil. The horse was plumb loco. Rage filled its expression. Its nostrils flared, and then it charged again, looking sure to trample the cowboy where he stood.

Boyd shifted his weight, effectively skirting the horse's path with an inch to spare as the beast rushed past him. A flash caught her eye in the flurry of movement. The cowboy's wide grin, as broad as the Nebraska sky. He was enjoying this. A tingle rose over her, raising the hairs on her arms.

Goodness gracious, this was better than the county fair. She hooted a cheer and waved her hat like the folks who'd pay a premium to see the bull riders stay on for more than eight seconds. Boyd Hastings was rider, toreador, matador, and acrobat all in one.

The animal circled the pen, slowing half-way around, bobbing his head and sizing up the instigator of its humiliation. Boyd turned his shoulder to the animal. He walked along casually, looking completely comfortable in his own skin. A slick of sweat broke out on Sadie's forehead where the band of her hat pressed. She swiped it away on her rolled-up shirt sleeve and couldn't tear her eyes away from the new cowboy.

A flick of hooves preceded the sudden rush aimed directly at Boyd, and only a heartbeat separated a ton of horseflesh from inflicting a cracked spine or shattered leg. Boyd leapt at the rail boards, using his arms to swing his body up to the top. Somehow his boots found the top rail, and achieving balance, he launched himself back into the arena, and onto the animal's back.

Spinning, the horse went down sideways in a heap, raising a vortex of dust. Sadie climbed the rails in a desperate attempt to see.

"*No mas*," Miguel's call reached her ears. But Teddy didn't end the match yet.

Sadie's heart thrummed in her throat. Scuffling rose from the cloud of battle and low utterances escaped the melee, indistinguishable as real words. Then the white front legs of the pinto emerged, rearing, pawing the air. He broke into a run, leaving the cloud behind. And there Boyd sat, clinging onto the animal's back, goading him onward as though they had the whole prairie stretched out before them.

They ran together like a driven gale, the horse's instinctual reliance on speed perhaps its only hope to save him from the *diablo* on his back. The sheer swiftness, with the horse whipping around the very edges of the circular enclosure, was breathtaking. All else faded except this amazing horse and rider conflict. Or was it a partnership?

A gust from their passing blew her hair back. Still clinging to the fence, Sadie blinked. Her fingernails had dug into the wooden rails, and she had to pull them back. She clambered down and stood in the patchy sod as the horse and rider rounded again in a slower pass, then circled slower still. A thrill swept through her that none of the other riders had ever inspired.

On the fourth pass the animal seemed to be responding to Boyd's voice and physical commands. It was clear who was in charge.

Boyd slid off in front of the foreman and let the stallion continue. Suddenly the direction changed, and the animal turned toward him with bared teeth.

"Look out!" Sadie warned.

Boyd stepped toward the charging stud, his arms raised in a menacing wave, and the horse veered away. The cowboy then walked alongside the fence again, a slow, steady gait, his head facing forward. To Sadie's utter amazement, the animal joined up with him stride for stride, matching the cowboy's pace with quiet calm. The horse drew nearer, and nearer again until Boyd could almost reach out and touch him.

Sadie could hardly believe her eyes. This loco, dominant stallion who had scared everyone else away, now followed the new hire around the ring like a puppy.

"He makes medicine, this music man." A familiar low voice rumbled behind her. She turned in recognition of her friend Two Sparrows. "The horse hears his music. Feels the rhythm inside of him."

Sadie smiled at the simple beauty of Two Sparrows' description, and the small miracle of a wild horse walking beside this mystery man. A music man with medicine. Maybe she heard his music too.

———

Slow clapping from the fence brought Boyd's gaze around to search for its source. The girl dressed in chaps applauded his approach to the gate, and she had a companion with her. A wiry young man with the coppery complexion of one the plains Indian tribes. His long black hair blew around his face and shoulders, concealing his expression.

Boyd grinned and slowed to a halt. The stallion walked up behind him and bumped him hard in the shoulder. Boyd ignored the animal, and it sniffed him, blowing a breath that pushed the brim of his hat.

"Did you like the show?" he dipped his chin to look the little lady in her eyes. They were the color of coffee-and-cream, the way he liked his morning brew. And they brimmed with warmth.

"Show's not over yet, Babyface," the girl replied with a giggle.

That's when he felt it. The horse grabbed his Stetson in its teeth and lifted the hat from his head.

"Ah, a jokester." A light chuckle rumbled in his chest, making a similar sound to the horse's nicker.

"I'll take that back, now." Boyd reached up and the horse swung its head in an evasive move, chomping down on the crown with a flattening bite. "Oh, no you didn't."

The three *caballeros* at the other side of the fence broke out in fits of laughter, and Boyd had to admit, it was pretty funny. Except, the hat had been a gift from his cousin Jake, back in Juniper, Texas. A going away gift when Boyd had left. He'd told his family he wished to pursue his dream of being a professional musician. If only that were the whole truth.

Now, the hat and his ambitions felt a mite flattened. And the stallion had a gleam in its eye that called his bluff. He shook his head and raised his arms. If that had been a lawman standing a few paces away instead of a horse, he would be surrendering. But in this instance, his raised arms meant to deliver a warning. The animal lifted its tail and trotted to the other side of the pen, waving his hat in its teeth like a banner at an Independence Day parade.

"How you gonna get your hat back, *el charro*?"

"I ain't figured that out yet, Miguel," Boyd shrugged with a grin.

"Offer him a fair shake."

The voice had come from Sadie's companion.

"A trade?" Boyd turned to face him. "Sure. Let's offer him *your* hat instead."

Sadie chortled. "Not what Sparrow meant. What about that apple Cookie gave you?"

"Good trade, music man." Sadie's friend smiled.

Boyd nodded. "Let's see if the horse thinks so."

He pulled the round fruit from his embroidered shirt pocket and held it up as though inspecting it. Hitching his hip and leaning against the fence, he crossed one leg over the other, striking a casual pose. Finally, Boyd lifted the apple to his mouth and sank his teeth into it. The bite made a loud crunch, and the sweet juice trickled down his chin.

The horse made a low rumble and turned its head, giving him the side-glance with its blue eye.

"You want some of this?" Boyd wiped his shirtsleeve across his chin. "It'll cost you."

Sven guffawed. "He's talkin' to a dumb beast."

Sadie tossed a reply over her shoulder. "That dumb beast probably understands English better'n you do."

Two Sparrows' face broadened in a wide grin, but Boyd hid the smirk that sprang up. That girl sure had a sassy tongue.

Chewing his bite of apple, he bided his time, and sure

enough, the animal's shifting gaze turned into sniffing the air, and then a slow, lumbering gait in his direction.

The stud looked almost penitent, hanging his head low, holding the stolen hat out before him. He stopped two paces in front of Boyd and dropped the Stetson to the ground, sniffing for his reward.

"Not so easy, Blue. Pick it up."

"Are you serious?" Miguel groaned. "You better take it while you can, *amigo.*"

Boyd brought the fruit almost to his mouth again, sparing an inch before he made contact, apple to teeth. The horse took another step toward him, extending its long neck, reaching out with a lipping action for the tasty prize.

"Back up. I want my hat." He raised his arms again and leaned toward the animal. "Back up, I said."

Light-stepping hooves danced sideways, respecting his space. Boyd scooped his hat from the dirt, slapped it against his thigh, and placed the half-eaten apple in the crown. He held it up and let the horse take the fruit.

"Good trade, Blue." Boyd managed to touch the animal's cheek before it swung its head and trotted away, chomping down the reward between crushing molars.

It was time to make an exit. Boyd shuffled to the gate that Two Sparrows held and slipped through the narrow opening.

"*¡Olé!*" Miguel joined them and pumped his arm, clapping Boyd's shoulder with his other hand. "How did you do that?"

"Whatever I did, I'll have to keep doing it until it sticks." Boyd shrugged off the praise with unassuming laughter.

Truth was, the physicality of horse breaking—and the shattering of an animal's will—left both horse and rider damaged. He had learned certain tricks from watching old timers along the way. Herd creatures naturally desired the company of others. Perhaps their instincts drove them to seek safety in numbers. Drawing on the animal's instincts took most of the struggle out of the thing.

McAllister sauntered over, the tall Swede flanking him.

"Fancy." The foreman hooked his thumbs into his belt and rocked back on his bootheels. "You fixin' to audition for a pony show? If I went in and tried to ride that animal, what do you think would happen?"

"You'd get busted off and given a swift kick for your trouble, is what." Sadie's matter-of-fact delivery cracked the tension. Snorts of laughter rose from Two Sparrows and Miguel. Even Sven's slow chuckling joined theirs.

The foreman's hairline reddened, turning his forehead into a big sore toenail. He slapped the fence rail with the flat of his meaty palm. "I want results, not a show. Get this horse ready to ride, or you'll be looking for a new situation."

Boyd stood tall, his chin lifted and his gaze steady. "He'll be ready, and sooner than it would take to half-starve and beat him into submission, the way some do it."

McAllister glared at Sven who continued to chuckle.

"Sorry boss," the taller man yammered.

"Let's go. We got those calves to brand."

"*Ja,* boss."

Miguel followed, tossing a light punch to Boyd's shoulder as he passed. "*¡Bravo!* I'd wager that's somethin' even Teddy's never seen before."

"Thanks."

The sassy tomgirl lingered with her Indian companion until the others distanced out of earshot. "Best be on guard with Teddy." Her gaze followed them, then turned to Boyd. "He's meaner'n a rabid coon."

"He doesn't like new ways." Two Sparrows spoke in a low, respectful voice. "Even when new ways are better."

A deep breath filled Boyd's lungs as these last two parted company.

If he got off on the wrong foot, it could spell sure trouble.

He mopped the sweat from his brow and set his jaw, turning back to the horse waiting for him in the paddock. *I'm done running away. I've got to make this work.*

3

Sadie's lingering thoughts about the new buckaroo drifted until they flitted away on the breeze. Walking alongside her Omaha friend she slackened her pace to match his slowing strides as they neared the calf pen, where the other three ranch hands had arrived ahead of them.

"Think he'll last around here, Miss Sadie?" His question probed her hidden thoughts and seemed to retrieve a piece of her mind.

"Hope so. The last few hires sure proved disappointing." She shuddered, recalling how one had been a wobble-jawed coffee boiler, always braggin' and boastin' but never around when there was real work to do. Then, the most recent one, a friendly young man, had been a thief. Or so Teddy McAllister had told the boss.

"Boyd Hastings seems to know what he's doing so far."

"With the horses, or with Ted?" If the foreman didn't like you, he'd find a reason to sack you. Unless someone with more influence took a shine to you first.

Two Sparrows shrugged. "He'll need to know how to handle both."

"Well, I have an idea how to help."

Her companion tilted his head to the side, his shoulder shrugging the colorful quills and beadwork strung in loops over his brown calico shirt. "So, you're going all out for this one?"

"I've a mind to."

"The season is right." He glanced up at the wild flowering vine climbing a near post, as bees populated the blossoms.

"Whattaya mean, Sparr'a?" She narrowed her gaze in a formidable squint, daring him to tease her.

"The time is right for you to build a nest like the birds and gather sweet nectar like the bees."

"Ugh." Sadie shook her head. "Bad enough Widow Garrity's been pressuring me. Now you?"

"The cook speaks truth."

She fisted her right hand. "If you weren't my best friend, I'd clobber you."

His eyes crinkled in humor. "Pairing up is the way of all creatures."

"What about you? I don't see you chasing any young squaws."

"Don't you worry about me, Miss Sadie." He gazed off in the distance, his eyes still merry and yet ... A hint of determination firmed his jawline "There's bound to be a certain someone out there preparing her garden for me."

"Good. I hope she isn't the jealous type." Sadie strode toward the gate where the garrulous chatter of Miguel, Sven, and Teddy saturated the sultry air. Giving a disgusted look, she nudged Two Sparrows with her shoulder, provoking his reaction. "I sure wouldn't want to work this ranch without you nearby. How else could I tolerate those oafs?"

He returned her frown with a grin. "I won't let any pretty birds come between us, Miss Sadie."

"Well, since you put it that way, I'd like your help with something. I need to convince Mrs. Garrity that I'm lovestruck so she'll leave me alone. And I don't aim to take her prescriptions for what's proper and what ain't. Catch my meaning?"

"What do you want from me?"

His umber eyes bored into hers, switching the lighthearted tone of their conversation to concern.

"Oh, relax. I don't plan to get all girly and kiss no one. I just want her to be convinced that me and the new buckaroo are a pair."

He shook his head. "Count me out, Miss Sadie. That would be lying."

"Not entirely. I want Boyd to stick around, and if we have a couple of pow-wows while Mrs. Garrity's watching, it might give her the impression she's already hoping to see."

"That's deceit."

She huffed. "Aw, Sparr'a, you're such a straight arrow. Listen, she's the one always pushing her ideas on me. Can't I plant one little idea on her for once? Hmmm?"

He pushed his arm straight toward her and splayed his hand. She stopped in her tracks.

"I'll help. But only by listening to what you say. I'll stand there and listen. But I won't agree or disagree. Those are my terms."

She clasped his outstretched hand and shook. "You've got a treaty, chief."

"Not funny, Miss Sadie." He lifted one eyebrow and gave a look of censure.

"Sorry. I don't mean to say the wrong thing. It just always seems to come out."

Two Sparrows shook his head and folded his arms across his chest. "Best we put our hands to work, now."

"I know. I'm a'comin'."

The open area in front of the barn milled with activity. Ranch hands came and went with tethered calves, and the air reeked of smoke and fear. The little ones bellowed, and in the distance, their mothers stomped and kicked fence posts and rails, calling for their young.

Sadie hated branding day. But she understood its importance. In the open range, identity and belonging could be sorted out without conflict by a simple mark. Rustlers could be prosecuted based on this recognized evidence of ownership. And claims were easily settled. It was a necessary bit of cruelty, and there was no other way around it. So, she clenched her teeth, hardened her soft inclinations, and strode up to the head of the enclosure to help hold the next calf. She would rather be the one closest to the animal in its moment of terror and pain, to sooth it with her soft voice and stroke the shag between its horn buds. Let Teddy and Miguel do the other parts.

Sven stoked the fire and thrust the branding iron into the coals as Sadie slipped into place at the head of a burly beef calf. The whites of the animal's eyes flashed as he tried to shift his head to look behind him, but the bars of his enclosure held him fast from turning. He stretched his neck, pointing his nose upward, and released an angry cry. Sadie's scratches under his chin and her soothing chatter seemed to do nothing to distract.

Sven brought the glowing hot instrument to the animal's flank, and the hiss of searing hide filled her ears. She steeled herself against the creature's bellows of pain, and placed her fingers on the latch, poised to release the calf into the holding pen where the other branded cattle were gathered. A salve of lanolin was applied to cover the burn so that flies would not infect the open sore. Then she tripped the latch to release him.

As soon as the metal clamp sprang loose, the calf bucked and twisted, smashing into the board on which she perched. Her boot slipped, and her leg dropped down into the tight enclosure just as the animal bolted forward.

A popping sound erupted near the curve of her chaps where she straddled the fence. A stroke of fiery pain shuddered up from her knee all the way to her hip. She sucked in a breath and released a scream.

Two Sparrows and Miguel were at her side in a moment.

Stars spun in her dim vision, but she resisted a swoon. "Is it broken?"

Miguel had her by the shoulders and Sparrow helped to lift her out of the tight enclosure.

"Something's busted, *Senorita*."

Sadie leaned on the two men's shoulders as her good foot touched the ground. She didn't trust her own strength to hold her up yet, but instead examined her leg all the way to the toe of her boot. Pressure throbbed down her thigh with every pulse, but the ache broke apart below the knee. Her leg was firm and straight. She touched her boot to the ground and waited for the snap, but none came.

"The fence." Two Sparrows pointed to the perch where she'd slipped. The rail had been split, taking the impact instead of her thigh bone when the two-hundred pound animal pitched a row.

"You're lucky, Miss Sadie. That would'a grounded you all season." Miguel lingered, bracing her beneath the shoulder to provide ballast. "Should we fetch your Pa, to be sure?"

"No. I don't need him telling me I can't work. Get me over to that trough and I'll sit for a spell."

Sparrow and Miguel practically carried her, her feet barely touching the ground as they moved across the yard.

"I ain't payin' you to flirt with the teamster's daughter," Teddy bellowed at them from the calf pen.

Sadie's stomach shrank. These ranch hands were like brothers to her, and the suggestion of anything else left her feeling queasy. "Why does Teddy have to be so crass?"

Miguel released her once she was settled on the corner of the trough. "I can run and get Mrs. Garrity."

"Heavens, no! Not that incurable worrywart."

"What about Boyd?" Sparrow gave her a wink and nod. Their conversation earlier apparently inspired the suggestion.

"Sure! He could bring me up to the house for the missus to patch me up. That way you and Miguel won't miss any more work."

Sparrow trotted off in the direction of the horse corral. Sadie thanked Miguel. "I appreciate your help. Now scoot before Teddy gets ornery. I'm good for now."

"All right Miss Sadie. But don't try to walk on it without help. I'll be right over there."

She saluted the way her Pa did occasionally, a holdover gesture from his war days. As she waited, the unyielding wood dug into the back of her leg, and the pain radiated through her hip again. She *hoped* she hadn't broken anything.

She braced her arms along the sides of the trough and lifted, slowly attempting to shift her position. A sharp jolt in her side stole her breath, and her arm strength faltered. Her balance tilted, and she slipped backward.

————

Splash!

Boyd arrived to the sight of Sadie tipping—boots up—into the water trough.

"Whoa, Nellie!" He broke into a run over the few remaining strides and reached in to fish the sputtering little lady out. He drew her up with both arms, cradling her wriggling, dripping form. Her cheeks glowed crimson, and her breaths came out in huffs of indignation.

She slapped at her sodden jacket with a growl. "Of all the confounded, silly, blamed ..."

"Careful, Miss Sadie. You're on the verge of cussing." He couldn't help a chuckle.

"Very funny, Boyd." Her brown eyes held a spark of fire. But not the kind that threatened to burn him. It lit something inside him for the briefest of seconds until he doused it like a candle dunked under water.

He cleared his throat, sobering. "You'd best get yourself a new kit." He started to carry her toward the ranch house.

"I can walk."

"I'm not convinced." He appraised her soaked hair, sodden jacket, and the dripping chaps snugging her form all the way down to her dry boots. "I won't have you falling into any more trouble on my watch."

Her pert mouth twisted into a scowl and she looked away, up the path. "Can you pass by the kitchen? I'll send Mrs. Garrity to fetch my duds."

"The cook? You sure she has the time?"

"She'll *make* the time."

Boyd set his jaw. Something about the cook's demeanor with this young lady concerned him. Sadie was a handful. That, he could already surmise, but he hoped the older lady wasn't unkind or churlish. Didn't Sadie have a mother to look after such matters?

He suppressed the inclination to shrug. "As you wish."

The aroma of cornbread, bacon, and simmering beans wafted out of the open window before he reached the double doors of the grub hall. As he stepped through, the Irish matron bustled toward him, her strawberry blonde bun frazzled beneath her mob cap, and her blue eyes a wild blaze.

"What's this? What's happened to my Sadie-girl?"

"I'm fine, Cookie. Mr. Hastings saved me from a mishap."

Boyd couldn't formulate words as fast as these two women, so he didn't attempt to provide clarification.

"You're wet as a river rat. What kind of shenanigans is this?"

Boyd shifted his stance, looking about for a way to restore the young lady to her feet and he to his proper place. He'd never held a dripping wet woman in someone's kitchen before, and he was quite at a loss.

"Set her over here, then." Mrs. Garrity cleared a bench away from the long central mess hall table.

"It's most likely not broken," Sadie's voice held a slight tremor, and she clutched him a bit tighter, gazing down her right side before he set her down.

"Broken? Begorrah! What have you gotten about, you whirligig in men's pants?" The matron stood with her arms out as though she would catch the girl up.

"I got tangled with a calf in the branding chute. But Mr. Hastings was kind enough to come to my rescue."

Boyd still couldn't manage to connect tongue to vocal cords, and he would have scratched his head in perplexity if both of his arms weren't so dubiously occupied.

"Well, it's a lucky girl you are to have such a fine lad lookin' out for you. And I'll not be forgetting the kindness, Mr. Hastings. I'll be telling her Da of your chivalry, to be sure."

He couldn't be sure, but he thought he spied a smirk break

out on Sadie's lips, but it was gone so quickly, he may have imagined it.

"Youch!" she yelped. Then she closed her eyes and exhaled a cleansing breath, as though to order calm over her expression and tone. "If you'd be so kind, do be careful as you lower me to the seat. My leg hurts something fierce."

"No, no!" The cook waved her arms in a manner like protecting food from flies. "That won't do a'tall. We must set her somewhere more comfortable." She bustled to the back of the mess hall and opened a door, beckoning him to follow. Down a short hallway, she opened another door leading to a private, modestly appointed room. Presumably the cook's quarters.

"Set her down on the bed. I'll fetch the boss's wife. She sees to all the sick and injured here."

"But what should I—" Boyd couldn't even finish his thought before the woman charged out the door and away. Was he really to be left alone with this young lady, her clothes clinging to her, her arms clutched around her form, sitting on a bed with wide, soft eyes blinking up at him?

The walls closed in on him, and his pulse thrummed against his throat. The humiliation of accusations and pointing fingers spun in his memory until a choking sensation caught his breath. He took a step backward, and then another.

Don't let one bad apple spoil the barrel. His rational reflections did nothing to stop the stampede in his head. Not all women were wicked, cunning schemers. Sadie wasn't the flirt that Matilda had been. And this straightforward cowgirl seemed incapable of the lies and insinuations Matilda had foisted upon him, spoiling his credibility as a serious-minded Christian man. What shame it must have brought on his mother. Even though his family surely knew the lie for what it was, it was still a serious accusation. Sadie would probably never conceive of making up a tale about this unguarded, innocent moment. But now, as then, how could he defend himself if he lingered in such a compromising situation, alone with a girl? She had already unfastened half of her chaps to remove the dripping wet gear so as not to soil Mrs. Garrity's bedlinens.

"I'll leave you in privacy," Boyd stammered, and bolted out the door.

4

W*hat in tarnation?*

Sadie crossed her arms over her bosom and snorted. What would get into a man to scamper away from a girl like a skeer'd rabbit?

She struggled out of the leather coveralls, freeing her throbbing leg enough to get a better look. The denim fabric of her pants had split at the outer seam. That accounted for the jolt she had felt. Another fraction of an inch and her leg would have been fileted like tenderloin. She heaved a relieved sigh. There was a scratch, but no blood. It would bruise, but it wasn't busted.

The clip of mincing steps approached from the outer hallway. Widow Garrity had made quick work of fetching help. A slower stride, covering one to the cook's two or three, jangled alongside with the unique tone of silver spurs. She knew the identity of the man before he turned into the room.

"I told you, Sadie, your Da would be fit to be tied. Well, here he is. What have you got to say for yourself, getting yourself half-killed today working alongside the men?"

The long, lanky shadow matched up to the figure of her father once he rounded the doorway. He reached a hand and placed it on the widow's shoulder. "Thank you, Mrs. Garrity. I'll take it from here."

The widow's chin jutted, being preempted from speaking her full mind, but she kept her silence, for which Sadie silently thanked Providence.

Pa's eyes leveled at her, and a muscle in his throat tightened then relaxed. He was as intimidating in his silence as he ever was in his hollering. His customary bawling out had earned him a reputation almost legendary. He'd had the fiercest temper north of Texas, that is, until Ma died, and he swore to be a reformed man so he would see Ma again in heaven. Ever since, he neither drank, nor cussed, nor brawled. And it was a rarity he even raised his voice. But those piercing eyes caught everything, even, it would seem, her beating heart beneath her skin. His gaze was so commanding that his mules dared not balk, with or without his use of an occasional rebuke.

Sadie's mouth went dry.

"Young lady, this incident has taken me from my work." He lifted an old, dented pocket watch from his vest and gave it a cursory glance. "I like to keep a tight schedule, as you well know."

"Yes, Papa."

"I've asked kind Mrs. Garrity to look after you in my absence, and yet, you seem to defy her good sense and advice."

That stung. Since when did he take the cook's side of things? Surely, he thought the woman's harping as petty as Sadie did. But nothing about his demeanor suggested he thought his daughter's situation either trivial or funny. She swallowed.

"Can I trust that you will take Mrs. Garrity's instructions from here on out as though they were from me?"

"Oh, but Pa—"

"No, 'but Pa's.' Sadie, you aren't a little girl anymore. You're a young lady. And you have to start acting like one."

She looked away, not out of defiance, but out of humiliation. She didn't want anyone to see the burning red rims of her eyes, nor the well of emotion that brimmed to the brink of spilling. Her own Pa, consigning her to this awful fate of ... of prissy girlhood. She wanted to stomp her boot and spit. But that would make her fool tears escape.

"Yes, sir," she murmured through a constricted throat.

"I can't hear you, gal. Speak up."

Anger dashed through her veins and gave her enough fire to find her voice. "Yes, sir. And did Mrs. Idle-talk also tell you about how the new hire helped me? He's a nice man, Pa, so don't let Teddy chase him away like the others."

Her father shifted his stance and consulted the widow with inquiring gaze.

"Oh, he's a fine young man, that one. Polite as they come. Carried our Sadie girl because she was complainin' of pain."

"Well, where is he now? I'd like to thank him."

Mrs. Garrity shrugged and turned about as though she had dropped him on the floor like one of her ladles. "He was here a minute ago."

"Never mind. I'll find him. And Sadie, do as the cook says. Rest that leg today. Maybe you should help in the kitchen. Mrs. Garrity can set you up on a soft chair and you can chop vegetables, or some such."

Pa turned on his bootheel and bounded down the hallway. Sadie tempered the vexation burning in her chest, threatening to singe her good sense. She might still be able to charm the cook and get her way, if she didn't let her tongue fly.

"My leg is getting better by the minute. Must'a bumped it. I'll head up to the house and get some dry duds, and I'll be able to get back to work in the flick of a cow's tail."

"Oh no, you don't, young lady. You heard what your Da said. He wants you resting, and I'll see to it that you do. Now I have a lovely frock right here that should be a good fit for you. You let me take those wet clothes, and I'll see that they get a proper scrubbin'."

The matron produced a gingham dress that she just happened to have hanging on a hook on the back of her door. Suspicion twisted Sadie's innards. It was a dozen sizes too small for the cook and looked to be brand new. The calculating woman had no doubt waited for such a moment to foist this on her.

"You'll look lovely in this peach color. Brings out the blush in your cheeks, dearie."

Sadie took the garment, chewing on the sharp words that she held in check. The widow won this round, but the next time, Sadie would not be so easily hoodwinked and outmaneuvered.

———

Sweaty palms and a fast heartbeat were no way to meet a new challenge. Boyd had to order his distracted wits into line. His cousins Jake and Caleb came to mind, and the recollection of their cool, steady ways brought about the same effect on him. Caleb was a lawman back in Juniper, Texas, and a great confidante. Jake's unflappable nature and ability to find the sunny side of things always put matters into perspective. He sure missed their company and wisdom. A pang of homesickness stirred in his belly.

Restored to balance at the comforting thoughts of kin,

Boyd faced down the mare snorting and pawing in the corral, and he summoned the needed gumption. He swung the rope he'd used to drive the animal around the circular enclosure and stepped into the game of earning the animal's trust like he'd done a few times already that morning with others.

The jingle of spurs and the sense of being watched gave Boyd pause, and he turned to look over his shoulder. The moment he broke his concentration, the silver *grullo* mare switched direction and came at him in an all-fired hurry. Boyd dodged the snapping teeth, but the mare's shoulder knocked him sideways into the fence. He clambered up the rails and out of her reach so he could assess the distraction and the nature of the visit.

A tall, lanky man with a whip of graying hair trailing from his Stetson stood by the gate, taking his measure. Boyd hadn't met him, but by the process of elimination knew he was neither the boss, nor any of the cowboys.

"Howdy." Boyd scaled over the top rail and hopped down outside the pen. He loped around the perimeter to meet the man. "Boyd Hastings," he greeted as he held out his hand.

"Fletcher Mitchell," the man replied beneath a drooping gray mustache, and met his handshake. "Sadie's Pa."

A cold dart sent a shockwave through him, but the man's whiskers lifted in a smile, dispelling Boyd's apprehension. He was not in Juniper anymore. This was not Matilda's Pa gazing at him through the crosshairs of a shotgun.

"Pleasure to meet you, Mr. Mitchell."

"Call me Fletch. That's what folks round here call me. I'm the mule man. I run deliveries for the ranch and help train the horses in my spare time. I reckon we'll be working together off and on."

"Well, I'll look forward to those occasions. And since I've got your ear, would you be the one I find to post letters for me?

I got family back in Texas that's probably wondering how I'm settling in."

"Sure, I'd be happy to carry your letters to town when I go. So, how *are* you settling in, Boyd?"

"I hope I'm meeting expectations so far. Trying to keep my nose clean and focus on my work. Not looking for any distractions, sir."

"That's the answer of a smart young man." Fletch grinned again, but he seemed to hold back a thought as he lifted his Stetson and scratched his scalp. "I hope you'll pardon my daughter's free-spirited ways, son. Since her Ma passed, I haven't had the heart to crack down and force her to face the expectations of adulthood. I think she'd like to stay a girl the rest of her life, but it's getting past innocent child's play at her age. So, I don't want you to misunderstand her ways. She's a good girl."

"I understand your meaning, sir. I only had the intention of looking out for her like a brother, but I'll keep scarce if that would suit you better."

"No need to be a stranger, Boyd. She knows her boundaries when it comes right down to it. And you strike me as a Godfearin' young man. The cook tells me you play some music?"

"Thank you, sir. Yes, indeed, I brought my banjo with me."

"Do you know any camp meetin' church songs, son? I'd sure love to have a bit of that here on Sundays."

"I'd be proud to lead a few rounds of hymns and spirituals. Who's the preacher in these parts?"

"That would be me. Just a man who owes a mighty debt to the Lord's grace. I'd be obliged to have a song leader join our meetin's."

Boyd shifted his stance. "I'm obliged. Good to know there are devout folk here."

Fletch walked a pace back to where the mare picked at a clump of prairie grass at the fence. He reached in through the rails and touched her glossy silver neck. She didn't even flinch at his touch.

"I've watched this one out on the range for a year now. She's a beaut'. Proud and spirited like my Sadie. But with the right approach, I know she'll make a fitting companion to someone special. Glad to see Zephyr's in good hands."

"Yes, sir." Boyd climbed the rails again to return to business.

He hoped his face hadn't gone ashen in his embarrassment at the man's obvious insinuation. What a change of circumstances. From the threat of a shotgun wedding for which Boyd had no blame, to the invitation to take an interest in this man's daughter, Boyd was ready to swear women off completely. They were nothing but trouble. At least wild horses were straightforward about their intent to wreck you. They held no guile about it. The flick of a tail or the flattening of an ear gave a hint of what was on their mind and in their intentions. Women with their wiles on the other hand ... Boyd could never read them. He would have assumed a tomboy was safe, but Miss Sadie apparently had more going on under that little Stetson of hers than he would have figured.

As Boyd re-entered the arena, Fletch called his parting words. "Be careful of that McCallister. He's an ambitious one and holds no compunction about trampling anyone in his way."

5

Peach tart. That's what Sadie felt like in the frock Mrs. Garrity had given her, with its creamy white ruffles and blushing squares of gingham. The ridiculous bustle on her derrière was bad enough, but frivolous puffy sleeves added insult to injury. If any of the cowboys filing into the mess hall said a word about her dress, she'd throw a ladle of piping hot beans at them. Sitting on a cushioned chair all day peeling carrots had made her as cross as a tethered billy goat.

She thought to avoid eye contact when Two Sparrows looked her way, with the stunned Miguel at his side. Instead, she met them both with a glare warning them not to dare comment on her attire. Her fiery look shut their gaping mouths and sobered their amused grins right-quick. They bowed their heads and dropped their gazes in deference and shuffled through the food line with nary a peep.

Sadie thrust her chin up, wielding her serving spoon to heave a dollop of beans on the plate of each ranch hand that passed. Cowboys moseyed past, some with wide eyes, but they kept their traps shut. Wise on their account. The torrid air in the mess hall seemed to cool a few degrees once her humiliation eased to moderate discomfort with each stock handler that passed by. It was almost as if she wasn't a sight to see in this dolly-belle getup. But she knew better.

She huffed a relieved sigh and settled into her seat. That's when a snort resounded from the doorway and echoed through the hall, filling the expanse to its beams.

"Haw, haw, haw!" The most obnoxious laugh followed, which could only have been generated in the cavernous lungs and oversized beak of the tall Swede.

"Looks like Sadie finally figger'd out she's a girl!"

The room quieted and shuffling boots stilled. The slick serving spoon faltered in her grip and the portion of beans she had just lifted fell into the coffee mug of a nearby *vaquero*. All eyes fixed on the pointing, hooting figure of Sven, making a perfect spectacle of himself. And her.

"Lady Sadie, all gussied up." Sven doubled over with another guffaw.

Teddy slapped Sven upside his blonde head. The opportunity to reach what would otherwise be too tall for Ted's squat stature must have tempted the foreman beyond what he could resist.

Sven pulled up, cradling the back of his scalp. "Yow! I was only teasin'."

"Show the lady some respect or next time you'll get your jaw wired shut."

"*Ja*, boss." Sven said no more. But Sadie didn't miss the subtle muscle that worked in Sven's set jaw, nor the way his blue eyes iced over.

A chill cut through the sweaty discomfort in her suffocating dress for a split second. But it was gone the next when she dodged Teddy's gaze lifted her way. Not quickly enough. Something in his expression made her chagrin turn to something else entirely. A cinch in her gut sent a ripple of nausea through her. She had never suspected to see hunger light McCallister's narrow-set eyes. And it wasn't for Widow Garrity's cooking.

She shrugged it off with a shudder, hoping never to see that sight again.

The cook intervened, mercifully. "Save room for dessert, boys. I've got cobbler comin' once you finish your supper."

Mercy, woman. Don't say peach!

Sadie slipped from the stool, hoping to escape the widow's notice in the busyness of serving the meal. She aimed to check on the percolating coffee, but she didn't get far.

"Oomph!"

That pesky black case caught her in the chest, sending her tumbling back.

"Oh, Miss Sadie, I'm sorry!" Boyd spun back around to face her. "I didn't expect you'd spring up like a jackrabbit." He extended his free hand to steady her.

"Saints above, what are you doing out of your seat?" Cookie raised her hands in exasperation. "Do I have to tie you down like a roped calf?"

A deep rumbling chuckle resonated, and a wave of excitement swept over her, tingling the fine hairs on the back of her neck. She blinked up at the new cowboy's grinning face hovering over her. Boyd's laughter had an unsettling effect on her nerves. Too much like the low burble of a brook, or the warm pop of corn kernels over a covered skillet. It caused sensations that confused her. All pleasant, and yet, putting her on notice.

"What's so funny, Slim?" She folded her arms over the frilly flounces on her bodice.

That baby-faced grin with dazzling white teeth threatened to wreck her bravado. She was sore-tempted to return the smile. But instead, she bit the inside of her lip to ensure that her feigned indignation held.

He chuckled again. "Just the image of Widow Garrity throwing a lasso over you. I can practically see it in my mind's eye."

"Thunderation!" It was all she could manage to exclaim before giving in to laughter too. "You got a wild imagination, mister."

He leaned in and winked. "You best get back up on your perch before she makes good on her threat." Before Sadie could object, his free arm guided her and helped her settle back onto the seat.

"You gonna keep swingin' that black club around, or are you actually gonna take that thing out and play something on it?"

———

Sadie's invitation to share his music lit a spark in him. "What would you like to hear?"

A snorting breath behind him soured the air with a whiff of stale tobacco and bad manners. Boyd turned to find McCallister's stubby figure standing square up to his Adam's apple. The foreman's indignation pounded a staccato rhythm from the toe of his boot tapping the floor to his short fingers drumming over his folded forearms. "You planning on holdin' up the line, Hastings? I'd like a chance to eat whiles the food's still hot."

Sadie huffed at the man's bluster. "Simmer down. You got enough hot air to keep the kettle a'boil."

Boyd bit back the grin that the girl's sass inspired. "After you, Ted." He swept his hand in invitation for the man to cut in line in front of him.

"Suit yerself," McCallister replied. He and Sven pushed ahead to the grub. "But quit your loitering. Sadie's got better things to do, and so do you."

"*Ja*, the boss don't like fraternizing with the *jungfru*."

Sadie balled her hands into fists. "Who d'y think you're calling a young frou-frou?"

Widow Garrity returned, bearing a sheet pan of bubbling cobbler. "Sadie, push that empty platter aside. I'll have you dish this out when the men come back with clean plates." The cook lifted her head to address the room. "That means you men best hurry up and eat if you expect to get some of this while it's still warm."

The other workers moved on to take their food to the long table, and Boyd stood before Sadie. She fixed his plate with a heap of beans and cornbread and then she looked from one side to the other. No one else was close by. "Why'd you skedaddle before, when I was waitin' on Cookie to come back?"

Now he looked from side to side. He didn't want anyone to hear his business. "I didn't think it was appropriate for me to be there."

"What, you afraid of me?" A hint of a grin hung on her pixie-like face.

He didn't want to answer that with a lie, and say he wasn't scared. Fact was, he was afraid of what others might think. And he had good reason. And maybe he was afraid of losing his good sense to the beguiling charms of a woman. One misunderstanding was hard enough to shake, but two would start to form a pattern. "I'm concerned with keeping my job and staying out of trouble. I don't want anyone to get the wrong idea ..." Honesty was the best policy. He hoped she understood.

"Whew! Well, that's a relief. I didn't want you to get the

wrong notions, neither." She leaned in as though she were handing him a new fork. "Can you keep a secret?"

Inwardly he winced. He ought not to be listening to any secrets from any girl. He took a step away, but she reeled him back in with a few slices of bacon for his plate. "Men ain't nothin' but trouble in alligator boots, 'cept as friends. But Cookie won't let up on me about catchin' a beau, and now I got my Pa expectin' me to listen to her. Let's let 'em think I'm sweet on ya, only you and I'll know better. Deal?"

Boyd's jaw dropped. Before he could overcome surprise at her bold proposition, a distraction mercifully stirred.

"Mr. Hastings." A rich baritone voice called over the general clamor of the grub hall. It was the ranch owner, the man who'd hired him that morning. The older, bow-legged man made his brisk way over to Boyd with his hand outstretched in friendliness. "I wanted to see how you're getting on so far. Miguel tells me you're a natural with the horses. Glad to hear it!"

"Thank you, sir."

"And Fletch Mitchell told me you helped his daughter Sadie here this morning. Fletch is an old friend. We go back to Chickamauga together. We both served under General John Bell Hood. Another fine Texan. I'm much obliged to you for looking out for the girl. Much obliged." He pumped Boyd's hand with an unexpectedly strong grip. Boyd had to set his plate down, so it wouldn't spill.

"You let me know if you need anything, you hear? Pleased to have you with us. Looking forward to your banjo pickin' and singin' too."

"Yes, sir, Mr. Marsh." Boyd barely formed the reply before the man's energetic steps bounded away.

He shook his head to regain equilibrium after the man's

rapid-fire encounter. He wasn't normally slow to the draw, but the day's whirlwind had caught his tongue.

"You'd be smart to sit with Two Sparrows." Sadie's voice interrupted his thoughts. "He's the only one knows our secret. He's safe. The others ... they're not so trustworthy."

"Our secret?" He blinked.

She raised her hands, palms up, as though she were exasperated with him. "That I'm not sweet on you. Remember? Just go along with it."

The widow returned to clear away the empty serving dishes and gave him a big smile. "If you keep on lingering around Sadie, there's going to be idle chatter about you two." She patted him on the shoulder, and his reflexive flinch caused him to knock a piece of bacon off his plate.

"Oh, Sadie-girl, be sure and fetch him some more. And save him some of the whipped cream for his cobbler."

"But you told me that's for Mr. and Mrs. Marsh."

"I have enough to spare for a certain, special young man." The matron winked.

Boyd's cheeks flamed. What kind of predicament had he landed himself in? And what would he tell his cousins when they wrote to ask him how he was settling in? They'd never believe this.

6

D*ear Caleb,*

*I didn't want to wait too long before I sent you a quick letter.
I'm settling in at a new ranch in Nebraska, not far from
Lincoln. It's a fine place with over 200 head of cattle. The
owner is a fair man, and I've been hired on to break horses.*

*How are things in Juniper? Please tell your ma and
stepdaddy I send my regards. I heard about Daisy. Hard to
believe after all these years you found her but she's gone.
Sending up a prayer that you got some sort of closure.*

*Speaking of closure, has Matilda Bostwick's situation
improved any? Has the real daddy stepped forward to claim
responsibility? I still have conflicting feelings about leaving,
even though I never even kissed her. I recognize the wisdom
of your advice to leave. Makes me feel like a coward, though,
knowing what idle folks think, and probably makes me look
guilty. But stepping in for a man who needs to find his*

courage was no life for me, and living a lie would only cause problems for her and the child in the long run. I hope you're right, that the truth will set me free. Right now, it feels like I'm balancing on a razor's edge, waiting for vindication.

I'll be writing to Jacob in a few days or so. It's still hard for me to call him Jake as he requests. Maybe Aunt Becky's way of using his proper Christian name ruined him to the sound of it, since she always hollered it when he was in trouble. Uncle James's patience still makes me chuckle in admiration.

Before I sign off, there's a situation that's got me a bit off my stride. Ever seen a sheep so turned around by a droving dog that it doesn't know its next step? Well, in this scenario, I'm the sheep and the dog is a relentless tomboy who won't leave me be. I'm not sure whether to be grateful for the welcome or if I should run for the hills.

Pray for your poor cousin! Haha. I'll send word again soon. Maybe by then I'll hear of some music venue where my talents can go to good use.

Love,
Boyd

No sooner had he tucked the letter into an envelope and secured it in his banjo case than the rustle of footsteps rounded the corner toward his quiet getaway. The sun reached low behind him from the western horizon, causing the east side of the bunkhouse to deepen in shadow. A breeze stirred, fanning his face with a welcoming evening cool.

Boyd lifted his gaze to greet the Plains Indian man who had

sat at the dinner table with him. Neither had conversed much but both had dug into their food with the gusto of laboring men. Two Sparrows, or Sparr'a as Sadie called him, lifted a hand in a wave. Boyd waved back.

"The others are curious about your music, friend. Come. There is room for you by the fire and a pot of coffee boiling." Sparrow reached to help lift him to his feet.

Boyd grasped his hand and stood. "Obliged."

The aroma of mesquite and juniper smoke wafted down the path from a clearing behind the bunkhouse. Swallows swooped to catch bugs in the waning light, and the crackle of the fire rose in Boyd's ears before its orange light appeared beyond the brush.

Low chatter around the campfire quieted, and one of the cowboys announced their arrival. "*El hombre de la música.*"

Boyd's grin widened, and Sparrow clapped him on the back. "The music man brings his medicine."

Miguel stood and gestured for Boyd to take his seat. "Set yourself down on that overturned barrel, and I'll fetch you some hot coffee, amigo."

"*Gracias*, Miguel." Boyd tipped his hat in gratitude.

"*De nada.*"

Boyd perused the clusters of ranch hands relaxing along split log benches or sitting in the hardpacked dirt, stretched out by the curling flames. A few nodded his way and resumed their conversations as he took up his seat. Taking his banjo from its case, he hoisted it to his lap and slipped the strap around his shoulder. He plucked at a few strings and adjusted the tuning pegs against his internal notion of what they ought to sound like, what folks called "perfect pitch." Satisfied at last, he cradled one hand along the neck, placing his fingers on certain frets.

A motif lit his imagination and took over his fingertips.

Translated through strings, it resonated through the instrument's round drumhead until a slow tune flowed out on the evening air. Subtle at first, the notes intermingled with the low sputter of the flames. A few of the men nearby shifted their postures, leaned in, and listened.

Boyd found his confidence, and his strumming and picking grew a bit livelier. Toes began to tap. Tired bodies awakened to the invigorating sound and hands then started to clap. Stomping ensued, and then dancing. Before long, his playing seemed a resounding success.

At the conclusion of the first ditty, Miguel returned, parting the crowd that had gathered around Boyd. He set down a tin mug in front of him. "I didn't forget, *Señor* Boyd. *Un café.*"

"Thanks, friend."

"I hope I fixed it the way you like it."

Boyd slid his finger through the mug handle and lifted it, swirling its contents around to observe the dark rich color lighten with the cream added into it. He smiled and drew it near to inhale the wonderful aroma. "Looks perfect. Thanks again."

His lips barely made contact with the hot, brimming, metal rim, when a feminine screech pierced the air.

"*Don't!*"

Boyd sucked in a breath, pulling a measure of the sip he was about to take into his windpipe. He stood, sputtering, and his coffee spilled, dripping down his shirt and leaving brown splatters across the pale skin of his banjo.

Sadie's unexpected appearance emerged from the twilight beyond the circle of the bonfire. She ran to him and thumped him on the back. "Oh, crimany! I'm too late."

She went in for a second swing at the space between his shoulder blades when he twisted and caught her arm. "What

—" he cleared his throat between coughs, "are you—doing, woman?"

"Hot pepper seeds!" She grabbed the mug still dangling from his fingers and dumped out the liquid. Then she held it up, inspecting the dregs of ground coffee at the bottom. Squinting, she looked up at him. Earnest concern poured through her wincing eyes, studying him as though expecting him to turn into a convulsing, wild creature.

He smacked his lips and rolled his tongue around the inside of his mouth, waiting for the fire of spice to sear his mouth. He blinked a few times. Nothing happened. Only the taste of coffee. Good brew too.

He frowned. "What made you think there'd be hot peppers in my cup?"

Sadie poured out the last of the dregs onto the ground in the light of the fire and kicked them with the toe of her boot, spreading them around. She released a sigh. "Guess I was wrong. I thought Miguel and the boys were playin' a prank like they always do."

He clenched his teeth. The stain on the front of his instrument might not come out, thanks to her meddlesome antics.

"Sadie," Boyd expelled a slow breath to temper his rising pulse. He ordered his voice to come out low and calm, though he wanted to bawl her out for the damage to his banjo. "I don't think it's going to work out between you and me."

Her eyes widened, and a grin quirked one side of her mouth. Then her lips stretched to a full smile, showing teeth as white as starlight. Sweet, infectious laughter bubbled out. "You cain't get rid of me that easy, pardner."

She flicked her hair behind her, the girlish braids of that morning now let loose in thick brown waves. They tumbled against bare skin where the dress's off-the-shoulder neckline revealed a milky complexion where the sun hadn't touched.

Nothing had touched those vulnerable, womanly places. The unbidden thought startled him, and he stepped away from her again.

She cocked her head to the side, and another smile teased at her pert mouth. She was all curiosity and wonder, as though she'd just discovered her power to catch a man's notice but didn't know what to make of it.

The girl was as unpracticed at feminine wiles as he was uncomfortable with his own susceptibility to them. A slow glint of recognition sparkled in her eye. She fluttered her lashes in a silly attempt at flirtation, and he shook his head and grinned at her innocence. She was back to being the kid sister, the one he could relax his guard around.

"Has Miguel really pulled a stunt like that?" He leaned toward her in conspiratorial conference. "Peppering up a fella's coffee?"

Her brows peaked and she raised her middle and index fingers. "Twice now."

As they shared a chuckle, Miguel approached them. "Don't believe her, *señor*. She's loco." A twinkle in his eye suggested mischief.

"Acknowledge the corn, ya liar." Sadie shook a finger at him. "That one kid was barely able to breathe, and the other talked with a slur for a week, his tongue was so sore."

"I'm *inocente*." The *vaquero* lifted his hands, palms up.

"It's all fun and games until someone gets hurt." Her scowl wrinkled her forehead and crinkled her nose. "You galoots better leave your mitts off'a this'un. Or you'll answer to my Pa."

"You've got it all wrong, *señorita*. Me and Boyd, we're

friends." He braced his arm around Boyd's shoulder. "*Hermanos.*"

The banjo strap slipped, and Boyd caught it with his free hand. "Well, brother, how about another cup of coffee, and a rag to clean my banjo?"

———

Sadie's gaze followed Miguel as he slipped away to where the coffee percolated. His silhouette reflected orange and yellow tones of the fire against the deeply shadowed background fading into night.

She shuffled her boots, taking a step closer to Boyd. "I'd sleep with one eye open 'round that one."

Boyd shook his bandana from his back pocket, spit on it, and rubbed at the coffee stains. "You'd best not be sleeping around him, or any of these men."

"What's that supposed to mean?" A flash of fire inside her shot the blood rushing to her head, and almost blinded her. Shaking it off, she shoved him with both hands. "You're pretty free with your tongue for a greenhorn."

"Sorry, Sadie. That didn't come out right. I'm concerned, is all. You're prettier than you realize, and naïve to boot. A dangerous combination."

She propped a hand on her hip and slackened one side of her stance. "I thought you said it wasn't working out between you and me." A teasing laugh broke through her words. "Sure sounds like a compliment to me."

"Well, take it as you will. It's the truth. And if you were my sister ..."

"Or your sweetheart ..." she winked at him, drawing his exasperation with teasing delight.

"Sadie, you should listen to Widow Garrity and keep yourself scarce around these cowpokes." His strong hand encompassed her wrist, holding her still, and he bent down from his height to meet her at her eye level. Swirls of tingling sensation emanated from where he touched her arm. Half-way to her brain, they sprouted wings and flew through the hollow cavity of her ribcage. Thrill, anger, delight, terror, and anticipation crowded around her heart, sending her senses reeling.

"Is this man bothering you, Sadie?" McCallister forced himself between them, ending the sizzling encounter.

She scowled, ready to cut Teddy down to size. But Boyd stepped back. He picked up his banjo case and placed the instrument inside it, clipping its fasteners shut.

"Mind your own business, Teddy. You're not my boss." She leveled him with a stern warning look. He didn't fear many folks in these parts, but he did have a healthy respect for her daddy. She'd wield that weapon if she needed to.

"Ain't ya gonna play some more, Boyd?" She shouldered past Teddy and caught the handle of his case with one hand.

"Maybe tomorrow. I'm bushed." He pushed his hair back from his forehead, and it set in a side part, high in the middle, showing off his handsome features.

"Suit yerself, then. See you at breakfast." She lifted his case and handed it to him, and their hands brushed. That cascade of sparks ignited back through her.

"You feel that?" She shook out her arm. Like lightening was about to strike.

He shook his head, backing up. "I'll walk you to your cabin, Miss Sadie. Is Sparrow still around?"

"He's sitting by the barn over yonder."

"I'll go get him, and we'll see you home."

His strides took him outside the circle of light, but a flutter on the ground caught her attention. A white sheet of paper wavered and tumbled toward the flame. Teddy stooped and picked it up. He held it up to his eyelevel, turning it toward the glow of the campfire. Sadie's neck craned to see what it was, and caught a glimpse of Teddy's face, twisted into a grimace. A sensation of heaviness, like the dropping pressure before a storm, hit her gut.

"Here, Sadie. Your new friend dropped this. I'm sure he'll want it back." Ted set it in her hand, sliding his palm across hers.

It reminded her of the time a snake had slithered over her bare foot, and she recoiled from his touch. At least he had the decency to give it back, whatever it was. She folded the paper and headed in the direction Boyd and Sparrow waited, eager to get away from the foreman.

7

Sadie's rapid approach alerted Boyd's protective instincts. He'd just asked Sparrow to join him in walking her home for the night. Now she made a beeline back to him. Had McCallister bothered her?

He met her halfway.

"Teddy said you dropped this." She called to him, still a few paces away, and a piece of paper fluttered up and down in her hand with each of her bouncy strides.

He took it and recognized it instantly—the letter he'd written to his cousin. But how did McCallister get a hold of it? And where was the addressed envelope? He'd tucked them both safely inside his case.

The jolt took him off his purpose, and it must have showed, judging by her wary look.

"Teddy grabbed it before it flew into the fire. It was blowing across the clearing. He saw it was yours and told me to give it to you."

"He did, did he?" Boyd didn't even try to hide the scowl on his face as he secured the letter into his vest pocket.

She shrugged and lifted her hands, palms up. "At least he saved it from burning up."

Or maybe he'd use it to blow Boyd's secret wide open.

"Well, I'll be sure to thank him." He forced his features into a neutral expression like the card sharks who never revealed their hands. "But first, your stop. Are you staying with Widow Garrity?"

She slapped her skirt at her knee and ripped a snort of laughter. "Oh, Jiminy. I'd rather sleep in the hoosegow!"

He didn't share that laugh. Jail would be exactly where he'd be sleeping if Ted McCallister exploited the information in that letter. He might have been there already if his cousin Caleb hadn't given him the heads-up on the girl's father's plans, to pin her wanton behavior on a naïve young man like him. Caleb had been incensed. And his Ma and Pa must be worrying themselves into gray hair over it all. Anger and shame would spoil his mood if he didn't direct his thoughts elsewhere and right quick.

"Babyface, I asked if'n you were gonna keep walking to the state line, or if you were gonna head back to the bunkhouse. I'm home now."

He halted at the cabin where she stood, not far from the main house, and on the other side of the compound from the men's quarters. She'd be safe here. "Oh, sorry. I'll say goodnight, then."

"See ya tomorrow, cowboy."

He tipped his hat. "Night, Sadie. Thanks for showing me around today."

Sparrow said his goodbyes and followed Boyd a pace behind. He jogged a step to catch up, once Sadie was safely inside her cabin.

"Your thoughts run like a slow, deep water. You're tangled on something beneath the surface."

Boyd turned aside to meet the perceptive gaze that studied him. Sadie had chosen her friendship with this young man wisely. He clapped his hat down over his head, having removed it in the presence of the lady. "Reckon I'll be all right, Lord willin' and the creek don't rise."

"Don't fear the flood, Boyd Hastings. The downpour uncovers what's buried."

Boyd contemplating Sparrow's meaning. The words sounded familiar.

For there is nothing covered, that shall not be revealed: neither hid that shall not be known.

The scripture rippled over him in waves of both dread and promise. If the truth were revealed, he would be vindicated.

"Thanks, Sparrow. I think I'll check on the horses before I turn in."

As they parted ways, a dark swell of doubt sank his buoying spirits. More likely, the version of the story that made him look guilty would be uncovered. Could he hope that this accusation would not be his ruination, and that a fresh start waited around the corner for him? If he were to find the right opportunity playing music for a show, it would put him in the spotlight. He'd risk notoriety. It was safer to skirt the shadows and drift outside of notice. But his stubborn heart refused to give in to playing it safe. Self-preservation was no prize if it meant sacrificing the things that made life worth living.

Like passion.

Boyd shook his head to dislodge the unbidden thought. Where had that come from? Passion was the last thing he should be thinking about. "Sorry Lord. *The heart is deceitful above all things, and desperately wicked.*"

He approached the corral where the small herd of unbroken horses stood in a cluster, their shapes outlined by a silvery thread of moonlight. He drew up to the fence and waited for the blue-eyed paint stallion to approach, which he did.

Boyd reached into his pocket to retrieve a few pieces of carrot he'd smuggled from the kitchen earlier. He held them out and the animal lipped them from his open hand.

Passion isn't a dirty word, Boyd. It's the mark of my calling on your life.

The familiar impressions on his heart that he had come to recognize as the counsel of the Lord sometimes emerged so clearly, they were almost like a voice. Like now. He bowed his head, humbled in the Presence.

"I may never make it to the big show, playin' for crowds, and that's all right, Lord. I'll lead worship for Fletch's Sunday meetings. And if that's all you have for me, it's enough."

A scuffle of a boot behind him turned him around. In the shadow, he couldn't discern who was there.

———

At last, alone in her cabin, Sadie couldn't wait to scramble out of the poufy-sleeved gingham nightmare. She unclasped the buttons that she could reach at the back of her collar and swiftly wriggled out from under the dress. The voluminous skirts proved a worthy adversary. She took up several arms-full and gathered yard after yard in her struggle to manage the encompassing wrappings. She hadn't figured undressing was this challenging. She'd be quicker untangling herself from that barbed *devil's rope* that surrounded the ranch.

Lifting the skirts over her head, Sadie discovered she hadn't unfastened enough of the ties holding the form-fitting bodice in place. She tugged, twisted and pulled, but it held fast, while the weight of the fabric pressed down on her neck, forcing her to bend at the waist to relieve the burden. And now she couldn't reach the ties.

"Oh, you *wretched* garment!" She twisted and pulled again. Nothing budged. "Blazes! I'm trapped!"

What a sight she must have made, with nothing on but her pantaloons from the waist down, and wrestling with a great fabric beast.

"Lord, have mercy," she prayed. "This is all Cookie's doing."

She stumbled against her bedpost and fell face-down on her quilted coverlet. Flopping like a fish in a net, she wriggled until she teetered on the edge of the bed and then dropped to the floor with a cabin-shaking thud.

A pop and the inimitable sound of cloth tearing brought sweet music to her ears and allowed her to take the first deep breath she'd drawn in hours. She pushed the rest of the textile entrapment off of her and sat, gasping, relishing her triumph.

"Yoo-hoo! Sadie, are you in here?" A gentle rapping at the door rushed in on her ears.

Sadie heaped the remains of the widow's garment into a ball, and pressing it to her bosom, she marched to the door in her skivvies.

"I'm returning your dress." She opened the door, flung the garment at the bewildered woman, and quickly shut herself in again.

The Irish tongue lashing, though muted through the door, still packed a wallop. Sadie stuck her fingers in her ears. Still somehow the phrase "I'll be telling your father about your appalling shenanigans" managed to penetrate through her sound blockade to deliver the righteous fear of God.

"Fiddlesticks." She flounced back to the entrance and opened it up again.

"*Begorrah!* You're practically naked, child! Get inside and be decent for once in your life." Cookie clutched her heart with her right hand, dragging the dress through the door with her left.

"You'll be the very death of me, Sadie Mitchell. This is not how to catch a husband. It's how you catch the devil."

Sadie folded her arms across the chemise's drawstrings at her chest and flopped into a chair. "What's the difference?"

"You're a sassy-tongued tart, and I've a good mind to take a buggy whip to ..."

Sadie's laughter diffused the scolding, and Widow Garrity lost her steam.

"Oh, my poor heart." Cookie patted her neckline, all drama as she sagged down onto the edge of Sadie's bed. "Can't you *try* to be the young lady that you are?"

"First of all, *you* just called me child. Second of all, my mother wore chaps and rode alongside Pa on the range." She pushed her bottom lip out for a second. "No one ever accused her of being unladylike."

"Your saint of a mother knew when to dress and act the part. She'd be appalled at what we've allowed you to get away with."

"My mother would be proud of me. She was fierce and independent, and ..."

"And she loved your Da. Don't be forgetting that." The widow's eyes flooded, and these weren't crocodile tears. Sadie would never question Cookie's love and loyalty to her mother. Even if the widow's gaze did seem to brighten when her Pa was near. Romance was silly enough without it getting downright ridiculous involving folks old enough to know better.

"Sadie, I'm taking this dress back with me to mend it. I'll be bringing others too. You're no child anymore. You're eighteen, now. Long past time you should be serious about your future. Now, that young man from Texas has fine manners. You could do a lot worse. And he's quite fair to look upon ..." Her blue eyes twinkled with mirth.

"Ugh!" The temptation to plug her ears again almost overtook Sadie, but she retorted. "I thought you only had eyes for my Pa."

"Oh, go on with you." Now it was the widow's turn to laugh. "You behave like a lady and make your mother smile down from heaven. You know, it'll be ten years next month she's been gone."

"You don't have to tell me." Sadie's chest felt like a cow had sat on it, and she relieved the heaviness with a long exhale. "I know."

"I've got a lovely frock for the sabbath for you. A bonny rose calico. Oh, you'll be a regular garden of loveliness!"

Sadie stifled a shudder. Gardens and loveliness were not in her dictionary. "How'm I supposed to ride and rope all tangled up in your rose calico lasso?"

Widow Garrity leveled her with her blue-bonnet eyes. "That's the point, Miss Priss. You're *not* supposed to. That's man's work."

Before Sadie could sputter a protest, the cook whisked the gingham dress away and retreated through the exit, shutting her in with her thoughts unspoken.

8

Boyd stepped toward the sound in the darkness. His muscles tensed, anticipating one of the pranks Sadie had alluded to.

"I thought I might find you here, Hastings."

Recognition coiled his defenses tighter. "Something wrong, McCallister?"

Ted emerged from the shadows and stepped into the moonlight. "You tell me. It's a real problem, what I read in your letter."

"Wait." Boyd thrust his hand out in front of him, palm out. "You read my private letter?" Pointing with his index finger, he pushed back the accusation. "That makes a problem for both of us."

For the first time, Boyd saw the man without his hat. Ted's hairline was receded, pallid under the silvery lunar glow. Creases where he furrowed his brow darkened. "You better watch yourself, Boyd. Last chiseler who came around didn't have half the reason for me to dislike him as you. And he didn't last a week."

"You don't know me to be judging me." Boyd bristled, finding it too easy all of a sudden to formulate what he really wanted to say.

"I know your kind, Hastings. Drifters. Shiftless. But you'd better keep your roving eyes in your head as far as Miss Sadie is concerned."

Boyd almost laughed at the accusation. He was no drifter, and he certainly wasn't shiftless. But did he have *roving eyes?* His rising temperature seared any humor with the temptation to retaliate. He throttled both inclinations with calm reasoning. He needed this job.

"I'll prove you wrong, McCallister."

"Boss!" Sven stumbled up to them in the dark, stepping across the moonlit path. His gangling limbs were animated with some sort of urgency. "A heifer got stuck in the barbed wire. She's cut up bad."

Ted took a step back from Boyd, from where he'd inched up on him almost nose to nose. He swung about to face the Swede. "She got a calf?"

"Due to drop any time, boss."

"Hastings, gather lanterns and the men and meet us up in the high pasture."

Concern replaced all animosity. "I'm on it."

"Bring rope and water buckets too."

Boyd set off immediately to the bunkhouse, praying under his breath all the way. Grateful for the interruption, he nonetheless chewed on the remnants of the confrontation. If the foreman thought to use the letter against him, he'd better dispose of it before he could.

Fletch Mitchell had promised to carry his mail. He could go try to hunt him down. But it would have to wait until the heifer was out of crisis.

Reaching the open door of the bunkhouse, he poked his

head in. "We got a situation in the top pasture. McCallister needs a few hands up there to help. There's a heifer caught up on the wire, due to calve. Bring water and lanterns. I'll grab the rope."

As he turned from the building, the low tone of Two Sparrows' voice met his ears. "Music man." The Omaha tribesman had stealth—Boyd hadn't even heard him approach. "What did Ted want?"

"You saw him?"

Sparrow nodded. "I watched from a distance to make sure he didn't ambush you."

"Thanks, friend." Boyd recalled seeing coils of rope hanging on the gate where the branding had been done earlier that day. He headed there and Sparrow stayed with him. "He somehow got ahold of a letter I was writing to my cousin back in Texas. Seems he's itchin' for a fight, to go and nose in someone's business."

"You didn't give him one."

Was the man asking or stating the obvious? "No, I didn't give him the satisfaction, but something tells me it won't matter much."

"The foreman could sack you, but he doesn't have more authority than the one who brought you here."

"You mean the ranch owner, Mr. Marsh?"

Sparrow stepped into Boyd's path. He stopped and Boyd almost collided with him. Sparrow squared his stance, his eyes like glittering coals in the dark. "There's a purpose bigger than Boyd Hastings that brought you here, *ikhága*. You make music, and the music makes medicine."

Boyd couldn't help twisting his mouth. *What in tarnation was that supposed to mean?* "All right." He shrugged. "Whatever you say."

Sparrow remained where he stood, so Boyd ducked around

him and resumed on his way to retrieve the rope. That kind of talk made him itch.

"You won't need that."

Boyd hefted the loops around his shoulder. "I was told to bring it."

"But you won't need it."

"We'll see." He heaved a loose coil over his arm and marched up the slope, following the flickering lanterns of the cowboys who had already started out to meet Ted and Sven.

As they approached the knoll where the men had gathered, the lowing of the cow rose in Boyd's ears. The sound was pitiful, and his heart moved at the pain and desperation of the tangled animal. Torches and lanterns raised above the site helped light the view. Her front leg had barbs piercing through her skin where the fence wire had been stepped over. The heifer lay immobile, trembling. A few men cut away wire where they could reach it while others held her in position.

Boyd set the ropes by the fence post and knelt down at the animal's head. The cow's eyes closed and opened. There, a tear glistened in the wavering light. He stroked the top knot between her ears, speaking and humming in low tones to calm her. At his touch, she lurched forward suddenly, and gathered her feet under her. Finally, the remaining strand of barbed wire came loose, and a cheer rose up. She stood, shakily, blinking, and Boyd stroked her head and continued his low little ditty near her flicking ear.

"How often at night when the heavens are bright
With the light from the glittering stars,
Have I stood here amazed and asked as I gazed
If their glory exceeds that of ours.
Home, home on the range ..."

"We need to get her down to the barn so we can stitch up those cuts." Ted directed with a pointed finger. "Slip the rope around her head and lead her while she's still on her feet."

Boyd reached for the rope and before he could grasp it, the little heifer strode with him, following him. Then out of the corner of his eye, the sight of Sparrow, his hands folded over his chest, stood, nodding at him and grinning. "Music man makes medicine."

Fletch Mitchell walked up on his left. "You have a real way with animals, Boyd. How did you come by your skills?"

He shrugged. Looking back at Sparrow, who was now laughing, he replied, "I guess it's a gift."

"Whatever it is, it sure comes in handy around here. Can you stay up and help me bring her calf tonight?"

"I'd be proud to, Mr. Mitchell."

"Call me Fletch, son."

Ted stood off to the side and let him pass, his jaw jutting sidewise and his scowl flickering in the lanternlight.

Gratitude flooded over Boyd. Whatever the source of this strange turn of events had been, it had given him an ally that even McCallister wouldn't challenge. And Fletch's invitation had helped him skirt his first night in the Dice House and any hazing they'd planned for him.

Thank God for small favors.

———

"Your Da will be wanting good strong coffee this morning, dearie."

Sadie yawned, half-hearing what Cookie had said. The persistent widow had woken her up even earlier than normal. Chided her about making herself presentable in these new duds. This day, Cookie had foisted a lemony yellow pleated work dress on her. Having to wear a skirt was bad enough but losing sleep to boot ... it set her teeth on edge.

"Strong coffee sounds good to me."

"Well then, missy, you'd best get a wiggle on and get it brewing. No one's going to do it for you." She flicked her hands up, clucking her tongue to shoo her forward to the kitchen.

"Ain't no cause to be mean, now," Sadie complained as they walked along together.

"A grown lady has no one to cook her meals and clean her house for her. You'd better get used to it."

She heaved a sigh as they strode through the door, and she trudged to the iron water pump, tin coffee pot in hand. "Where was Pa all last night?"

"Bringing a calf, so I hear." The widow's eyes beamed with affectionate light.

"Why was he needed for that?" Sadie topped the container with fresh water and returned to the cookstove. Her boots kept catching the hem of her gown, and she stumbled more than once. Her long sleeves, which flared at the shoulder and tapered to form-fitting wrists, chafed at her skin.

"The cow had trouble, I guess. Your Da sure has a soft spot for God's creatures ..." The widow shook her head and breathed out a soft, lilting laugh.

Yeah, Pa spends more time with his mules than with people since Ma died.

"Coffee's on." She blew at a strand of hair which dangled down from the middle of her forehead. She hadn't mastered pinning her hair up yet. Maybe she'd never grasp the art of such frivolous things.

Widow Garrity stood for a moment, her hand on her hip, her gaze examining Sadie up and down.

Oh, no.

"What, now?"

"You're growing up a fine young lady. Your Ma would be proud."

"I'm only doing this because you're making me." Sadie cut her eyes away, tamping down the lump in her throat at the mention of her ma. This time of the year always did it. And leave it to Cookie to take advantage of her one vulnerability.

"You look like her, you know."

"I look like her *more* in my regular clothes." Her bottom lip curled in petulance, and she had no intention of making a pretty face if the Queen of England suddenly appeared and demanded it.

"Oh, but you don't remember. She loved her pretty things. She had silks and embroidered linens, and—"

"China teacups, too, I suppose. That's nice. But when Pa went away on the trail, who do you suppose kept the horses, and the cows, and the farm going?"

"Your Ma, of course. She was of strong stock."

At least they could agree on that.

Boots scuffled at the entrance to the grub hall, and Sadie turned to see who their first patrons were.

"Well, look who the cat dragged in." She'd seen half-chewed mice looking better than the two sleep-walking figures who practically fell into their seats. Both Pa and Boyd could use her strong coffee, not to mention a shave. She had the sudden itch to rake her fingers over the stubble on Babyface's jaw. She smoothed her apron over the folds of her skirt instead.

"How's the cow and calf?"

"It's a girl," Pa replied. "But the heifer didn't make it."

A murky stirring in her belly brought up fresh tightness in her throat. The thought of senseless death was enough to make one sick.

Boyd lifted his gray eyes up to meet hers. Tiredness carved deep shadows beneath his long-lashed gaze. Puppy-dog eyes.

Sadness. She swallowed again, aware of the lump forming at her own throat.

"I'm sorry, fellas. I'm sure you gave it your best." She placed her hand on Pa's, and for good measure, let her other hand fall on Boyd's forearm. And blamed if those sparks and shoots didn't sizzle through her again. She whisked her hand away into her apron pocket and stepped away.

"Want griddle cakes with your brew?" She turned halfway back, getting their order.

"That sounds good, Sadie." Pa fiddled with his handkerchief and his pocketknife. Looked like he was cleaning something off, and she'd rather not know what.

"You, too, Babyface?" She couldn't help herself. Her grin gave way to playfulness.

The man's complexion burnished. His cheeks flushed beneath his tan, making him fairly glow. Was that embarrassment? Did cowboys blush? She breathed a little huff of laughter.

"It don't make us married if'n I fetch you breakfast. At least, not here in the grub hall like this."

"Sadie!" chorused both Pa and the widow with sonorous disapproval.

Then, Boyd laughed. It was the most wonderful, free sound. A deep, belly laugh. "You do beat all, Miss Sadie." The cowboy's eyes crinkled in mirth that warmed her from the previous stirrings of grief—over her ma, over the heifer ... over her fading independence. "Sure, I'd be obliged for some griddle cakes. Thank you kindly."

Maybe acting the part of the little lady had its perks after all. Sadie hurried to fetch the men their breakfast.

She had no sooner slid their plates and cups before them when it seemed the floodgates opened, and the rest of the workers hustled in. Cookie zipped around, juggling a coffee pot in one hand and a platter of biscuits in the other. The griddle was livid with spits and spatters of bacon and scrambled eggs. Sadie took over at the stove.

"Could it be the apron, *Señorita* Sadie?" Miguel tipped his sombrero. "Your smile is brighter this morning."

Though tense and alert for an untoward remark, she refrained from rolling her eyes. She knew the *vaquero* well enough to understand his intentions were friendly. "And good morning to you, too, Miguel."

"I'd marry her this minute if she cooks as good as she looks." Sven rubbed his hands together.

"She's not interested." Sadie replied with an impersonal pronoun, but the shiver down her spine was very personal.

Laughter rose and quickly sputtered out as Teddy swaggered his way into the line, cutting in front of several others. "Sadie, can I speak with you?"

"Now? I'm in the middle of helping Cookie."

"She can get along fine without you. Always managed in the past." Something brewed behind his eyes. Something dark and angry.

"Make it quick." She set the wooden spatula down at the edge of the cookstove and filed after him outside the building. A cool breeze drifted over the prairie and lifted the heavy air of the kitchen from her. But it did nothing to lift her annoyance at being interrupted from her work.

"Sadie, you've known me since we were kids. You know I wouldn't steer you wrong."

"Probably not. At least not intentionally."

"You didn't read that letter last night, did you?" It was an accusation, not a question.

"Of course not. It wasn't mine to read."

He had the nerve to huff at her. "Well, there was something in there that would have set you straight. If you knew the type of character the new hire's hiding behind that flashy grin and Texas charm, you wouldn't be giving him the time of day. He's—"

"He's what, McCallister?" The deep voice sent a chill up her spine. Sadie hadn't heard him approach.

"Pa!"

"Sadie, go on back and help Mrs. Garrity."

"Yes, sir." As she hastened to the kitchen, she cast a quick backward glance. Teddy had his head hung, his face ruddy and his thick fists clenched at his sides. Pa must have been bawling him out, but in that quiet, restrained way of his that Sadie found even more unnerving than his old angry rows.

Though in some way it was quite satisfying to see him get his comeuppance, she almost felt sorry for Teddy. Surely, he was only trying to warn her. Of what, though? She'd have to come out and ask Boyd later. She'd try to catch him alone, when he went to check on the new calf.

9

Boyd had devised a schedule with Fletch for the newborn calf to feed from a milk bladder every couple of hours. Meanwhile the search was on for a foster mother from among the herd. Orphans rarely survived, and the constant need of round the clock feedings posed a strain on the manpower. Boyd held the newborn against him, imparting his body warmth to stave off the unseasonable chill of the spring morning. The red-and-white calf suckled eagerly, almost butting the bag of warmed milk out of his hands.

"Hey, pardner. Mind if I take over?" Sadie popped her head over the stall half-door. "I used to help my Ma with the newborns."

"I'd be obliged for the help, Miss Sadie."

She slipped into the stall, thick with straw for the baby to bed down in. "Did you get your letter off to your folks back in Texas?"

His eyes remained on her, even as his hands worked to transfer the animal into her care. "Your Pa said he'd take it into town with him this morning. Already off and away."

"Good."

Why was she inquiring about the letter? Had she read it too? No, he saw the whole exchange. Ted handing it to her, and Sadie walking straight over. "What did McCallister say to you this morning?"

Her lashes did an involuntary flutter as she struggled to meet his gaze. This time it wasn't put on, that sweet, girlish affectation. But it was endearing.

"He said something about your character being in question." She narrowed one eye. "Now, Teddy's a lot of things. Bossy. Arrogant. But he's not a liar. Why would he say that?"

Boyd remained by the calf's side even after Sadie had assumed a workable position with it, one arm wrapped about its chest and one arm holding up the milk. In truth, he had nothing to run from, and nothing for which to feel ashamed, and yet the impulse to do both assaulted his better judgment. He rolled his shoulders, trying to relieve the pressure of holding a prolonged burden.

"I was writing to my cousin. We're close. Like brothers. He's a sheriff and knows me better'n most anyone."

She held his gaze and waited for him to continue.

"He's the one who told me it might be best to leave Juniper. Now, music's always been my aim, and all of that's still true, but there was a rumor about me that would have destroyed my family. My cousin's working on finding the truth, and he needs time to clear my name."

"A rumor."

"Yes. I told your Pa all about it last night, while we worked side by side. He thought it best not to tell anyone else about it."

"Does Pa believe you?"

"Yes. He said he did."

"Then that's all I need to know." She smiled a conspiratorial smirk. "Teddy's just jealous of you, you know."

Now that was not what he had expected to hear. "Jealous? Of me?" The man practically ran the ranch for Mr. Marsh. It was an enviable position. Job security, authority, respect ... Boyd couldn't imagine what the man could possibly see in him to be jealous.

"He's liked me since we were both kids. And he thinks I like you."

"Miss Sadie, I don't want any trouble with him. I reckon I best be getting to my chores, now."

"The fact is, Boyd, I do like you. You don't treat me like a scarecrow in a skirt."

"Huh? A scarecrow?" She was hardly that. In fact, he had a hard time not noticing the pleasant ways she filled out her clothes, whether denim and chaps or her pretty work dress.

"Never mind. Seems some men don't think womenfolk got anything but stuffing in their heads."

She pursed her lips like she would spit. The effect, like a pucker for a kiss, was oddly captivating.

"Even if Teddy was the last man on earth, I wouldn't marry him. I ain't the marrying type. I don't need a man."

"I see." He raised his brows, crediting her with both a sound mind and an honest will, refreshing to him. "Then what *does* Sadie Mitchell want from life?"

She looked away, as though the barn walls opened up a vista that only she could see. A wistful light overtook her coffee-and-cream eyes. "I want to be independent. Ride my own horses, rustle my own ranch, raise my own livestock. Or maybe travel. Or ..." The light in her eyes dimmed, the spell broken. She returned her focus to him, searching him for connection. "I just don't want anyone telling me what to do."

He nodded. Even chuckled. He respected her honesty. "But have-to's are a fact of life. Don't know where we can run where we don't have expectations put upon us."

"You found a place. You didn't have to stay where folks misunderstood ya."

Their gazes locked, and her sincerity pushed past a wall he hadn't realized he had erected. "You're right, Miss Sadie. I did. And I ask the good Lord every day if I did the right thing."

The calf pushed away, finally full. She stood and dusted off her skirts, letting the baby drift about the stall until he plopped down in the thick straw for a nap. "Well, I think you did. Sparr'a tells me you belong here. He says you got a purpose to fulfill."

"Maybe." He shrugged and stepped back behind the half door of the stall. "I'm still hoping to find a show to join up with. I reckon I'll leave the timing of all that in the good Lord's hands."

"Sadie, Boyd, come *pronto*." Miguel's voice held uncharacteristic urgency "There's a stampede, and we need every rider."

Sadie sprang to the door, which Boyd had drawn open for her, and they both swept out of the stall. She led to the tack room. The working horses were all claimed by other riders and being saddled. Sadie's Appaloosa mare would be waiting, but what was Boyd going to ride? They hadn't assigned him a horse yet.

"Grab that bridle hanging above the grain bin. You'll have to take one of the Mustangs. They're half-trained bang-tails, barely green-broke, but if anyone can handle 'em, it's you."

She hoisted her mare's tack and led the way to the corral.

"Sadie, how're you goin' to ride with that dress on? It's not safe to ride side-saddle on a cattle roundup."

"If'n you're the squeamish type, then turn yer eyes away. And besides, this ain't no side-saddle."

"It's not my place to argue with a lady. But I'll ride with you to run interference, and you can't stop me from doin' that much."

Laughter bubbled out of her, partly in admiration of his pluck, and partly to mask her nervousness. She'd never ridden in a confining dress, and a tingle of caution rose over her arms in prickles of gooseflesh. "That's if'n you can keep up, cowboy."

Her mare stood waiting for her with ears tilted forward, ready and eager at the gate. Sadie pointed at the corral opposite, motioning to Boyd to select a mustang out of that group. "Let me know if you need a hand."

"I ain't no bushwhacker. I'll manage."

"There's a crackerbox saddle over yonder on that barrel."

"No, thanks. I'll ride bareback."

More gooseflesh rose over her skin. He was a daring one. "Suit yourself. It's your neck."

As she slipped the bridle over her mare's nose and behind her ears, she marveled that Babyface had no trouble wrangling a big bay into its headgear and had started to lead him toward the gate.

She made haste to draw her mare's girth strap and cinch the saddle tight. "Come on, Dixie. Let's go round up some orn'ry cows."

She met Boyd in the avenue between fences where he stood with his horse waiting for her. She gathered up the reins in her hand and stepped up onto the bottom rung of the split rail. Placing her boot into the stirrup, she swung one leg over. Her dress bunched over the saddle horn, and there was no helping it that her bloomers' lacy ankle-cuffs showed.

What would Cookie say now? Too bad. Her daddy wasn't there to order her down.

Boyd hopped up onto the horse's back from a standstill,

and reined the animal about, seeming not to see her unmentionables. But a bright red splotch appeared in each of his cheeks.

Sadie kicked Dixie into a run and passed Boyd and his chomping horse in a fury of mane and tail.

Clouds of dust in the distance showed where the herd had broken through the barbed wire. Near about where she'd heard tell where the heifer had gotten tangled up. *Didn't anyone repair the fence?*

Boyd approached on her right, riding hard to take the lead. His red handkerchief flashed at his collar, whipping in the brisk wind created by his horse's fleet pace. His chiseled profile struck her with a sense of awe. He rode like a figure in a Frederic Remington *Harper's Weekly* sketch. His image captured every imagination she'd ever entertained of what Pa must have looked like when he was young, riding on the open range with Ma.

Her heart took winged flight.

This was freedom.

Exhilaration raised that gooseflesh again. Wave after wave swept over her, racing over the prairie with this strong, capable cowboy who somehow slipped past her and took the lead.

She could no longer deny the strange pull in her belly every time she looked at him. Was this what folks called magnetism? She was wrecked with it. Smitten.

Hiding her grin, she tucked her chin into the high buttoned collar of her dress and goaded Dixie into longer strides. The cattle herd thundered directly ahead, and shouts of other riders rose in her ears above the roar of pounding hooves. The chalky dust in the air choked with each breath, and she kept her head down.

Lassos whipped overhead to her left and right. A few riders pulled up short on their mounts to slow the runaways. Boyd wove in and out of the surging steers, cutting them out of the herd one by one with the bulk of his horse's body. He was a physical rider, and his instincts were sharp. She was mesmerized.

Dixie's stride stumbled. A scream gusted from Sadie's lungs as her horse wobbled, threatening to go down in the stampeding herd, taking her with it.

10

Surging animals flanked her right and left, and she dared not look to see if they were bovine or equine. Sadie braced herself as the ground sped up to meet her. At the last stroke, an arm reached about her waist and lifted her. She was pulled back up, and she grasped onto the safety of her rescuer. Boyd smiled down at her, drawing her to his chest. She clung to him for several rough strides until he managed to pull her away from the chaos.

The herd plunged past them, and once again in the clear, he set her on her feet. "You okay, little lady?"

She shoved her hat down on her head, hiding her wide-eyed terror with a feigned bravado. Standing square, she pushed her shoulders back, countering the force of the ripple of wind in her skirts. "Shucks. I'm solid as Fort Knox."

He tipped his hat and goaded his mount forward. "Stay there and catch your breath. I'll fetch your mare."

Pressing one hand at her waist and her other at the crown of her hat, she took his advice and gulped the air until her head stopped spinning. She couldn't have been more addled if the cowboy had kissed her.

With a sidestep and a quick tug at her skirts, she managed not to swoon.

———

Sadie's appaloosa had already pushed away from the madding herd and found a patch of prairie grass to graze. Boyd reined his mustang over to the mare and grasped her leather reins. She batted one wily eye at him and after chomping one last bite of grass, she lifted her head, coming along with him willingly. The shouts of cowboys and the thundering of hooves fanned out as the herd was driven apart to break its momentum. Several steers had been roped and were now being led back toward the ranch. The herd slowed and came to a standstill, while a few followed the roped steers in a procession toward home. The stampede was effectively over.

Picking his way around tall clusters of indigo bush and sage, Boyd's horse started as a cluster of cowboys flashed past, among them Teddy and Sven. They were the only ones still in a hurry, and curiously, riding hard in the opposite direction.

A few yards from where they'd just come, a yearling bull scrambled to its feet, its swishing tail drawing Boyd's attention to an oozy brush burn across its flank. Angry, wounded, and pawing the ground, it flung huge clods of dirt back toward him. But its attention was fixed forward, swinging its long-horned head in a display of aggression.

His blood instantly chilled. Beyond the animal, a figure in a billowing skirt held her arms out, backing up slowly.

Sadie.

"Hey!" He shouted to get the bull's attention. Releasing the appaloosa mare's reins, he spurred his mustang toward the menacing bovine, but the half-trained horse balked and raised its head against the bit.

"Git'yup!"

With a bellow and a sideways twist of its head, the angry steer fixed its stare on Boyd. The rims of the animal's eyes flared red against the pale white ring around its dark center. Slowly, it turned its hulking body to face him.

Yeehaw and thank the Lord, he had succeeded in drawing the threat away from Sadie. Relief filled him when, out of the corner of his eye, he caught her mare trotting past and Sadie catching her by the reins. She hurled herself, skirts and all, into the safety of the saddle.

His green horse continued to contest his commands. Though he spurred and pushed the animal's head down, the mustang thrust its back legs out in a leap and a buck, followed by an immediate rear and caper. Boyd clung onto the horse's back without the aid of stirrup or horn and managed to stay astride.

A flash of sunlight reflected off the polished horns of the steer. In a rush, the arm-wide rack streaked up at him in frontal assault, and the collision of hundreds of pounds of bull against the withers of his horse threw Boyd backward through the air. Before he could utter a shout, the crushing impact of ground slammed across his back, and searing heat filled his ribs and chest. He gasped for breath.

Sadie!

Please Jesus, let her be all right.

———

"Dixie, h'yah!" Shouting, Sadie drew the syllable out as she slapped the mare's spotted haunch and crouched low in the saddle to blend her weight with the horse's movement.

She drove the bull with frenzied vocalization and flapping arms away from the mustang which stood between it and Boyd's fallen body. As far as her baby-faced cowboy, she had lost line of sight where he lay. But if she could make the bullock chase her and Dixie, she could lead it to one of the other *vaqueros* and neutralize its threat.

Ahead, she spied Sparrow riding down on her like a Comanche war party, whooping and hollering with a few buckaroos waving lariats behind him. One loop snagged the animal's horns, and another caught the animal's rear leg. The riders pulled their mounts up short, drawing their ropes taut. The plunging beast fell a mere stride behind Sadie's mare.

Dixie side-stepped while Sadie waved away the cloud of dust raised from the commotion.

Sparrow rode up on her right side. "Are you hurt?"

She shook her head. "Boyd." She pointed to the clumps of sage where the mustang still stood, a gash on the animal's chest streaming bright crimson in the sunlight. "He fell over yonder."

She led the way, asking her mare to break out of a trot into a canter to cover the distance.

The mustang stood with his head hung, his tail swishing away the flies. As Sadie moved closer, she discerned the cut on the animal's shoulder was thankfully not a gore, but more of a glancing scrape. The horse needed care, but the injury didn't appear to be life-threatening.

Further on, another streak of red riveted her gaze. Boyd's body lay sprawled, face-up, and a blaze of scarlet slashed above his collar.

"Oh, no!" She threw herself down from Dixie's saddle. Her

feet hit the ground at a run, and she fell to her knees in the grass beside him, her skirts settling in a semicircle.

Her eyes blurred through a well of emotion and she blinked several times. That scarlet slash at his throat ... it wavered in her vision like looking through blown glass until distinguishing features—his chin, his neck, bandana, and shirt collar—came into focus. "Oh, gracious. It's your red bandana!" She wiped her eyes and laughed at her own silliness, even as her pounding heart sought to burst through her chest.

"Babyface?" She touched his stubbled cheek, and a gasp parted his lips. The sky-high, soaring excitement of riding alongside him moments ago erupted into a thunderhead of doubt and worry. She'd tasted freedom tucked in at his wing. Now she plummeted back to earth, wondering if she even wanted to fly, if he should be unable ... if he ...

She trailed her fingers to trace his firm jaw. No obvious cuts or bruises marred his handsome face or body. But he wasn't getting up.

Sadie waved to Sparrow and another ranch hand in the field beyond. "Help me get him back to the big house."

Before the men could climb the rise and reach them, she leaned her head down against Boyd's ribs to listen for his heartbeat. A rustle at the back of her head sent tingles, as his fingers swept through her hair.

"Sadie. You're okay." His hushed voice sent a thrill through her like the wind whispering over the tawny prairie grass.

His nearness nearly overwhelmed her, awash in his masculine scent of sage, cedarwood, and leather. She jerked her head away in self-composure, sensing the approach of the other cowboys. "You crazy buckaroo. That bull could have killed you!"

His hand fell away from her loose hair, and a half grin lifted his expression, though a wince of pain remained. "Don't I get a kiss for my trouble?" His teasing wink weakened her resolve to dash to her feet.

She held her position leaning over him and lifted one brow in quizzical wonder. The bold bronc buster lifted himself in an unexpected surge of strength and—to her shock—stole a peck on her lips.

11

At the approach of riders, Boyd scrambled to pull himself to his feet but a crippling pop in his back knocked him to the ground again. Sparrow and an older Mexican cowpoke came alongside.

"Eh, *muchacho*, don't get up. You need a *travois*." The man conferred with Sparrow for a moment and mounted his horse again, riding off to gather the materials for a litter.

Sparrow leaned down to meet Boyd's gaze, his brows bunched in concern. "That was no accident, *ikhage*. Teddy drove that steer right at you."

Boyd gasped to catch his breath through clenched teeth, fighting to regain his voice. "McCallister deliberately set that wounded bull on me?"

"I saw three men wrangling a longhorn across the chaparral. Ted joined up with them, and he directed them to drive it up here."

"Didn't they see Sadie? Why would they put her in danger?"

Sadie watched from her mare, quiet. Her silence seemed

uncharacteristic, and Boyd wondered what she was holding back.

The older *vaquero* returned, bringing Miguel with him. They set the poles and woven fabric in place. Then the men lifted Boyd up onto the stretcher.

He clutched the sides, barely able to keep the pain slivering through his back and ribs from overwhelming him. He was pretty sure he'd busted something, and he drew short, shallow breaths until he grew dizzy.

"*Hola, amigo.* José told me what happened. I'm sorry I wasn't here to help." Miguel's expression held no teasing for once.

The *vaqueros* exchanged a few sentences with one another in Spanish, and Miguel turned back to face Boyd. "Teddy must have wanted me out of the way. He sent me back to repair the fence where the herd got out."

"Was it the same place the heifer got tangled up?"

Miguel nodded.

"Why wasn't that fixed last night?" Sadie kneaded her pinched brows with her fingertips.

"It was." Miguel replied, carrying one end of the travois Boyd was riding. "I fixed it myself. But it was fresh cut again when I got there."

"Cut? How can you tell?" Boyd lifted his head and met Miguel's gaze.

"It was a clean slice top and bottom, and the poles weren't pushed."

Boyd reclined and closed his eyes, contemplating the bewildering likelihood that someone had set a sabotage to cause the stampede.

The next thing he saw was a beamed ceiling and Sadie and Cookie standing over him, staring down.

"Got the wind knocked out of me."

"Sure did, pardner. In spectacular form." Sadie's free jaw suddenly clamped shut with Cookie's blazing blue-eyed glare. Sadie backed away under the matron's censure. She stood to the side and folded a blanket half-way, then rolled it into a tube.

He would have chuckled at her teasing if there wasn't what felt like a hot poker wedged into his right side. What had he managed to do to himself, falling off that mustang? He shifted his bedcovers, to make sure they hadn't left one of those sheet-warming pans with hot coals in there. Lifting the quilt, he grasped the state of his undress from the waist up, and quickly set the blanket back down over him. The area where he felt the worst pain was bruised up like he'd gotten a right and proper lambasting.

"That bull sure gave you Jessy. You *and* your horse. Dunno which of you's worse off." Sadie set the rolled-up blanket behind his head to prop him.

He settled back into the cushion, and it eased the fire in his rib. "And the bull?"

"Mr. Marsh told me to cook a beef roast tonight." Cookie raised her chin, looking the other way.

"So, Mr. Marsh knows what happened?" A twist of dread kinked in his gut. He hadn't been here two full days, and he had already landed on his back. But for how long?

"He's heard how you rescued Sadie and took the brunt of it like a regular soldier," the widow replied. "Says he'll be back when you're feeling better, to pour you a drink himself."

"That's right kind. But it'll have to be coffee, ma'am." Boyd lifted his shoulders in a shrug, but the hitch in his rib left him gasping.

"He's called for a doctor from town. Worried your rib might have splintered." Sadie leaned in and pulled the blanket-cushion smooth. "You best lie back and be still, Babyface."

He obeyed. After a moment passed in silence, an unresolved question stirred. "Sadie, did McCallister see you?"

"I couldn't tell. The dust was pretty thick. I dodged out of the way and let them pass. But they up and left the steer there, with the lasso still around him."

He replayed the moment in his mind's eye. She had been on foot, and her horse had been down the trail behind him. It was possible McCallister hadn't seen her. Boyd, on the other hand, would have been easy to spot. He would have stood out with his dove gray Stetson and red bandana astride the tall mustang.

McCallister had warned him. This was deliberate.

"Can I talk to Fletch?"

"He's driving the mule train to Lincoln. Won't be back until the first of the month." Cookie's tone held a lament that seemed out of place for anyone except a near relative. Or close friend.

"Well, how 'bout you ladies wrap my ribs up nice and tight, and I'll get about my business."

Cookie raised both hands to her forehead, aghast. "Not on your life, sonny. You'll go nowhere before the doctor claps his eyes on you." She tightened the blankets covering him until he could scarcely wiggle his shoulders.

"You'd make a good warden, ma'am."

Sadie giggled. "That, she would."

Cookie shook her head in exasperation and slipped out of the room, leaving the door open wide. "For propriety," she said, and then continued down the hall.

Sadie sat in a chair by his bedside. "Miguel told me they found a cow who might take in the orphan calf. Seems she lost hers in the stampede. It was a newborn."

"That's hopeful."

Boyd studied her dark, curled lashes and the way they

deepened the shadows of her eyelids. The girl didn't have a bad angle. The best part of it was that she had no idea that she was a real beauty.

"I guess they've got to make the mama cow believe it's her own by putting its pelt over it. Seems kinda cruel. Like it ain't worth lovin' and bein' accepted on its own merits, it's gotta dress up and pretend to be something other than itself."

"It's a fallen world, Sadie. So much isn't as the Creator intended. But if I see anything in it, I see a second chance. I see hope where there could have been rejection, loneliness, and even death."

"Why, Boyd? Why is there so much rejection? So much loneliness and ... and death?"

Her lashes grew dewy with unshed tears, and he pushed the widow's restraining covers away so he could take her hand.

"It's like the scapegoat in the Bible. All the wrongs, the lies, the meanness of the world. There had to be a payment for it." A sudden itch made him squirm as he contemplated the sacrifice of an innocent man for the sins of another. Had he refused the cup of suffering that the Lord had measured out to him? Had he run from a calling to lay down his life for a fatherless child? The scapegoat took on the sin of the people and carried it away.

But all *he* had done was run.

———

Sadie sat forward. Mental dominoes fell, pushing down other thoughts in succession. "So, one calf had to die to give the other a chance to live."

Boyd nodded. "Remember Adam and Eve, how they lost their innocence and needed covering? It was the first mention of death in scripture when God clothed them in animal skins."

Lost innocence. She rested against the back of the upholstered chair, folded her hands in her lap and looked down. That's how she felt. What she used to say and do no longer felt right, like her eyes had been opened. "Maybe Cookie isn't wrong after all. Reckon I shouldn't go around acting like a wild thing anymore. Maybe it's time I got domesticated, act like a lady."

She blinked as though the action could help her connect the string of her feelings and make a pearl necklace with them.

"New clothes." She lifted a slip of fabric from her yards of skirt. "Maybe I do need a new identity."

"Whoa, don't run yourself off like some prairie wolf. I like the Sadie I know."

"Thanks, Boyd. But my selfish ways got you hurt today. If I had stayed back, listened to others, none of this would'a happened." She stood, gathering her skirts, and bustled out of the room before he saw her cry.

She fled from the guest cabin into the privacy of the back pasture, where she nearly collided with Widow Garrity. The matron returned, carrying a big old black case. The banjo.

Sadie gulped down her tears. "I didn't know you were holding onto that for Boyd." The buckaroo was probably worried about it.

It was a thoughtful act. A kindness that spoke of consideration and an artful touch. So like Cookie. Always there for folks with a smile of welcome, a hot cup of coffee, and a savory plate of food.

"Bring it in to him." The widow placed the handle in her hand with a knowing smile. "I'm guessing he could use a friend, alone in a new place, and now ailing besides."

The dam burst and Sadie wept openly. The matron's embrace drew her to her shoulder.

"Now, now. It'll be all right, dearie." She held Sadie until she regained composure. "He's a long way from home. Why don't you show him a sense of belonging right here?"

The widow nudged her back down the hallway toward the lonesome room where she'd left him. After clearing her throat and pressing her free palm to her cheek to feel for any leftover tear streaks, she stepped through the door.

Boyd's smile swept away the cobwebs of any lingering doubts. "Thank you, Sadie. I was just wond'rin' what happened to you—I mean, to my banjo." He looked sheepish but readily accepted the gift, and her company.

"Would you," he began almost shyly, then started again with a quiet simplicity. "Would you hand it up to me?"

"Sure, Boyd. But won't it hurt your ribs?"

"It would be a comfort to have it close."

She took his prized possession out of its case and lifted it to him. A sense filled her at his expression that she had seldom felt, except perhaps gazing on a misty sunrise over the prairie, or watching an eagle skim the surface of the Platte River. She sat at his bedside and closed her eyes. Almost without notice the soft picking of musical notes drifted between them. Serene, heartfelt, beautiful. Her heart ached with a strange emotion that his music stirred in her.

"What'aya call that'un?" she asked with a purling reverence in her voice.

"I ain't given it a name, Miss Sadie. Reminds me of happy times and folks I care about."

"Sounds like it should be 'Lonesome for Home.'" She breathed a wistful sigh.

"Or maybe, 'Home is Where You Are.'" His gray eyes met hers and then he looked back down at the strings and the placement of his fingers.

Her face warmed, and the sensation spread to her fingertips and toes. "Yeah, I like that name."

Footsteps approached the entrance to the room. A knock on the doorframe preceded the appearance of the ranch owner, Mr. Marsh, and the city doctor with his black bag.

Sadie stood. "I'll step outside." She moved slowly toward the door, glancing back.

The white-whiskered man with Mr. Marsh stooped over Boyd and set about his examination, saying nothing. Sadie blushed and turned away, imagining the cowboy's determination to hold back his pain in her presence.

Mr. Marsh joined her, and they strolled together outside. "Hard fall. I hear he stepped in to protect you."

"He did." She nodded. "I hope he's going to be all right."

Mr. Marsh removed his Stetson and pushed back his thinning hair. "We'll do whatever it takes to get him fixed up. Don't you worry, Sadie."

Before he turned back, she thrust another thought at him. "Where's Teddy? I was hoping to talk to him about something."

"Oh, he came to me just before Boyd came in. Asked if he could take leave. Said he had some business to attend to. He left half an hour ago."

Sadie gasped as though the air had fled. "Did he say where he was bound, Mr. Marsh?"

"He did. Said he was aiming to catch a train to Texas."

12

Sadie paced the floor of her cabin. The sun had set hours ago, and the distant hoot of an owl reminded her that she was missing sleep. But she was as wide awake as a black fish with round, staring eyes, trying to see something that she might have missed in the events leading up to this accident. But it was no accident, of that she was certain.

Teddy couldn't leave it alone that she had kindled a friendship with the new cowboy. Had he driven all the other recent hires away because she liked to talk to them and set them at ease? Jealousy really was a green-eyed monster.

One thing made her grateful. Boyd hadn't heard Mr. Marsh say anything concerning Teddy. And she wasn't going to tell him. He didn't need that worry on his head. But she had to do something. She couldn't stand the feeling of helpless anticipation of what Teddy was about to do. He knew a secret about Boyd, and since his stunt with the bull had only cemented her concern and affection for Boyd, he must be resorting to an even more dastardly plan to discredit and harm him.

She needed to know the secret about Boyd that her Pa knew. And something told her that Widow Garrity might have an idea what that was. Still fully dressed, Sadie snuffed out her light and tiptoed to the cabin door, bound for Cookie's room.

She wrapped once, twice, three times. "Cookie, it's Sadie. Open your door."

Shuffling and muttering inside carried to Sadie's eager ears. She smiled. The woman loved her too much to leave her out on the stoop. She'd tell her what she knew.

"Come in here or you'll catch your death of cold, out in the middle of the night with no coat." The widow scolded her with the affront of a henhouse visited by a fox in the night.

For the first time, Sadie heard affection instead of fuss. She stepped in and let Cookie close the door behind her.

"Now, what are you about at this unearthly hour?" Her blue eyes were gentle and concerned.

"I'm worried about Boyd." She shrugged. How else could she explain it? It was true. And a good way to start, to win the shrewd widow over. Clever fox, indeed.

"Oh, of course you are, dearie. Don't fret. I'll fix us a pot of tea, and we can set down and talk."

"Thank you, Cookie."

She followed the matron out to the kitchen and helped fill the kettle while Cookie set the stove flame. Next, she reached into the cupboard and retrieved the tin where sometimes leftover cakes or pastries were stored. And the small jar of tea.

A lantern sent rays of light through the room from a small table by the stove. Cookie brought the tea and sweets plus two cups as a whistling cloud of steam rose from the kettle.

The woman poured hot water into a teapot and fixed two tea balls, setting them gently into the porcelain cups. "Your Ma left me this tea set. For safekeeping when you set up housekeeping."

"I thought they looked familiar," Sadie's reply sounded low and wistful, even to her own ears. "I reckon you're the closest and best thing to a mother that a motherless girl could ask for all these years, Cookie. Thank you for always being there for me, even when I didn't necessarily want you to be."

A soft chuckle shook the widow's plump frame. "You've almost been the death of me, but I would do it a thousand times again."

"I know you and my Pa are close."

The widow lifted a cagey brow. "You have eyes in your head, and a nose that seems to sniff out enough trouble for yourself without concerning yourself with others."

Now Sadie laughed. "I'm glad he has someone looking out for him."

"Do you, now?" Her smile was full of mirth. "Well, that's a relief."

"Has he talked to you about ... about Boyd?"

Mrs. Garrity opened the confectioner's tin and lifted a plate of ginger snaps from it. "His name has come up, yes."

"Don't be coy. I need to know what Pa has said to you. The cowboy's life might depend on it."

She paused in mid-nibble and set down the cookie. "What do you mean, girl?"

"I mean, Ted McCallister has a secret he's planning to use to destroy Boyd. He's gone to Texas to stir up trouble, and I need to know what that secret is."

"Your Da told me in strictest confidence. And the thing is, Sadie, he's gone to Texas himself to learn the truth. I wasn't going to tell you, but you asked. You can be sure your Da will get to the bottom of it. And keep Teddy in his place."

Sadie buried her face into her open palms, her elbows propped on the table. After a moment, she met the widow's gaze. "How bad is it, Cookie?"

Mrs. Garrity reached out and took her hand, drawing it down to the table. "I think we should pray."

————

A creak on the wooden floorboards caused Boyd's eyes to shutter open from a dead sleep. But the dark of the late, night hour shed almost no light into the room. It almost made no difference to open or close his eyelids. So, he closed them, and listened intently. A heavy tread. Male. Slow, long strides that neared.

And a smell ... pickled herring?

Boyd suspected who it was but didn't want to speculate as to why Sven would be sneaking into his room in the middle of the night.

"What do you want, Iversen?"

A scuffed halt. Shuffling of indecision and attempted retreat.

"Good of you to come by and check on my condition, Sven. No need to lose sleep on my account, though." His voice dripped with sarcasm, and he half-hoped McCallister's sidekick would retaliate. Even with a busted rib, he could handle the oaf.

"When does Doc say you'll be up and around?"

"Come on in and I'll show you."

"Nah. Before I get back to the bunkhouse I wanted to tell you, McCallister's gone down to Texas to find out what you done. If I was you, I'd tuck tail and run while you got a chance."

Blood rushed to Boyd's head, and pain or no, he pushed himself half out of bed. "You and Ted set that rogue steer on me, and it almost killed Sadie. That's the only thing you should be worrying about right now. When her Pa gets back, you'd better have some good answer for him, because he's gonna have a lot of questions."

Sven cussed under his breath, and with a grunt, he turned and left.

Waves of pain rippled up and down Boyd's body, and he slowly drew his legs back up into the bed. The thought of McCallister sniffing around his hometown made him want to retch up Cookie's good broth.

Maybe Sven was right. Maybe he would be better off hitting the trail now before the law returned with McCallister. He couldn't face more disgrace, especially in Sadie's eyes.

A commotion outside jarred his thoughts.

"Sven? What are you about, coming out of Boyd's cabin at this hour?"

Widow Garrity's voice, with its hints of Irish brogue, could be mistaken for no one else's.

"Yeah, what do you think you're doing, sneaking around in the dark? Now you're caught."

That was Sadie!

"I've a mind to rouse the Marshes out of their beds and have them ask the questions."

Smart girl.

"I was checking in on him, Miss Sadie. I thought I heard him yell."

"Boyd? Is he all right?"

A commotion of scuffling feet and Mrs. Garrity's protests ensued, and his door burst open. "Babyface?" Sadie rushed to his side.

"Sadie Mitchell! Mind your reputation, girl." The widow floundered to light the lantern at his bedside. She huffed and sat in the wooden chair by the door as the impetuous and endearing girl forged ahead.

Sadie stood beside him, studying him head to toe. He was

mostly covered in blankets, so she settled her gaze on his face. "Are you all right?"

"Doc says it'll take a few weeks, but I'll be back to ropin' and ridin' again." He couldn't help but grin at her. Her hair was disheveled, half slipping from an upswept knot. Her dress was wrinkled, and her face careworn. She was the purtiest thing he'd ever seen.

"Sven didn't do anything foolish, did he?"

His grin faded. *Sven.* The news and threats he spoke soured even this sweet visit.

"Miss Sadie, I've got to tell you everything, so you'll know my side of the story if folks come around accusing me of bad things."

She folded her hands at her waist, and he motioned for her to take the extra seat by his bed.

"When I was back in Texas, there was this girl. Matilda. She had all the boys on a string. A real coquette. I admit I was one of them, admiring her from afar. I was barely twenty-two years old at the time. Pretty wet behind the ears. She asked me to come help her. Said her daddy was away, and no one else was around. She made it sound like one of the horses was down in its stall. I naïvely followed her into the barn alone. When I realized there was no horse, no crisis, I wondered what she really wanted with me. She cornered me and kissed me and said she was in trouble and I was the only one who could help. I asked her what sort of trouble, and she started to cry. I should have run away, gone to fetch the pastor, or tried to find her ma. But instead, I thought to comfort her, and I wrapped my arms around her and held her until she would stop crying."

He pounded his fist into his open hand.

"I was so blamed stupid. I should have known what that would look like. And sure enough, her daddy appeared and assumed that whatever she was crying about, I was to blame."

"Oh, Boyd. But you don't mean she was in *that* sort of trouble, do you?"

He nodded. "And the tricky part is, it could have been a number of fellas. Her daddy is a wealthy ranch owner. Always hiring new men, a steady flow of visitors."

"And they thought you would take responsibility."

"I was going to. But my older cousin, a lawman, talked me out of it. Her father pressed charges, and my cousin Caleb, the one I wrote that letter to, told me to lay low until he could figure out who the real father was."

"Is that what Teddy thinks he's got on you?"

Boyd nodded again. "Yes, ma'am. And Sven just told me McCallister's gone down to Juniper to alert the authorities of my location."

"They won't find you here."

"What do you mean?"

"Not if we hide you in Lincoln. My Pa has friends there that would put you up. And besides, ain't you hopin' to find a way to play your music? A big city like that could be a connection."

"That's askin' too much, Miss Sadie. I won't make you an accomplice. I'm done running. Whatever comes, I'll face it like a man. I'm innocent, and the Lord will vindicate me."

She sighed and bowed her head. "It ain't right."

"It *will be* all right." He reached out and pressed her slender hand in his. "Thank you for believing me."

"I'm goin' to town as soon as I can. I can't sit by and watch you get railroaded. I'll hire Pinkertons if I have to!"

13

After a few days making arrangements, and half another to travel, at last Sadie and Cookie disembarked a stagecoach in Lincoln. Everywhere Sadie looked, there was movement. Noise. Life. The streets cut neat squares between lawns and closely spaced buildings. An endless parade of coaches, buggies, horsemen, and pedestrians dazzled before her sights. Cookie's smile was contagious, and Sadie's cheeks pinched with the wideness of her own grin. Leaving the ranch for a visit to town was a rare treat.

"Where should we go first?" Sadie craned her neck to see as far down the boulevard as she could. Bakery, pawnshop, dentist, mercantile, tannery, and boots ... so many painted signs hung over doors that her eyes boggled.

"We should start at the diner, I think. We can make inquiries there and refresh ourselves after the long ride."

Her tummy rumbled, reminding her she hadn't eaten since the night before. "I can set with that."

They found a dark-stained wood table with a white diamond cloth, set beside the window overlooking the street.

Sadie sat herself and ordered a ham sandwich with a sarsaparilla to drink, while Mrs. Garrity ordered a cup of chicken noodle soup, tea, and toast.

The waiter had no sooner brought their orders when a commotion erupted outside. Whooping and hollering, a great stampede of horses and riders, mules, wagons, and even a few dandies on Penny-farthings turned the street into a spectacle. Sadie stuck her head through the curtain to gawk.

A banner in bold colors advertised the group as *Pawnee Bill's Historic Wild West*.

A herd of longhorns and a few bison tramped up the road hemmed in by whistling and shouting cowboys ending the procession like the caboose of a train.

Sadie slipped from her window seat and scampered out the door to the boardwalk. A man with a handle-bar mustache passed by, handing out printed handbills advertising their show. She took one eagerly and examined it.

"Say, Mister," she reached out and grabbed his sleeve. "Are you looking for a ballad-writing musician to join your troupe?"

The man paused and removed his hat, giving her a slight bow. "A pretty face is always an attraction, miss. Do you sing?"

Sadie laughed. "Oh, no, sir. I sing like a horse with the strangles. I'm talking about my friend, Boyd. He's a virtuoso on the banjo. He writes his own tunes and sings like a canary. Well, a cowboy canary." She batted her lashes.

"We're looking for a lady, mainly, to draw in the cowboys. We're all stocked up on men. Unless he can ride broncos."

"Oh, he can do that, yessiree."

"And what about you? Can you ride?"

"I can ride, rope, and rustle near about anything. I'm not so sure I'd be clear to travel, though, without my Pa's permission. But my friend Boyd ... well, he's got a busted rib. It'll take some time to heal, if he was to show you what he can do on horseback. Could he audition to see if you like his music?"

"I'll tell you what, little lady. If you're willing to audition with your friend, I'll make an allowance for him."

She grasped his hand and pumped it. "You got a deal, Mister!"

"What's your name, ma'am?"

"Sadie Mitchell. What's yor'n?"

The man bowed his head again to her and set his hat back in place. "Pawnee Bill, at your service."

Her jaw dropped. "You're—you're him?"

"Gordon Lillie's my real name, but yes'm, I'm the proprietor. I hope to see you at the show, Miss Mitchell."

"You sure will, Mr. Lillie. I mean, Mr. Pawnee. I mean Mr. Bill, sir."

He chuckled. "See you tonight, then." The gentleman cowboy continued up the boardwalk handing out playbills to the townsfolk.

A tingle of excitement not unlike the feeling of Boyd's kiss coursed through the hand that held the pamphlet and traced up her arm.

Could this be destiny?

"Sadie, what did you just promise that man? We won't be in town long enough to see any show." Widow Garrity strode up beside her, plump hands pushed onto ample hips.

The tingling dispelled, and dizziness crowded in to replace it. "I could stay back and catch the next stagecoach ..."

"No, you can't, Missy. No young lady should be lingering about without a chaperone. And you know I can't stay because I've already left the ranch without their cook for one day ..."

Sadie kicked the toe of her leather boot into the road, sending a plume of dust up from beneath her skirts. "I've been plumb-willing until now to go along with what you say,

Cookie Garrity, but I've had it up to here—" she cut her hand across her chin— "with your rules."

The widow squared off with her, her cheeks darkening with a sure storm brewing in her Irish head. "Now you listen here, Sadie—"

A tall man slipped up behind Cookie and placed his arm around her waist. Sadie did a double-take as she realized who it was.

"Liza Kate Garrity, I didn't expect to see you and my Sadie here when I stepped off the train."

"Pa, you're back!" She stood up on her tiptoes, clapping her hands together.

"Nice to see both my girls," he replied, and winked at the widow who had instantly calmed and settled in his arms.

"Don't that beat all." Sadie hung a half grin as she cocked her head in a gloating gaze at them. "I knew it."

"I brought back gifts, and news. But first, let's eat. I'm famished."

Sadie followed as Mrs. Garrity and Pa led back to the diner. A rising impatience threatened to bust her stays. She halted at the door. "Did you see Teddy down there? What lies is he telling about Boyd?"

Pa paused, holding the door for Cookie. He looked back at Sadie. "I'll let him answer. He's inside with someone I want you to meet."

The bandages over Boyd's middle had worked wonders over the past week since Sadie had left, and the doc's visits confirmed he was making a quicker recovery than anyone would have expected. It was a relief to stretch his legs and mosey out, looking for her return. But if anyone should ask, he'd insist he was bound for the mustang pen.

A familiar squeal sounded a greeting from the blue-eyed pinto as Boyd hung at the fence-side. He fished in his pocket for a sugar cube he'd saved from his coffee that morning. Flattening his palm, he let the stallion take it with a sniff and a lipping chomp.

Another squeal and the horse raised its head, reaching for his hat.

"No trade." He doffed his hat and hid it behind his back to remove the temptation, then reached out and patted the white-and-bay cheek through the slats. These visits would hasten the process of breaking the animal to saddle, though it might be a while before he could mount up himself.

"Boyd Hastings! Is that really you?"

His heart bucked in his chest. His rib pain almost knocked him to his knees as he twisted around to affirm the source of the familiar voice.

It couldn't be.

But it *was* her, sauntering in a garnet-red dress over the dirt path toward him, her arm linked in Ted McCallister's. Both had their gazes fixed on him.

He'd like to have jumped out of his boots, but a strange calm settled over him, filling him with a notion to listen and not light a shuck out of there.

"Hastings," Ted stopped a few paces away, lifting his head in address. "I'm guessing you already know who this is."

He swallowed and found his voice. "Matilda." He nodded in acknowledgement of her presence, breathless in the searing heat like flames licking at his feet, his face, his lungs. If he were wearing his hat, he didn't know if he would have been able to take it off or not, as he normally would in the presence of a lady. What she'd done had made him doubtful. But something about her had changed. The slant of her beguiling eyes, and the curve of her cunning smirk, had given way to softer lines and gentler expressions. She stepped forward, closing the gap between them. She stretched out both hands and grasped his. He was too stunned to pull back.

"I've come to say my peace, and it's high time I did. You left me with the biggest regret of my life, and it's time to make things right at last."

14

"Cat got your tongue, Hastings?"

McCallister's imperious tone somehow muted in Boyd's ears, as though he had fallen under water. The foreman's laughter clapped with a sudden force, startling Boyd back to clarity.

"She said you're not to blame, and she's sorry about all the lies."

Something about the words "sorry" and "lies" riveted his focus back to her.

"You admit it, then? It was a lie all along." Boyd's voice regained strength. He wanted to shout in jubilation.

"I admit it, Boyd. It was a terrible thing I did, and I've regretted accusing an innocent man ever since. I came here to ask your forgiveness."

Invisible shackles popped open and tumbled down the backs of his arms and legs. He could stand tall again, weightless. "Of course, I forgive you. But who is the real—"

"Does it matter, Hastings?" Ted interrupted. "Maybe God means to provide for the lad in another way." The foreman adjusted his string tie and shifted his stance—in new boots with platform heals. McCallister was dressed in his best bib and tucker. Trying to impress.

Boyd raised a brow.

Matilda bowed her head and gazed up meekly at Ted. "Sidney's a good boy. He could use a strong example in his life."

McCallister seemed to grow a foot taller under her encouragement. And here he'd thought Ted had ambitions for Sadie. Could he have misunderstood McCallister's protectiveness for jealousy?

"I hope you and Sadie can forgive me, too, Boyd." The foreman mopped the back of his neck. "I confess I tried to run you off at first, but I swear I had nothing to do with getting you hurt. Mr. Marsh found wire cutters in Sven's bunk. He's been booted off the ranch. Dismissed."

"I can't say I'm sorry to see him go," Boyd confessed.

"Sadie and I grew up together, and I've always watched out for her. The fact that I was looking so hard to find fault everywhere else but right next to me is humbling. Again, Hastings, I'm sorry I misjudged you. Thank you for stepping up and saving her life."

"Sadie's a one of a kind. I'd do it again in a heartbeat."

McCallister grinned. "Well, I hope you won't have to, but she sure is a handful. If you hope to break that will, you're in for a wild ride."

He chuckled at the foreman's hooting laughter until a hitch in his ribs drew his hand to brace himself.

"Well, anyway, Boyd. No hard feelings?"

"No, Ted. We're square." They shook hands.

Releasing from the hand clasp, McCallister gave a parting remark. "That Fletch—he really went to bat for you. He'll tell you all about it, but he had a good conversation with your kin.

Mr. Mitchell brought news from both of your cousins and your family back for you."

————

So much had happened since Sadie had prayed with Widow Garrity, the night Boyd had gotten hurt. Back from Lincoln almost a week, she fairly burst with eagerness to go to him and tell him all she had experienced, all she felt.

But Pa ... He'd made a bargain with her. She could set up an audition for the show for Boyd if she agreed to leave the cowboy alone until after Sunday service. Pa reasoned that a man with such a shock to his system needed time to recuperate —in more ways than one.

Seemed the more she tried to put Boyd from her mind, the more he stuck like a cactus quill. The song that Gordon Lillie's wife kept singing in her practice sessions had become engrained in Sadie's mind and emblazoned on her heart.

My love is a rider, wild broncos he breaks,
Though he's promised to quit it, just for my sake.
He ties up one foot, the saddle puts on,
With a swing and a jump he is mounted and gone.
The first time I met him, 'twas early one spring,
Riding a bronco, a high-headed thing.
He tipped me a wink as he gaily did go;
For he wished me to look at his bucking bronco.
He made me some presents, among them a ring;
The return that I made him was a far better thing;
'Twas a young maiden's heart, I'd have you all know;
He's won it by riding his bucking bronco.

Her heart ached with a tenderness completely new. There was no relief for it until she could see him.

I'm in love.

She must tell him.

But she couldn't do that yet. So, instead, Sadie prayed.

Praying was a thing Ma had done with her. A childhood custom, a bedtime ritual. It had faded from her with the same inevitability as losing the exact recollection of her Ma's voice itself. And though Pa had been leading Sunday meetin' every week, Sadie had trouble connecting with the God he spoke about. His sermons about trusting and obeying were geared more toward recalcitrant cowpokes than her. Surely.

But when Cookie had taken her hands to pray, everything had flashed across her mind as though she could see her life on display before her like shadow puppets on the wall. All at once, she could see how stubborn, ornery, and bullheaded she had been. Resisting the kindness and constant care of a good woman. She should be proud to take after Cookie, who had been like a Ma to her these past ten years.

And not only Cookie, but also, Sadie had been resisting the Lord. The One who had always been there, always protected her, always waited for her to see Him. Hear Him. Surrender her will to His.

Tucked in under His wing she determined to stay, he One who offered real freedom.

Pa had brought back a letter from Boyd's cousin. She couldn't wait to bring it to Boyd and tell him everything. Sunday still seemed so far away. She could barely stand it.

Pawnee Bill had agreed to come to the ranch for Sabbath service and hear Boyd's playing. He wanted to listen without Boyd knowing it was an audition. Said he could learn a lot about a man who offered his talents first to the Lord, rather than another run-of-the-mill showman.

That resonated with her.

And what would she do if Mr. Lillie were to offer Boyd the position? Would he take it and ride away with her young maiden's heart?

Trust and obey.

She'd have to learn to do that in the next twenty-four hours' fiery crucible.

————

Boyd took his evening meal alone in his room that night. Mr. Marsh and Fletch Mitchell insisted, referencing his need to make a full recovery. It had been nigh on two weeks of rest, and he was going a mite stir-crazy. Especially with the uproarious laughter echoing across the compound from the grub house. Sounded like a celebration.

A secret amble down the lane would find out what all the excitement was about. But he reviewed his circumstances. He remained by the good graces of the owner, since he had yet to earn his stay with only a few days' work. No, he'd stay put as he was told, though it vexed him to feel so separated from what seemed like high festivities.

He hadn't much of an appetite. Sadie hadn't come by to see him since the first night he'd been injured. Was she angry with him? Had he missed an important cue, or forgotten to thank her for leading the bull away?

Maybe it was Matilda. Had he made a mistake telling Sadie everything? He expected too much of the girl to trust him and believe his innocence. She barely knew him, after all. Though to him, the days since meeting her had become a new lifetime. Time enough to believe again, feel free. To experience an unexpected wonder in her presence that kindled something he'd never dared to let himself feel after Matilda's lesson had left him so full of self-doubt. He suspected what some folks would call it. But how could it be, after only a handful of moments together?

Each day she remained distant gnawed at his gut worse than his rib pain. Could he have misunderstood this girl's intentions too? Just when he thought she might be worth risking his heart, his future, on?

He stood from his bedside chair and paced to the window. A bright moon rose over the roof of the mess hall, and lights shone through every opening in the building. Figures passed by the windows in what sure seemed like dancing. He strained his ears to pick up any hint of music, but there was none. There was clapping, though. More an ovation than a steady rhythm.

He fixed his walking stick in hand and drew to the door, overcome by temptation. As he stepped out, he nearly collided with a stealthy figure coming up on the door.

"Music Man. You made medicine." Sparrow's form materialized in the light by his open door. The Plains Indian pointed to him, apparently referencing the fact that he was up on his own two feet.

"I give the good Lord the credit for that, friend."

"I came to bring you news. From Sadie." Sparrow pushed forward, and Boyd had no choice but to turn back inside the cabin.

Sparrow waited for him to take a seat before he did the same.

Boyd prompted him. "From Sadie, you say? Is she unable to come herself?"

Sparrow stretched his legs out before him, settling in quite comfortably. "Your people make courtship rituals so complicated. Why shouldn't a maiden make it known to a warrior that he is acceptable to her?"

"What are you saying, man?"

Gentle laughter. "I'm saying that the cook and Sadie's father have made her unavailable to you until you pass a test of your worthiness."

Boyd scratched his chin. "Is that what Sadie told you to tell me?"

"No. Sadie told me to tell you she will see you at church tomorrow, and to bring your banjo."

Boyd stood, a jolt of nervous energy coursing through him, though he couldn't rightly say why. "Is that the test?" He paced across the room and back. "I already figured on goin' because Fletch asked me to."

"Then you're prepared."

Boyd gave Sparrow the side-eye. There was something the man wasn't saying. "What was all that hootin' and hollerin' about tonight?"

"A happy couple has announced their engagement."

"Who?"

"Fletch and Widow Garrity."

Boyd slapped his hat against his thigh. "I knew it!" His grin broke through, expelling his jitters. "That must make Sadie happy."

"Tomorrow is a hard day for Sadie. Ten years ago, her mother left this world to fly to the next."

The weight of that information settled in his stomach. "Then, this news is bittersweet at best."

Sparrow shrugged. "It is the season for finding one's mate. Even a mourning dove will pair again if his mate has passed."

They sat in silence for a full minute, the native man seemingly deep in thought. "And speaking of pairing, that woman who came back to town with Fletch and McCallister?"

"Yeah?" Boyd was almost afraid to hear what Sparrow would say about her. His powers of discernment were keen.

"She brought a traveling companion. A Coushatta maiden. She spoke with me, and we share many common thoughts."

"What'dya know? That's a fine development. What's her name?"

Sparrow flashed even rows of white teeth. "Sparrow Hawk."

Boyd laughed so hard, he had to stop and press at the hitch in his side.

"Oh, no. You're a goner!"

"I am Two Sparrows, in case she catches one."

"Well, good luck, *ikhage*—my friend. It seems tonight is full of celebration."

"And there is more, Music Man. Our foreman is moving to Texas with that visiting woman. They are getting married once he gets her father's permission, which under your people's courtship rituals, seems very likely."

Boyd thanked God under his breath. "Congratulations all around."

So much change was happening all at once. If only it could be Sadie and he who were celebrating. What did their future hold?

"I reckon I'll see you in the morning, Sparrow. Thank you for coming by. You've been a bearer of good news."

"Good medicine tomorrow, Music Man. Your purpose is being fulfilled, and in one week, you will scarcely recognize your life."

A chill swept into the room as Sparrow opened the door to leave. Outside the crickets and wild dogs made night songs, and Boyd was left alone to contemplate the portentous words.

15

Sadie examined her reflection in the looking glass, wearing the rose-colored calico dress that Cookie had selected for her. It softened the tanned complexion she had earned under the broad Nebraska sky, bringing out the blush that seemed to blossom at every thought of a certain banjo-playing buckaroo. Vanity was not one of her normal sins, but this morning, she had trouble tearing her eyes away from the transformation she had undergone in a such a short time. She scarcely recognized the pretty girl staring back at her. And her curls and frills didn't even make her want to spit.

"Don't be late to meetin' dearie," Cookie called through her door with a brace of knocks. "I'll walk over with you. Are you ready?"

Sadie opened the door and let her in. "Did I forget anything?" She searched the knowing gaze of her mentor for any hint of disapproval. All she saw was beaming pride.

"Oh, you're ready, dearie. Ready indeed." Her womanly chuckle communicated a conspiracy of delight. But then she sobered. "Your Da asked me to give you these. He's held them for you until now, and he said you would know what they are."

She lifted a hand and cupped Sadie's cheek before dropping a parcel into her open palm. Two glittering earbobs, in a rosy quartz floral pattern. Her Ma's. And a perfect match for the dress she wore. Not a coincidence. The result of a clever and thoughtful lady's planning.

"Thank you, Cookie." Her eyes blurred and she blinked the tears away. She wouldn't allow sadness. Not on this beautiful morning so full of promise with a golden sun rising on the wide horizon.

"She's smiling down on you, dearie. Beautiful, and all grown up. Let's see how they look."

Sadie fastened the clips in place, one on each earlobe. They sparkled from her reflection in the mirror. Such a pretty effect. She enjoyed the flash and glitter.

Music rose before them as they walked toward the clearing where they'd had the bonfire. A gentle strumming on Boyd's stringed instrument created a hushed, reverential processional as the faithful gathered onto split log seats, or some on stumps, or even sitting in the dirt. She tried not to focus on Gordon Lillie, who stood off to the side unobtrusively, his head bowed in genuine veneration. It was easy to forget "Pawnee Bill" and all he stood for when she realized the man was a seeker, same as each one present.

Her Pa stood next to Boyd, humming along on his harmonica to the familiar strains of a hymn, "Rock of Ages." Every voice joined the chorus, but Boyd knew all the stanzas. A few others sang with him as he led out the lyrics with a tempo and melody, clear and strong.

Boyd's next selection was livelier, and not one Sadie knew, but she picked up the refrain and risked caterwauling to raise her heartfelt praise. At times, Boyd seemed lost in the music and words, enraptured in the moment. She almost grew irksome that he hadn't looked her way. But mostly she was proud to see before her a man who took his convictions to heart and wasn't afraid to show it. He possessed a fine singing voice, but it was his passion that set him apart. His expression, with eyes closed and face lifted, was compelling, and made her want to sing with feeling too.

When the song had reached its crescendo and slowed to a satisfying conclusion, Boyd launched straight into his last hymn. He sang the words without accompaniment at first, steady and hushed.

> *There's a land that is fairer than day,*
> *and by faith we can see it afar;*
> *for the Father waits over the way*
> *to prepare us a dwelling place there.*
> *In the sweet by and by,*
> *we shall meet on that beautiful shore ...*

Many voices joined in, and the honied tone of his instrument rounded out the sacred sounds. Rich and full-bodied, the music washed over her like a healing balm, and she savored its beauty.

Beauty, she could now see, was a many-faceted thing. Nature was beautiful in all of its mystery and grandeur. A man's strength was beautiful, rendered in the service of others, and a woman's delicate allure was beautiful, offered with a pure heart. Love was a stunning balance between it all.

And God was there in the midst.

———

When the song concluded, there wasn't a dry eye in the crowd. Boyd's eyes included. He strummed the resolving chord and allowed it to resonate as he cleared his throat and drew a sigh, savoring the sweetness of the presence of the One they worshipped.

As he took the banjo strap down from around his shoulder, he searched the assembly to find Sadie. Her eyes shone, gazing at him, and his heart swelled at the sight. She was moved too. And then he knew. He had found his purpose. To provide the opportunity for a lost little maverick to find her way back to her heavenly Father. There could be no doubt now. God's peace filled her gaze.

He made his way over and sat with her, Mrs. Garrity nearby. Her Pa remained standing, addressing the crowd with a reading from the book of Hebrews.

Boyd would be lying if he were to say he heard a word of the sermon. All he comprehended was the beating of his own heart sitting next to the prettiest gal he'd ever laid eyes on. When service was over, he would waste no more time, and propose.

But as soon as Fletch spoke the benediction and the congregation responded with "Amen." Sadie jumped up and took his hand.

"Come with me. There's someone I'm dying for you to meet."

He didn't even have time to grab his instrument but barely managed to find his footing to keep up with her.

"Mr. Boyd Hastings, I'd like you to meet a new friend. Mr. Gordon Lillie." She stepped back and made way for the two to regard one another.

"Pleased to meet you, sir." Boyd shook his hand. "Are you visiting the area?"

The gentleman's mustache lifted in a grin. "You could say

that, son. But this church service felt more like home than a side stop along the road. I was particularly drawn by the songs, Boyd. Anyone capable of the depth of expression that you showed to the audience that matters the most would be someone I would welcome to sing for me."

Boyd blinked and cocked his head. "I'm flattered, but I'm afraid I don't understand, sir."

Sadie hopped up on her toes. "Mr. Lillie goes by another name, Boyd. Have you ever heard of Pawnee Bill and his Wild West show?"

Boyd's jaw dropped, and he had to gather his wits to respond with something other than addled awe. "Yes, sir, Mister." He pumped his hand again, clasping with both of his. "It's a real honor, sir."

"Come and meet my wife, and we can discuss what life is like traveling with a show troupe. If you're interested, you can sign a contract right away. We run a tight schedule, and we're moving out this afternoon. So, I'm afraid you'll have to make up your mind immediately."

Boyd followed, barely touching the ground as he passed. After a few paces, he turned, but Sadie was gone.

16

A wind swept the prairie in a dirt devil so big, and so fast, Sadie was caught up in midair. Or so it felt. Though the clearing in which she stood still teamed with people, she could have been a million miles away for the sudden sense of aloneness she felt. Boyd looked back once as he walked along with Pawnee Bill, and the conflict in his eyes told her all she needed to know.

He was leaving. He would take the offer, and she would never see him again.

Just like Ma. Ten years ago, to the day.

A lump formed in her throat, and hot, humiliated tears threatened to spill. This was what she got, letting her fool heart take in the notion of a man being a welcome intrusion in her life. She always figured fallin' for a feller would be a nuisance to her freedom. She never imagined that a man could take her very breath away and leave her gasping like a fish pulled out of the water. Helpless.

One tear steamed down her cheek, then the other. She

fisted her hands, and turned away, head down, stomping toward her cabin. She'd run over the devil himself if he got in her way.

Oof!

A wall had stepped in her path, and she bounced back. It was the wide chest and broad shoulders of a certain familiar figure, but this time he wasn't wielding his big black case

"Sadie? Aren't you gonna come and talk to Mr. Lillie with me?"

"Why should I?" She choked. "To hand you over to him and watch you ride away with my heart? I want to be happy for you, Babyface, but I guess I'm selfish. Since you don't need to run from your past anymore, I thought maybe you'd stay and take the job of foreman. But I wouldn't let you do that now. This is what you were born for. I ain't gonna stand in your way."

He stood there, his head cocked to the side, his puppy-dog eyes searching her. "Sadie, *you* made this possible for me—you set this whole thing up. Didn't you?"

She nodded, trying to bite her lower lip so she wouldn't blubber. "Take it Boyd. Don't look back."

"You silly girl." He chucked her on the chin. "I was going to propose to you today." His wincing gaze spoke of that same conflict that made her think he was leaving.

Would he stay after all?

Before she could respond, he took her in his arms and kissed her. "Marry me and come *with* me."

She gasped, fearing a full-on swoon.

"I couldn't help but overhear ..." Pawnee Bill strutted over to them. "My dear Miss Mitchell, you could sell raincoats in the desert." He chuckled. "Would you consider a position as sales manager and talent agent?"

Travel. For pay. With Boyd.

It all seemed too good to be true. But lately, she was beginning to believe in miracles.

"Let me look at that-there contract, and maybe me and the mister can work something out."

EPILOGUE

B oyd stretched out in the wagon, Sadie by his side. The first day of their honeymoon behind them, before them stretched a horizon blazing with the glory of a prairie sunset. His ribs were slowly recovering from laughter, celebration, and enough dancing to cut a rug. Now it was time to relax. In the last gasps of light, he worked out a letter to his cousin.

Dear Jake,

I got a letter from Caleb today, and all is well in Juniper County—or was as of this past week. As you probably know, Caleb has left Juniper County and won't be returning to Colorado, either. Caleb sold his place in the Texas hill country and bought a ranch in South Texas. He and his wife Lucy are living there now. But that's not the big news. Lucy just gave birth to twins, Caleb and Cathy, and they hope to have many more children—but maybe not all twins.

I have finally found my happily ever after. Seems the Lord has delivered answers to my prayers in a big heap. I'm no longer a wanted man, since Matilda cleared my name. I rejoice in that, but even more congratulations are in order. I have gotten hitched myself, to a great gal named Sadie. She and I may show up in your town one of these days, as we have been hired on to a traveling show. Pawnee Bill and the Wild West has given us a chance to recreate the days of the open range, and of swarms of buffalo thundering across the prairie, at least one show at a time. I am the happiest man alive, I reckon.

I hope you and your missus are likewise happy and fine. Give my love to Anabelle.

Your newlywed cousins,
Boyd and Sadie Hastings

The End

ABOUT THE AUTHOR

Kathleen L. Maher has two novellas in BARBOUR BOOKS' collections: *Victorian Christmas Brides* and *Lessons on Love*. Author of Genesis Award-winning *The Abolitionist's Daughter, as well as The Chaplain's Daughter, No Man's Daughter,* and Amazon top-selling novella *Bachelor Buttons*, Kathleen lives in an old farmhouse in upstate New York with her husband of twenty-three years, their children, and a small menagerie.

A
PANHANDLE
SUNRISE

KATHI MACIAS

Scrivenings
PRESS
Quench your thirst for story.
www.ScriveningsPress.com

Against the colorful backdrop of an early Texas Panhandle ranch, the tension that develops as two cowboys vie for the love of the rancher's lovely daughter creates an engaging and exciting romantic tale. Insight into the concurrent spiritual journeys of all three as they navigate the choices they face makes this a sweetly satisfying novella in another compelling story by Kathi Macias.

— MARTHA SINGLETON, AUTHOR/EDITOR

Such a beautiful picture of how, no matter how far away we are from the Lord, He still speaks to our hearts. Loved it!

— DEJAH EDWARDS, AUTHOR/SPEAKER

A Panhandle Sunrise is a Christian romance novella which takes place on a cattle ranch in the Texas panhandle. It is a sweet, enjoyable story and a relaxing, easy read.

— CRYSTAL LINN

To my beloved husband, Al, with whom I viewed my very first Panhandle sunrise. And, of course, to Jesus, my Savior and eternal Sunrise ...

1

Summer 1892
Double-Bar J, just outside Amarillo, Texas

"Beautiful sunset, wasn't it?"

The soft melodic voice caught Jake Matthews by surprise, but he managed not to show it. "I s'pose," he grunted, keeping his eyes focused on the corral gate, even as he brushed away the melancholy he so often felt at the sight of a sunset.

Anabelle Floyd, the ranch owner's daughter, had captivated Jake's attention from the moment he first set foot on the Double-Bar J in the early spring of 1889. And yet, after three years, he and Anabelle had never had more than a brief, cursory conversation. Jake told himself it was his fault, but he simply couldn't get past the lump that formed in his throat every time he got anywhere near the petite twenty-one-year-old with fiery red hair and green eyes.

"Looks like you're are about done there," Anabelle noted.

Did he hear irritation in her tone? Scolding himself for being rude, he turned to face her. Thankfully, he was once

251

again able to conceal his emotions as the sight of her in an ankle-length blue gingham dress with her hair done up on top of her head nearly took his breath away. He couldn't help but wonder if she could hear the pounding of his heart.

He cleared his throat, though the lump remained. "I, um ..." He nodded. "Yep, I'm about done here." He realized he still had his wide-brimmed, once-white hat on, so he yanked it off his head and held it by his side, hoping his dark hair wasn't sticking up in all directions.

"So I see." Glancing from Jake's face to the gate and back again, Anabelle smiled, sending a lightning bolt down his spine. "Besides, it'll be dark soon. Why not quit for the day and join us out back? Daddy's goin' to light one of his campfires tonight, and, as you know, everyone's invited." She tipped her head slightly to the right, a playful glint in her eyes. "That includes you, Jake Matthews. You will come, won't you?"

If she'd asked him to walk *through* the fire instead of sit next to it, he couldn't have said no. "I, um ..." He swallowed. "It's been a long day, and I ... uh ... I still have a couple of things to do. Besides, I'm kind of tired—"

Her laugh interrupted him before he could finish his thought. "You can't be that tired," she insisted. "And you couldn't possibly have that much left to do." She took a step closer. "We won't be out there that long. The other hands have an early day tomorrow, too, but they're comin'." Another step. "Come on, Jake. Join us, please. Daddy just wants to lead us in singin' a few hymns, deliverin' a short devotional thought, havin' a word of prayer, and then we can visit with each other for a little while before callin' it a day." Her smile turned playful. "Besides, you've come to a couple of our campfires before and survived just fine."

Jake's cheeks flamed, and he was glad for the deepening darkness around them. "Yes, sure ... of course," he managed to say. "Just give me a minute to go wash up a little. I'm ... kinda dusty." He lifted his hat and brushed some dust from the brim as if to emphasize his point, then immediately regretted it as Anabelle coughed and backed up a couple of steps.

"I'm sorry," he said. "I didn't mean to ... I didn't think ..."

Her face wasn't as clear as it had been moments earlier, but he was still able to make out her grin in the fading light. "That's perfectly all right," she said. "I was born and raised in the Panhandle, remember? I'm well acquainted with dust. Besides, that's Double-Bar J dust you're wearin', cowboy—my favorite kind. Now go wash it off if you must, but then come and join us. Please. I won't take no for an answer."

"Um ..." He nodded. "Okay, sure. I'll be right there, as soon as I—"

She nodded. "Good. I'll be watchin' for you."

Jake stared as Anabelle headed toward the back of the house, disappearing into the darkness even before she turned the corner. There was nothing he wanted more than to walk toward the campfire with her right now, but he needed to take care of a couple things and wash some dust off his face first. He hoped he wouldn't make a complete fool of himself in front of Anabelle, her father, or the other ranch hands who called the Double-Bar J their home.

———

The campfire was blazing by the time Jake sauntered up, trying his best to appear nonchalant, even as he scanned those already in attendance to find the redhead who had personally invited him. He spotted her almost immediately and wished he had the courage to join the half-dozen ranch hands already basking in her presence, obviously captivated by her every word. And then she laughed, the sound a joyous melody washing over Jake like a gentle spring rain. Before he could convince himself to move a little closer in her direction, Jasper Floyd, Anabelle's father and owner of the Double-Bar J, stepped up onto a makeshift wooden platform that elevated him a couple feet above the others, commanding everyone's attention.

"Welcome," he called, his booming voice loud and clear. Jasper was a big man—tall, heavyset, and strong as a bull. Jake had seen him hoist a stray calf and carry it back to its mother without blinking an eye. The man might be in his fifties, but he could keep pace with the best of his cowhands when necessary.

A slight movement caught Jake's eye. Anabelle was motioning him to join her. He nodded and smiled but stayed where he was. It wasn't so much that he didn't want to become part of her doting entourage—though the thought did dart through his mind—but he didn't trust his legs to carry him across the hundred or so feet that separated them.

What's wrong with me? I've stood up to rustlers and coyotes, even a pack of wolves when they threatened the herd. But one little woman turns my legs to jelly, and I can't say anything intelligent to save my life. Why does she even bother with me? It's not like she's lackin' for attention.

He tore his eyes away as Jasper's voice pulled him back.

"Thank y'all so much for comin'," the big man said. "Before we get started, most of you have been around a while now and have joined us for our little informal meetin's out here, but a couple of you are here for the first time." He nodded in the direction of two new hands, who nodded in return.

As the recently appointed foreman, Jake had hired them and so far was pleased with their work. They were relatively quiet and kept to themselves, which was fine with him.

"And, in fact, we have one more new hand I'd like to

introduce." Jasper glanced at Jake and smiled apologetically. "Sorry this is comin' as news to you, too, Jake, since hirin' and firin' are your job. But Clint Jordan's an old family friend, so when he showed up this afternoon and said he needed a job, I hired him on the spot." He turned back to his right then and motioned for someone to join him.

A little rankled at the public announcement of being bypassed on the hiring of this new hand, family friend or not, Jake watched closely as the tall blond, spurs jangling, made his way up to the platform to stand beside Anabelle's father. *Anabelle.* Jake glanced in her direction, but the new guy held her complete attention.

"Howdy," Clint said, removing his perfectly creased hat. With the man standing in the firelight, Jake couldn't help but notice his teeth shone nearly as white as his hat. "I'm glad to be here and look forward to gettin' to know y'all."

Jake grunted. Why did he suddenly feel threatened by this Clint guy? They hadn't even met yet, and already he sensed trouble.

He shook his head. *Knock it off. You're just imaginin' things. Like Mama used to say, "Don't go borrowin' trouble. There's always plenty to go 'round."*

Jake snuck another glance at Anabelle, only to find her smiling as she gazed intently up at Clint. Just how good a family friend was this guy? It was obvious he and Anabelle were already acquainted. And though Jake couldn't be sure, it appeared the newcomer was much closer in age to Anabelle's twenty-one years than he was. At thirty-one, Jake suddenly felt ancient. He slunk away and headed for the bunkhouse. He wasn't in the mood for singing or praying.

Jake retreated, looking forward to licking his unnamed wounds, but he'd forgotten that Cranky, the old-timer who'd worked on the ranch for as long as anyone could remember, would be there. Cranky knew everything there was to know about everything and everybody connected with the Double Bar-J, but he claimed he wasn't much for mingling. Hence, his absence at the campfire get-togethers and other such events.

When Jake opened the door and stepped inside, Cranky looked up from his self-imposed task of polishing his belt buckle. For the life of him, Jake couldn't imagine why a man who obviously despised baths could spend so much time cleaning and polishing his spurs and belt buckle. He was always working on one or the other. He'd once told Jake you could tell a lot about a man by the condition of his spurs and buckle. Jake had tried ever since to be a bit more careful about those two items, but he knew the shine on his didn't begin to match Cranky's.

The old-timer's slightly rheumy eyes settled on Jake. "Back already? Sounds like the singin's just gettin' started out there. What'd you do, sneak out early?" He shook his head. "Can't say I blame you. Ain't no point in those get-togethers, far as I can see."

Jake considered telling Cranky it was none of his business. After all, technically, Jake was his boss, despite the old man's seniority. Still, Jake's mama and daddy had taught him better than to be disrespectful to anyone, particularly someone of advanced age.

"Nah," he said, his conscience tweaking him over what he tried to convince himself was a harmless white lie. "Just don't care much for singin', I guess. Besides, I'm tired."

The old man nodded, the creases softening in his leathery face. For a moment, Jake considered asking him how old he was, but thought better of it and went straight to his bunk, turning his back to his elderly roommate.

"Tired, eh?" Cranky sighed loudly. "Yeah, I s'pose that's as good a reason as any. My old bones been wantin' to call it a day for a while now."

Cranky paused, obviously waiting for Jake to answer. When he didn't, the old man said, "Well, I guess that's about it. I've said all that needs sayin', so I believe I'll hit the hay and get some shut-eye."

Without turning, Jake nodded, looking forward to pulling off his boots for the first time in about fifteen hours. "Me too," he said. "See you in the mornin', Cranky."

The old man didn't answer, but Jake imagined he'd be snoring up a storm any minute now.

————

Scarcely twenty-four hours later, Jake stood outside the bunkhouse and watched as breathtaking streaks of orange and purple painted the night sky. He had awakened that morning, after Clint's public introduction at the campfire the night before, trying to shake off the hazy remnants of a dream that clearly included images of both Clint and Anabelle. Throwing himself into his work, he had done his best to put his dream out of his mind. Although he'd managed to get a lot of fence mending done, he wasn't as successful at banishing the two from his thoughts.

Despite the weariness of a twelve-hour workday, he knew he wasn't ready to sleep. He was about to head over to the barn and check on the horses when a deep voice he had heard only a couple of times interrupted.

"Jake Matthews, hold up. You got a minute?"

Jake's jaw muscles twitched, but he forced himself to turn

and look into the perfectly chiseled, tanned face of Clint Jordan. "Clint. What can I do for you?"

His smile appeared genuine as he spoke. "Oh, nothin' special. I just thought, since you're the boss around here, I should formally introduce myself."

Jake tensed. "We were introduced at the campfire last night, and I met you again later at the bunkhouse, not to mention we worked the fences together most of the day. Besides, I'm not the boss," he said, his words measured. "That would be Mr. Floyd. But then, you already know that, since y'all are family friends, right?"

Clint chuckled. "Well, I s'pose technically that's true, but you're the foreman. In my book, that's the guy who's in charge of what really matters. Know what I mean?"

Was the guy trying to flatter him or play with him? Jake squinted to better see Clint's expression. Although Clint was friendly enough, Jake sensed a hint of warning deep down in his stomach, the kind he'd felt just before he came up on that nest of rattlers one morning out on the back forty. Heeding that warning had enabled him to dodge the venomous strike that came seconds later. Was Clint Jordan a snake, or was Jake judging him unfairly because he resented the man's long-term relationship with Anabelle and her father?

Jake started to explain that he hadn't been foreman long and only got the job because the two more qualified hands turned it down, but he thought better of it. "Okay, if you say so. Well, I need to get goin'. I was just fixin' to go check on the horses."

"In the barn?" Clint's smile widened, if that was possible. "Hey, don't worry about it. Save yourself a trip. I just came from there, and they're all fine."

Jake's jaw twitched again. He wasn't sure what bothered him most at that particular moment—Clint's condescending attitude or his ever-present smile. Maybe Jake imagined the condescension, but the smile could not be denied.

"I believe I'll head on over there anyway," he said, forcing a smile of his own. "But thanks for lettin' me know everything's okay at the barn."

"Sure thing," Clint said, then shrugged his shoulders. "Tell you what. I'll walk on over there with you. It'll give us a good chance to get better acquainted, know what I mean?"

Jake didn't care what Clint meant. He wanted to be alone for a bit, especially after spending the last couple of minutes with the handsome newcomer who rankled him at every turn. He sighed and set out for the barn, their spurs clanking in unison as they walked.

2

Dust stung Jake's eyes as he raced back to the ranch, three hands riding hard beside him. They'd been working on one of the farthest sections of fence when the dust storm hit.

Should've seen it comin', Jake thought, scolding himself. *Bein' busy with the fence is no excuse. These guys depend on me to pay attention to this sort of thing. If my mind hadn't been on. ... other things ... we could've headed back before it got this bad.*

Anabelle and Clint. For the past few days, they were always together—never one without the other unless Clint was out working with him somewhere on the ranch. *Even today, Clint got himself assigned to some cushy job with Mr. Floyd, helpin' with somethin' up at the main house—no doubt somewhere near Anabelle.*

The dust grew worse, and though the men had their scarves pulled up over their noses and mouths, their eyes were exposed to the flying grit. More than once, Jake wondered if they were headed in the right direction, but the horses knew their way back to the barn, even if they, too, could scarcely see.

For that reason, he gave his steed free rein, knowing the others were doing the same.

About the time Jake found himself nearly despairing of ever making it back, the horses drew up and stopped just outside the familiar barn. Jake heaved a sigh of relief and dismounted. The four men led their exhausted rides inside and rubbed them down before heading back to the bunkhouse. The storm was still blowing at full force, possibly worse than when they'd arrived a few minutes earlier. If Jake's hat hadn't been held in place with a leather strap under his chin, it would have been long gone. He wondered how much sand had accumulated in his hair and was glad it was Saturday, time for their weekly baths that evening.

"I see you finally made it back," Cranky said a bit gruffly as the men stepped inside.

Jake ran his fingers through his hair, flinching at the filth. He nodded, hanging his dirty, battered hat on the nearest peg. "Just barely. I was beginnin' to wonder there for a while." He shook his head. "I should've seen it comin'."

The men who'd arrived with Jake chimed in, assuring him they didn't blame him, since they hadn't noticed either. Jake questioned his qualifications for being foreman. *If anything would've happened out there ...*

Cranky interrupted his thoughts. "If y'all think this storm is bad, you ain't seen nothin' yet," Cranky said, a slightly faraway look in his eyes. "Why, I recollect one storm so bad you couldn't see your hand in front of your face—and that was *inside* the house." He chuckled. "Now, let's see. I think it was back in ..."

Jake grinned. The old man, despite his reputation of living up to his name, had already succeeded in lightening Jake's mood, and he appreciated it.

The storm ended, and the entire crew had spent the late afternoon cleaning up the mess it left behind. Even Cranky had pitched in, though it wasn't long before he started complaining about his rheumatism acting up.

"Every bone in my body hurts," he grumbled, more than once. The others smiled. Cranky would complain for a while and then wander off to the bunkhouse for a nap. Whatever the old man's age, it was obvious he'd been at the Double-Bar J long enough to consider it his home. Jake figured that afforded him a few privileges, including living up to his name on occasion.

By the time they all turned in for the night, Jake could relate to Cranky's complaint that every bone in his body hurt. But at least the storm had passed without causing any permanent damage, and for that Jake was grateful.

Before dropping down onto his cot, Jake spotted a letter with the familiar script waiting for him on his pillow. He smiled, pleased his mama had written to him and pleased that Anabelle had carefully placed the letter where he'd be sure to see it. Delivering mail to the ranch hands was a small task but one the beautiful redhead handled with grace and thoughtfulness—as she did with everything else. By the time Jake kicked off his boots and plopped down onto the cot to read his mail, he was smiling with anticipation.

"Dear Son ..."

His heart warmed at those two simple words. He'd never realized how much he would miss his family—and yes, even the town of Juniper—until he left there more than a decade earlier to build his life. *Not quite five hundred miles from home, but it might as well be a million. Who knows when I'll be able to get back there for a visit?*

Jake cherished every letter he received from home, knowing how brief and unexpected life—and death—could be. He brushed away the thought before the lump in his throat could push the tears into his eyes. Jake was very careful where and when he showed his emotions.

"I pray this letter finds you well," his mother had written. "Your daddy and I are doing fine, though it seems we never get caught up with all that needs doing around here."

The words struck his heart like a hot poker. Was she hinting they needed him to come home and help? If so, should he go? He was just getting established on his own as foreman at Double-Bar J. And though he doubted he had a chance of winning the affections of the rancher's beautiful daughter, he couldn't imagine giving up completely and hightailing it back home. *Especially now*, he thought, as a vision of the handsome but annoying Clint Jordan floated into his mind. Dismissing it, he turned back to his letter.

"It's been far too long since you've written to us, son. I pray you're all right. You know, your cousins Boyd and Caleb write to their mothers much more regularly."

Ah, the hot poker was back with a vengeance. All of a sudden, his mother was holding up his younger cousins, Caleb and Boyd, as examples of good sons. She wasn't purposely trying to hurt him, but she could be quite adept at laying on a guilt trip when she wanted to.

Caleb and Boyd. Haven't heard from either of them in a while. I wonder what they're up to. He realized he would undoubtedly find out if he finished reading the letter. Since their mothers were Jake's mother's sisters, and the three women all lived within a few miles of each other in Juniper, they had likely filled her in on their dutiful sons' news.

Sure enough, as he finished the letter, he learned Boyd still lived and worked in Lincoln, Nebraska, nursing his dream of breaking into show business with his banjo playing. *Humph. What's pickin' a banjo got to do with show business? Anybody can play a song or two on one of those.*

Of course, that wasn't true. As far back as Jake could remember, Boyd had carried his old banjo wherever he went, always ready to pick and sing for anyone who asked. Jake had tried to learn a couple tunes himself, but in spite of Boyd's patient assistance and encouragement, Jake had given up fairly quickly.

He read on. Sure enough, all was well with both Caleb and Boyd.

Jake sighed. It had been years since he'd been back to Juniper, and he couldn't even remember how many weeks it had been since he'd sent a letter back home.

The familiar sound of Cranky's snoring interrupted his thoughts, and Jake realized he'd better get to sleep. As always, he had an early day ahead.

He dropped the letter on the floor beside his cot and rolled over to catch some much-needed shuteye.

3

Anabelle sighed. It had taken the better part of the morning to clean up the last of yesterday's dust storm, and now a violent spring rain promised to turn the dirt surrounding the house and other buildings to mud. Even as she rushed to spread large cloths in front of the doors, she realized it was inevitable she would soon be cleaning dirty floors.

She shook her head as she laid down the last cloth. *Maybe I should listen to Daddy and see about hirin' someone to help with the cookin' and cleanin' around here, but after all the stories I've heard over the years about what a hard worker my mama was, how can I not try to live up to her reputation?*

A reputation was about all Anabelle had to hang on to when it came to her mother. The woman had been beautiful and kind and honest, accolades attributed to her by anyone who was acquainted with her prior to her death twenty-one years earlier. *But she was also tiny and feisty,* Anabelle reminded herself. *A redhead who was a lot like me—or at least, that's what Daddy always says.* A slight pain pierced her heart as it always did when she thought of the mother she had never known. And though she had long since made peace with the fact that her mother's death was not her fault, knowing Olivia Floyd died giving birth to her did not help ease Anabelle's pain.

The front door creaked open behind her, and she turned to find Clint Jordan's tall frame filling the doorway. She scarcely noticed his smile as he removed his hat and stepped inside, the brim dripping water and his boots tracking mud.

"Wait," she cried, holding up her hand to stop him. "The floor ..."

He grimaced and pulled back, signaling he had recognized his mistake.

A minute sooner would have been nice, she thought. She forced a smile. "Never mind. It's just water." *And a little mud.*

Clint's face reddened. "I'm sorry, Anabelle," he said, his deep voice tinged with regret. "I should've thought ..."

Anabelle shook her head and waved away his apology. "Not a problem. That's what mops are for, right?" She smiled to reinforce her words. "What can I do for you, Clint?"

He frowned for a moment, as if puzzled. "Oh," he said, his expression clearing up. "Your daddy. He sent me to see if you still want to go into town for supplies today or if you'd rather wait until ... after the rain." The red in his cheeks deepened with the last three words.

He really is a dear. And having known him most of her life, she was certain he meant no harm traipsing into the house without first removing his boots or at least considering how he might keep from muddying up the floors. *That's just the way he is,* she reminded herself. *Well-meaning but not always the most thoughtful.*

An image of Jake Matthews flashed through her mind, as it did so often these days. Would he be any different? More thoughtful, maybe? Less? She sure wished she had a chance to find out, but every time she got near him, he clammed up. *Is he just not interested? Sometimes he seems like he is, but then ...*

"Anabelle?"

Clint's voice interrupted her thoughts. What was it he had asked her? Oh yes, the trip into town she had mentioned to her daddy the night before. She glanced past Jake through the open door at the rain that had yet to let up. "No," she said, shaking her head. "Not today. Hopefully, tomorrow will be better."

"Are you sure?" Clint asked. "'Cause I'd be more than happy to drive you—or just go into town myself and pick somethin' up if you need it right away."

She smiled. "I know you would, Clint. And I appreciate it. But I don't need anything badly enough to risk either one of us goin' out in this weather. Let's wait and see what tomorrow looks like."

Clint nodded. "Okay. Then I'll head on back to the barn and check with your daddy to see what else I can do. But just let me know," he said, turning to leave. "I'll help any way I can."

She watched the door shut behind him, knowing from experience he meant what he said. He would most certainly do anything and everything for her, as he always had. She was well aware there was nothing else her daddy would like more than for the two of them to get together. But as kind and helpful as Clint was—*Not too bad to look at either,* she reminded herself—she couldn't think of Clint Jordan in any way other than as the big brother she never had.

"I wish he'd find someone else," she muttered. "Someone who'd love him and appreciate him for the catch he is. But that someone just isn't me."

She headed toward the kitchen to retrieve the mop. Clint hadn't made it far enough into the house to make much of a mess, but she was determined to wipe up even the few drops of water and mud he left behind. After all, she was certain that's what her hard-working mama would have done.

———

The cloudburst hit as Jake rode out to check a distant fence line. He hadn't seen a cloud in the sky before he left, but as often happens in the Panhandle, the rain snuck up on him. In minutes, he was drenched and scolding himself for not bringing his slicker, which now hung, dry as a bone, on a peg near his bunk. He considered going back to get it, but he was already over halfway to his destination, so he pressed on.

It's my own dumb fault, he lamented silently, gently spurring his horse onward. *I get after the boys for not wearing theirs and then forget mine.* He made a mental note not to mention it to the others when he returned, especially since he'd be showing up looking like a drowned rat.

The torrent eased a bit as he neared the fence, and he hoped that would be the end of it. Having lived his entire life in Texas, however, particularly the last three years in the Panhandle, he couldn't count on it.

The downpour had slowed to a drizzle by the time he reached the fence line. Sure enough, a portion of the fence was down. *Good thing I got out here when I did. This hole's nearly big enough for a heifer to squeeze through.*

Jake had repaired the fence and swung his leg across his horse to hoist himself up when he heard a faint cry. He froze at attention, perking up his ears to hear it again. As desolate as this patch of land was, that didn't mean something—or someone—couldn't be out there in need of help.

Baaaw...

There it was again, and this time Jake recognized the sound. He climbed back down from his horse and returned to the fence, then parted the barbed wire so he could slip through to the other side. He followed the sound for about twenty yards to a rain-washed gully. Sure enough, there it was—a stray Herford calf, its legs stuck in the mud and its white face peering up at him as it bawled again.

"I got ya, little critter," Jake murmured, moving slowly toward the calf so as not to spook it. He was determined to get the animal out safe and sound and home to the rest of the herd. It was important to keep the animal calm.

Half an hour later, Jake sat astride his horse, the muddy bovine tied down in front of him, as they headed for the barn in what was once again a downpour. The closer they got to home, the harder it rained, and the louder the calf bawled. Jake didn't mind the rain so much now, since he had not only fixed the fence, but he had rescued a calf. And that, for a cowboy like him, amounted to a very good day.

The rain had ended and the bawling calf had been safely returned to its mother by the time Jake headed back toward the bunkhouse and spotted Anabelle on her porch, draping wet cloths over the porch railings. He couldn't help but smile at the sight of Anabelle, her cheeks flushed as tendrils of unruly red hair framed her lovely face. As he stood watching her—as unobtrusively as possible—she shooed two ranch hands away before they could enter the house.

"Can't y'all see I'm tryin' to get things cleaned up here?" She plunked her hands onto her hips. "I'll never get done if y'all keep traipsin' in and out."

Visibly chagrined, the strapping young cowboys slunk away, and Jake chuckled to himself. *Sure am glad I wasn't the one fool enough to try to enter the house in wet, muddy clothes.*

Whatever errand had required the two young men to go to the house would now have to wait until their clothes were dry, their boots free of mud, and Anabelle finished straightening up after the storm.

The beautiful young woman glanced up then and caught Jake's eye before he could turn away. His cheeks flushed. Hopefully she wouldn't think he was staring at her—even though he was. He tipped his hat, smiled and nodded, then turned and headed as nonchalantly as possible to the bunkhouse. Would he ever have the nerve to walk right up to her and start a conversation—one that would hopefully lead to at least moving their relationship to a more personal level?

He sighed. He sure hoped so, but left to his own clumsy devices, it didn't look promising.

From the corner of his eye, he caught movement—familiar movement. He turned for a closer look. Clint Jordan, clothes and boots immaculate and dry, headed for the house, where Anabelle still stood on the porch. No doubt Clint wouldn't get scolded as the others had.

Jake stepped into the bunkhouse and pulled the door shut behind him.

4

J ake greeted the announcement of a church social with mixed emotions. True, it would be a nice getaway from the familiarity of the ranch and its daily demands, but it would also be a test of his nerve. Would he have the guts or gumption to ask Anabelle to be his date for the function? And what if he worked up the courage to ask and she said no?

He wrestled with the question as he made sure all was well with the horses in the barn before retiring for the night.

"Atta boy," he said, patting Blaze, his favorite steed, on the neck. Though the horse technically belonged to the ranch, Jake considered it his own because it was the one he rode nearly every day.

"What do you think, boy?" he asked, running his hand down the horse's right flank. "Should I take my chances and ask her to go with me to the social, or just play it safe and sit this one out?"

Blaze nickered, as if he were chuckling at the question. Jake imagined Blaze wouldn't let a little possible rejection stop him from going after a pretty filly if he spotted one. And though

Anabelle certainly wasn't a filly, she was without doubt very pretty.

Determined to push the church social from his mind, he moved on from stall to stall until he was assured the horses were all bedded down for the night. It wasn't necessary for him to perform this task, especially since at least one of the ranch hands had already seen to it earlier. Still, he always slept better when he personally checked on the animals.

Finished with his self-imposed task, he headed for the door, pausing to tip his hat to Blaze as he walked by. "See you in the mornin'," he said, then walked out into the cool spring air.

Enjoying one of the last temperate evenings he would experience as summer closed in on them, he almost succeeded in forgetting about the church social until he approached the main house on his way to the bunkhouse. He froze as he heard Anabelle's voice, soft but clear.

"You're right," she said. "It does seem the storm has moved on, so we should head into town tomorrow and stock up on supplies. Thanks for the offer to drive me. I hope Daddy didn't force you to make it."

Jake frowned. He couldn't see the porch from where he stood, and because he was in the shadows, he hoped Anabelle couldn't see him either. He should no doubt turn around and head to the bunkhouse by a different route, but he couldn't tear himself from the conversation happening just a few yards away.

Who's she talkin' to? It didn't take long to find out.

"Anabelle, you know your daddy doesn't have to force me to spend time with you. Actually, there's nothin' I'd rather do. But then, you know that too."

Anger and jealousy crept up Jake's spine, and he clenched his teeth to bite back any words that might try to escape. He had no right. None. He had never expressed even the slightest desire to spend time with Anabelle, scarcely spoken to her beyond a polite "howdy." So where did he get off being jealous of a guy who had apparently known Anabelle for years and had the courage to tell her how he felt?

"I, um …" She hesitated before continuing, and her voice dropped a notch. "Yes, Clint, I do know that."

Jake held his breath while he waited for the conversation to continue.

"Well, since that's the case …" Clint cleared his throat. "I, um … I was wondering … I mean, I just heard about the church social in town next week, and I wondered if …" He cleared his throat again. "Would you … would you consider going with me … as my date?"

Jake clenched his jaw tighter. He couldn't listen for another moment. Whirling on his heel, he stalked away, wishing he had done that the second he first heard their voices. When would he learn? Why in the world would he think he had a chance with a woman like Anabelle?

————

Anabelle hated being pushed by Clint, though she wondered if his pushiness was simply a product of her not responding more forcefully to him over the years. She had known for quite some time she would eventually have to make her rejection of anything beyond a platonic relationship between them crystal clear. It had been obvious since their teens that he had a crush on her. It had also been clear—to her, anyway—that she did not return his feelings. She had tried on more than one occasion to help him understand she considered him a friend or possibly a big brother, nothing more. And when they lost touch for a few years, she assumed he had finally understood and moved on.

But now he was back, and it seemed they had made no progress in clarifying the boundaries of their relationship. The last thing she wanted was to hurt this kind man who had never been anything but nice to her.

"Please, Anabelle," Clint said, going on to encourage her to accompany him to the social and stressing her need to get away, at least for a few hours, from her many responsibilities at the ranch.

"You may be right," she admitted, though she scarcely heard him speak as she found herself, once again, thinking of the handsome yet shy ranch foreman, Jake Matthews. If only he would ask her to the church social ...

"Say yes," Clint implored, interrupting her thoughts. "You won't regret it."

She focused on his perfectly chiseled face, the shock of blond hair feathering over onto his forehead. Any other girl would ...

But I'm not any other girl. I'm not attracted to his good looks, no doubt because I've known him nearly all my life. And going to the social with him would only encourage him all the more. It wouldn't be fair to him ...

She told herself that was the reason she was resisting his invitation, but she couldn't deny the cowboy from Juniper had a lot to do with it as well.

"I ... just don't think I can," she said, wishing her voice were more forceful. "I ..."

He held up his hand, interrupting her before she could say another word. "You don't have to give me an answer tonight. Just think on it, will you?" He lifted his eyebrows questioningly. "Please?"

Anabelle did her best to swallow the lump in her throat,

but it was stuck beyond budging. Not trusting herself to speak, she nodded, receiving a hopeful smile from Clint in return.

As she watched him walk away into the night, her heart tore. How much easier life would be if she could simply change her feelings toward Clint. Would her future be less complicated if she didn't feel such a strong attraction to Jake? She imagined so, but she had no idea what to do to make that happen.

———

Jake scarcely nodded a greeting to Cranky as he entered the bunkhouse and made a beeline for his cot. Right now, he should be the one named Cranky, rather than the crusty old cowboy busy polishing his spurs.

A letter lay waiting on his pillow, and he snatched it up as he kicked off his boots and plunked down onto the bunk. He glanced at the handwriting on the envelope and realized this letter wasn't from his mother, but from his cousin Boyd. He and Boyd were more like brothers than cousins, and he looked forward to hearing what Boyd had to say.

He stretched out his legs and crossed one foot over the other as he ripped open the envelope, then chuckled at the brevity of Boyd's message. *You might be short on words,* he told his cousin silently, *but at least you took the time to say them.* As he read, he resolved to write back before the week was over. After all, he still owed a letter to his mama too. He'd best get busy.

"Dear Jake," the letter began.

It's been awhile, cousin. What's up in your corner of the world? I hope everything's going okay. Not much new here. Just a couple of banjo-playing gigs that pay almost enough to keep me playing and hoping for a break somewhere down the line. Meantime, I got hired on as a bronco buster on a ranch outside Lincoln, something I imagine you're plenty familiar with.

Jake grinned. *Yeah, I'm familiar with most anything that has to do with horses or cattle.* His grin faded. *It's women I can't figure out—one of them in particular.* He shook his head and returned to the letter.

Anyway, I'm doing fine and hope you are too. Haven't heard from Caleb in a while. Guess I'd better drop him a line.

You and me both, Jake thought, doubling up on his resolution to write not only to his parents and Boyd but to Caleb too. They were, after all, the only real family he had. He went back to reading the letter.

Before I sign off, I have to ask you one thing: You still insisting on being called Jake?

The letter ended with a happy face and Boyd's simple signature.

Very funny. And yes, I'm still goin' by Jake. Don't see any reason to go back to bein' called Jacob. Mama agreed to callin' me Jake when I got a little older and begged her to. Can't say the same for my cousins. They teased me about it for years, especially after I admitted I changed my name 'cause I thought it'd make me sound manlier and tougher, and girls might like me better. He shook his head. *Not sure it made any difference then and probably doesn't now, but I've gone by Jake for so long I can't see changin' back after all these years.*

Thinking of Anabelle and Clint pierced his heart, and he

swallowed a groan. *Nope, bein' called Jake instead of Jacob doesn't seem to matter now either—not when I'm up against somebody like Clint Jordan.*

He tossed the letter to the floor and rolled over to face the wall.

5

It had been a long week. Jake simply could not get the church social out of his mind. All the ranch hands, even Cranky, were going. They all had the day off, and they'd taken their weekly bath early in the afternoon so they could be at their best when they got to town in a couple of hours. Jake figured he'd be the only one left behind on the Double-Bar J.

Somebody's got to stay here and look after the animals, he told himself as he brushed Blaze's mane. *It wouldn't be responsible to run off and leave the place wide open to anybody that might stop by.* He'd repeated those words several times, and though there was a ring of truth to them, his heart wasn't convinced.

Especially when he'd watched and listened to all the hullabaloo as everyone got ready to leave. He hadn't seen the men so excited since Christmas.

"I don't know 'bout you, but I've got my dancin' shoes on."

"Shoot, I could dance circles around you, dancin' shoes or not."

"I hear there's gonna be a kissin' booth. Y'all think that's true?"

"This is a *church* social, so I wouldn't count on it."

"Well, I can dream, can't I?"

"Ugly as y'all are, you're gonna need more than dreams to snag a kiss from anybody but your horse!"

The laughter and good-natured ribbing had continued in the bunkhouse as Jake slipped out the door and headed to the barn. He imagined the men all assumed he would accompany them to town, but that's because they didn't know how he felt about Anabelle and the fact that Clint would be taking her to the event. There was no way he wanted to lay eyes on the two of them having fun together.

"Not very nice of me, is it, Blaze? If Anabelle's happy, I should be happy for her. But I gotta admit, I'd rather have her bein' happy with me instead of Clint Jordan."

The horse nickered and stomped a hoof. It was probably to shake off a fly that kept landing on Blaze's flank, but Jake chose to believe it was because his faithful steed shared his feelings about the ranch's latest hire.

"You're a good friend," he murmured as he continued the grooming far beyond what was needed. "Maybe the only real friend I've got here. That's why I know I can tell you anything, and I don't have to worry someone else will find out."

In spite of himself, he chuckled at the absurdity of his words, then turned as he heard the barn door open. It was Jasper Floyd, the ranch's owner and Jake's boss.

"Mr. Floyd," he said, stopping his grooming to tip his hat. "I hadn't expected to see you down here at the barn."

Jasper smiled as he approached. "You might be surprised at what I do and where I turn up on the Double Bar-J. I built this here barn with my own two hands, you know."

Jake nodded. "I figured as much. You're a hard-working man, Mr. Floyd, and I know this place didn't build itself."

"That's for sure." The man stopped a few feet from Jake

and his horse. "But what I want to know is, why are you down here with the animals? You should be back at the bunkhouse with the rest of the hands, gettin' ready for the big wing-ding in town. You know you have the rest of the day off to attend, right?"

Jake struggled to answer, wanting his words to be just right. "Sure, I know that. And I appreciate it. But I figured one of us has to stay and keep an eye on things. Might as well be me."

Jasper chuckled and shook his head. "Sometimes you're too responsible," he said. "When I said *all y'all* could take the day off and go to the social, I meant what I said. *All y'all* can go. I'm gonna be here, lookin' out for things the way I did in the old days. And I'd say your horse is about as groomed as he's gonna get. So why not head back to the bunkhouse and get ready to head into town? You been workin' hard and deserve the day off."

Jake opened his mouth to protest, but his boss waved him off. "Now go on, git. That ain't a suggestion—it's an order."

It looked like Jake was going to the church social in Amarillo whether he wanted to or not.

———

Summer was quickly making itself at home in the Panhandle, with several weeks of heat yet to come. Like most everyone else in town, Jake hoped a cooling breeze would come up soon, though too much wind would stir up blowing, swirling dust, and no one wanted to see that happen. So far, the heat was bearable, and the crowd swelled as more people arrived to enjoy the festivities.

Jake had considered hiding out in the bunkhouse all evening rather than come into town and risk running into

Clint and Anabelle. But he'd dismissed the thought as quickly as it had come. Jasper Floyd had ordered him to go to the social, so he was here. What was he supposed to do now?

A throng of boys, just old enough to hang around the event without their parents, raced by, whooping and hollering as they sailed past. Not far ahead, Jake spotted a gaggle of teenaged girls, sporting their finest and giggling as they eyed the eligible young men in attendance.

"Hey, Jake, we wondered when you'd get here!"

Jake turned toward the familiar voice and came face to face with two of his ranch hands. They were grinning from ear to ear, mischief sparkling in their eyes.

"So did y'all find that kissin' booth yet?" Jake asked.

The two men burst out laughing. "Not yet," said the one known as Slim. His name fit the tall, lanky cowboy. "But if we do, want us to let you know where it is?"

Jake chuckled and shook his head. "No thanks," he said. "I'm fixin' to go find me some lemonade." He took off his hat and wiped his sweaty brow with his shirt sleeve. "Gettin' mighty warm here this afternoon."

The two men didn't answer. They were already on their way, quite possibly on the lookout for a nonexistent kissing booth.

Jake moved on and soon spotted a lemonade stand. He bought a cup to take with him and went on to explore the rest of the premises. He didn't get far before he laid eyes on the most beautiful woman he'd ever seen. Anabelle, of course, but she looked even better than usual. Her long red hair hung loose down her shoulders and back. A green ribbon, matching her long dress, held the hair back from her face. Best of all, Clint didn't seem to be anywhere around. Was it possible she had come without him?

Jake took a tentative step toward her, even as his heart

hammered in his chest. She looked up, and their eyes met. A smile spread across her face. This was it. Time to make a move ... before it was too late.

And then it was. Too late, that is. Clint Jordan appeared out of nowhere, sauntering up to Anabelle with a drink in each hand. Lemonade? Punch? Jake didn't know and didn't care. Once again, the handsome young cowboy had beat him out for the chance to be with Anabelle.

Jake spun on his heel and turned back the way he'd come. He didn't much care that Jasper Floyd had told him to go to the social. He'd come as ordered, but now he was heading back. He figured he wasn't the toughest bull in the herd, but he sure knew when to accept defeat.

————

I knew he'd come. I knew it! I just wish he'd asked me to come with him.

Their eyes met, their gaze held, and her heartbeat quickened. *Maybe I should have asked him instead of waiting for him to ...*

"Here's your punch, Anabelle."

The familiar voice interrupted her thoughts. She blinked and turned her eyes to the voice's source. Of course. Clint. Always Clint. Why had she let him wear her down and finally convince her to come with him?

She sighed, forced a smile, and reached out her hand to take the offered cup. "Thank you, Clint. You're very thoughtful."

"Always." He smiled. "When it's for you."

Anabelle took a sip, knowing she should say something more but wanting only to check and see if Jake was still watching her. She cut her eyes to where he'd been standing seconds earlier, but he was no longer there.

"Everything okay?"

She turned back to Clint. Had he noticed how disappointed she must look? Determined not to be rude, she took another sip of the sweet red liquid. "Sure. Everything's fine, thanks."

He slipped his hand under her elbow and gently steered her forward. As they walked, Anabelle scanned the crowd. *Surely he didn't leave already. He must still be here somewhere.*

Clint was talking to her again. She looked up at him, wishing his expression wasn't so adoring. "Excuse me?"

"I asked if you're hungry. There's a place right over there that's selling corn-on-the-cob and turkey legs."

He appeared hopeful, but she just couldn't bring herself to eat something quite so ... big. "I was thinking of something a bit lighter," she said, trying to force a smile into her voice.

Clint appeared confused for a moment, but then he looked out over the surrounding booths until his face lit up with a smile. "Homemade ice cream," he announced, pointing at a booth a couple hundred feet away. "How does that sound? Would you like some?"

Though she would rather be having ice cream with Jake, she had to admit that ice cream was one of her favorite foods. "Sure." She nodded. "Why not?"

Clint beamed as once again he placed his hand under her elbow and steered her forward.

Anabelle was glad she'd made her longtime friend happy, but she chided herself for giving the man false hope. He'd had a crush on her when they were younger, and ever since he showed up at the Double Bar-J a few weeks ago, he'd made it perfectly clear that his feelings for her had not changed. If anything, they had intensified, and Anabelle knew she was going to have to tell him she did not share those feelings, nor was there much chance she ever would. The question was, how was she going to make the situation clear to him without breaking his heart?

As Clint ordered their ice cream, she heard the band launch into their first song. She could already see couples gathering at the nearby wooden plank dance floor. Swallowing a groan, she realized exactly what would be next on Clint's agenda.

6

Jake had been up since before dawn, determined to put all thoughts of a certain redhead with stunning green eyes out of his head. It was obvious she and Clint Jordan were fast becoming an item, and Jake imagined there was nothing Anabelle's father would like better. It was time for Jake to cut his losses and move on.

Not that he had any plans to leave the Double Bar-J. It was a great place to work, and Jasper Floyd had just made him foreman. *I wonder if he would've given it to Clint instead, if he'd shown up here just a few weeks sooner ... But he didn't,* he reminded himself, shaking off the insecurities that taunted him. *I got the job, and I'm gonna prove I can do it.*

Hoisting another bale of hay into the wagon he used around the ranch, he hopped onto the driver's seat, picked up the reins, and clucked at the two horses standing in front of him. Empty feeding troughs awaited, and the cattle were already complaining.

Minutes later, he was unloading those same bales and pitchforking them apart so he could spread the hay throughout the seemingly endless line of troughs. It was a long, backbreaking, tedious job, and he could have insisted on having a couple of the ranch hands do it instead. But he was the one who was up early, needing something to do to keep his mind off Anabelle and Clint. Unfortunately, though he'd thrown himself into his current task, it didn't seem to be helping.

The *clip-clop* of approaching hooves snagged his attention, and he turned as the horse and rider drew up a few feet away. It was Cranky, his hat low on his forehead to block the burgeoning mid-morning sun.

Jake stopped distributing hay and eyeballed the old cowboy. He never ceased to be amazed at how well the arthritic sixty-something could still sit astride a horse and ride with the best of them. The other ranch hands were quite a bit younger than Cranky, but they'd all come to respect him. It wasn't because he was their senior, but because he seldom took advantage of his age and shirked his responsibilities, passing them on to the others.

"Hey, Cranky," Jake called as the old man gingerly swung his leg around and off the horse, onto the ground. As always, his belt buckle and spurs glinted in the sunlight. "What's up? Everything okay up at the ranch house?"

"Yep," Cranky grunted, the only answer Jake would get to that particular question. So what was on the old man's mind that brought him out to the feeding troughs? He considered asking him outright, but experience told him the old man would clam up. Better to let Cranky's thoughts unfold at his own pace.

Cranky dug in and scattered the now loosened hay into several troughs, moving down the line as he went. Jake didn't have to give him any direction. No doubt the old man had more experience as a cowboy than Jake had years on this earth.

"Noticed you had another letter on your bed."

Cranky's matter-of-fact statement caught Jake by surprise. Another letter? From his mama or one of his cousins? Had to be one of the three, since no one else wrote to him. Still, that didn't qualify as a reason for the old man to ride out and tell him about it.

"Good to know," he said, keeping his eyes on his work. They'd be done soon enough, and then he could head back and check out the letter himself.

"Miss Anabelle brung it in this mornin' right after breakfast. Seemed like she was lookin' for you."

Jake doubted that, remembering what he'd seen at the church social the day before.

They worked in silence for a few moments, then Cranky said, "Seen her in there lookin' for you before."

Really? Jake straightened up and studied his companion. Cranky might be old, but no one had ever accused him of being senile. Was there a chance he was right? "So ... what are you tryin' to say?"

Cranky paused and returned Jake's stare. "I ain't *tryin'* to say anything. I'm sayin' when Miss Anabelle comes into the bunkhouse to deliver mail, she always looks in the direction of your empty bunk."

Jake shook his head and went back to work. The sooner they finished, the sooner he could stop listening to such nonsense. "I think you're imaginin' things, Cranky."

"Maybe. Lord knows I do that on occasion. But I don't believe this is one of them occasions. I think she's sweet on you."

A lightning bolt shot down Jake's spine, even as he strained to convince himself the old man didn't know what he was talking about. Most everything in him wanted to believe the cowboy's words were true, but the rest of him was busy listening to warning signals. Why set himself up just to get let down again?

"I'm about done here," he announced. "You can go on back to the ranch. I'll meet you there."

Cranky shrugged and walked back toward his horse. "Okay by me. But if I was a young buck like you and somebody told me a beautiful woman like Miss Anabelle might have a crush on me, I do believe I'd do whatever's necessary to find out if it's true." He shrugged again and climbed back on his horse. "Suit yourself," he said and rode away.

———

Jake knew the minute he laid eyes on the envelope that it was another letter from his mama. Guilt stung his heart as it always did when he thought about how long it had been since he'd gone home for a visit. *At least I wrote Mama and Daddy a letter after her last one to me. She must have written back the minute she got it.* If he hadn't followed through on writing to her, the guilt might have been unbearable.

It was nearly lunchtime, but he figured he had enough time to read the letter before going to eat. He made his way outside, letter in hand, to a shady spot behind the bunkhouse. Hunkering down on a large rock, he opened the envelope and pulled out the two pages flowing with his mama's beautiful script.

"We were so pleased to receive your letter," she'd written. "I pray for you daily, and I know the good Lord takes care of you, but I always feel so much better when I see your handwriting assuring me you're okay."

Jake smiled. Only a mother could find a reason to feel good about seeing his awful handwriting. He read a few more lines, then stopped cold when he came to the end of the first page.

I'm so sorry to have to tell you this, son, but your daddy has been injured. It happened when he was chopping wood the other day. You know we've had that old axe longer than we've had you. But up until now, it's worked just fine. This past Tuesday, the axe head flew off just as your daddy was swinging it down to split a big log. The axe itself didn't cause any harm, but the axe head smashed straight into your daddy's face. We're pretty sure his nose is broken, and his face is a mass of bruises. The worst part is he can't see anything out of his right eye. When Doc came out to see him yesterday, he said it could be temporary. We're so grateful to God it wasn't worse. He could have died, you know.

The words washed over Jake like a flood, taking his breath away at the thought of his mama and daddy having to deal with this situation on top of everything else. This time the guilt grabbed hold of his heart and nearly squeezed the life right out of it.

Tears pooled in his eyes, not so much for what his parents were enduring, but for what his mother had said about being grateful to God the accident hadn't been worse. *Grateful*, Jake thought, anger fueling his emotions. He supposed they were grateful his daddy hadn't died, but being blind in one eye certainly didn't make an already hard life any easier.

Should I go home? It sounds like they need me, even though they'd never say so. It'd mean quitting my job here at the ranch—and leavin' Anabelle behind. Then again, it's not like I have any claim on her. She seems happy in her relationship with Clint, so maybe I should use this as an excuse to head back to Juniper.

His mind conflicted, he read on.

I know exactly what you're thinking, son. Should you quit your job and hightail it back home, back to Juniper and the beautiful hill country you haven't seen in so long? Should you give up the life you're making for yourself and come home to help your parents? Well, let me answer those questions right now. No, do not come home. Your daddy and I are perfectly fine. We have wonderful neighbors, as you know, including your aunts and uncles. Everybody has pitched in, and we're doing just fine.

I'll write again in a few days and let you know how your daddy is coming along. For now, just sit tight where you are. The only thing I ask is that you pray for us, as we pray for you. Never forget, son, God is there for us, and He loves and cares for us more than we care for one another.

Tears once again bit his eyes, but he refused to let them overflow onto his face. It had been so long since he'd prayed about anything, and he wondered if he even knew how anymore.

———

Jake had no intention of attending the campfire that evening, and yet he found himself there, sitting a bit apart from the others and listening to the songs. He even caught his toe tapping a couple of times as he stared into the firelight to keep himself from staring at Anabelle. Of course, he couldn't help but notice she was sitting next to Clint.

What did you expect? Any fool could see they're practically an item, as my mama used to call "almost engaged" couples. Well, fine. Maybe that's how it's supposed to be. They've known one another for years. They're both good-looking and about the same age. How do I compete with something like that?

His shoulders slumped. *I don't,* he admitted, *and I just need to accept that. All the more reason to head on out of here and go back to Juniper where I belong, where my mama and daddy need me.*

Jasper Floyd's voice snagged his attention then, and he realized the singing had ended. He seldom paid much attention to the brief message his boss gave at the end of the campfire meetings, but tonight was different. He found himself wanting to stay and listen, though he wasn't sure why.

"When we think of Abraham," Jasper said in his booming voice, holding up his Bible, "we think of a guy who was a giant when it came to faith. The book of Hebrews, chapter eleven, has a list of so-called 'giants of the faith.' And of course, Abraham is listed right there with 'em, one of the greatest of the greats."

Jake hadn't thought of his childhood Sunday School lessons in quite a while, but suddenly they came flooding back. The stories about "Father Abraham" had been among his favorites.

Not that it makes much difference in my own pitiful life. My faith could never match up to Abraham's. Truth is, I can't think of anything I'd have in common with the man.

Mr. Floyd went on. "Now some of y'all may be thinkin', what's that got to do with me? He was a giant of the faith, and I'm not even close."

Jake sat up straighter. Had his boss been reading his mind?

"But if we look close at verses eight to twelve, we see Abraham was considered a giant of the faith for one reason: he believed what God told him, and he obeyed." Jasper grinned. "That's the hard part, ain't it? Believin' God and doin' what He tells us. Most of us say we believe in God and even believe what the Good Book says about Him. But if we don't do what He tells us, our faith is as worthless as an old beat-up bucket with holes in the bottom."

A few of the men chuckled and murmured words of agreement. Jake caught himself nodding. A beat-up bucket with holes in the bottom described his faith perfectly.

"But here's the thing," Jasper said. "Abraham didn't live in a palace. He lived in a tent out in the middle of nowhere, where God sent him. He left his comfortable home behind and moved on because that's what God told him to do. And God didn't let him build a new home while he wandered. He kept him living in a tent. Have you ever wondered why? I mean, surely the poor guy got homesick at times, right?"

A picture of his home back in Juniper tugged at Jake's heart. Yes, he understood being homesick.

The ranch owner lowered his voice just enough that his listeners, including Jake, had to lean forward to hear him. With his Bible open in his hand, he said, "The answer is in verse ten. You see, Abraham wasn't destined to find another home here on earth. He was looking 'for a city which hath foundations, whose builder and maker *is* God.'"

Jasper let that sink in for a minute, then said, "That's what we need to be lookin' for too—a city whose builder and maker is God. Because that's an everlastin' city, where we'll live with our great Creator and Savior, and with the angels, and with all those who chose to believe in God here on earth. That's the only place that'll ever satisfy our longing and do away with our homesickness. Heaven is the place where we'll live forever in joy and peace.

"My prayer is that y'all will choose to live there too. But there's only one way, and that way is Jesus. He said in the gospel of John, chapter fourteen and verse six, 'I am the way, the truth, and the life: no man cometh unto the Father, but by me.' Y'all can't get to that heavenly city where the Father lives unless you come by way of the Cross, where Jesus died for y'all and for me. There's no other way. Jesus said it Himself. Now either y'all believe Him or you don't. And if y'all say you believe Him, then you have to obey Him, as Abraham did."

He paused again, as thoughts and emotions swirled through Jake's mind and heart. Why was he fighting against them?

"Now it's time for me to bid all y'all goodnight. But before I do, I want to ask you to come up here if y'all want to be sure you have a home in heaven. We can talk and pray together."

When one of the new hands stepped up and Jasper turned his attention to him, Jake took advantage of the moment and slipped away. He wasn't ready to bare his soul to anyone, including his boss. He'd been raised in a Christian home, and he considered himself a Christian. However, he believed faith was a personal thing, and that's the way he intended to keep it.

7

Though the flickering fire light didn't reach far enough to illuminate Jake's face, Anabelle sensed he was deeply affected by her father's words. *Why do I feel that way, Lord? It's not like he's doin' anything special—just sittin' there, off by himself, pretty much like he always does. So why do I feel like somethin's different about him tonight?*

The whisper to her heart was silent, but the words echoed in her mind long after she heard them. *Because I'm calling him to Myself.*

Anabelle gasped. She wasn't in the habit of hearing from God, but there were occasional exceptions—and this was one of them.

Oh, Lord, she prayed silently, *what should I do?*

Pray for him. I'll do the rest.

Tears pricked her eyes as she looked around at the others in attendance, as if she thought they, too, might have heard God's message to her. Of course, no one had.

And then, as her father drew his message to a close, she

looked back to where Jake had been sitting. He was gone. Had he responded to her father's invitation?

Her eyes turned toward the makeshift wooden stage where her father had been standing as he spoke to those gathered together to hear him. He was still there, speaking with the ranch hand who had come forward. Sadly, it wasn't Jake.

Her heart sank. She was sure God had told her He was calling Jake to come to Himself. Had Jake said no to God?

The group was dispersing now, so she joined them, scanning in all directions for some sign of Jake. There was none.

She decided to head to the bunkhouse to see if she might catch him before he went inside, but she'd scarcely taken a step when Clint appeared at her side.

"There you are," he said, smiling down at her. "Been lookin' for you. I wanted to sit with you during the campfire, but I got hung up finishing some things in the barn, so I was late, know what I mean?" His grin widened, if that was possible. "But I'm here now, and I'm thinkin' it's a perfect evenin' for a walk. Care to join me?"

Not really, Anabelle thought silently, then scolded herself for her sarcastic attitude. It wasn't Clint's fault she was preoccupied with thoughts of Jake Matthews.

She forced a weak smile. "Sure. But just a short one."

Clint nodded. "Of course. I know it's gettin' late, and we all have an early mornin' tomorrow."

They headed in the direction of the bunkhouse and beyond. As they passed by, she caught sight of Jake standing in the doorway. If only she weren't with Clint, she could stop and talk with him. But even as the thought crossed her mind, Jake's expression changed, and he turned and stepped inside, closing the door firmly behind him.

Jake sighed as the first hint of dawn peeked through the window above his bunk. A rooster announced the new day. It had been a long night with little sleep. *It's gonna be a rough one, workin' all them hours as tired as I am. And even after thinkin' about it most of the night, I still don't know whether to go home and help my parents or stay here and fulfill my commitment to Mr. Floyd. But until I know for sure what I'm gonna do, I owe it to my boss to get up and give it my best shot.*

As he pulled himself from his bunk, the thought crossed his mind that he could ride into town and go to church, as some of the others did. *Mr. Floyd tells us all the time we should honor the Sabbath and spend the day at church and then restin' in the afternoon. But I'd feel like a hypocrite if I took advantage of that offer, so I'll just stay here and work. No better way I know to pass the time than just plain ol' hard work.*

He slid his feet into his boots. His eyes felt like he'd just been through another sandstorm, but he forced himself to stand up and head for the door. After hearing Cranky snore all night, he wondered how any of them ever got any sleep around there.

Sheer exhaustion. We're so tired when we hit the bunk, we don't hear much of anything.

A strong cup of coffee might help, but he didn't want to wake the others earlier than necessary by making some strong brew right there in the bunkhouse. He knew Anabelle often made a big pot of coffee early in the morning and set it out on the porch. *No doubt it's too early for that, but it can't hurt to check.* He ignored the voice whispering in his ear that he was hoping to run into the lovely redhead as she set the coffee out, though he knew it was true.

There was no sign of coffee or Anabelle when he got to the

porch. Still, he figured it couldn't hurt to sit and wait for a few minutes. It wasn't like he had anything pressing that needed to be done in the next hour or so.

He settled into a chair just near enough the porch railing that he could lean back and rest his crossed feet on it. He was facing the wrong way to catch a good view of the sunrise, and he was too comfortable to turn around. *Besides, you've seen one Panhandle sunrise, you've seen 'em all. Not like back home, where the sun peeks over a hilltop just before spreadin' its warmth across its gentle slope.* A pang of homesickness tugged at his heart, and he thought of Jasper Floyd's words the night before.

Abraham obeyed God and left home. How does that relate to me? Sure, I left home, but it didn't have anything to do with obeying God. I needed to get out of Juniper and make a life for myself. Sure been bouncin' around a lot since then—until I landed here at the Double Bar-J. This here's the closest thing I've found to a new home since I left Juniper ten years ago.

He shook his head. *All the more reason I shouldn't just up and leave—not after Mr. Floyd showed his faith and confidence in me by makin' me foreman. But what about my mama and daddy? Don't I owe them more than I owe Jasper Floyd and the Double Bar-J?*

He started when he heard the back door open behind him.

"Why, Jake Matthews! What are you doin' here so early?"

Jake nearly catapulted out of his chair and spun around to face the redheaded woman of his dreams. Sure enough, she was as beautiful as ever, dressed in a pink dress with her hair pinned up on top of her head.

"I, uh ..." Jake paused and cleared his throat. "Sorry, Miss Anabelle. I couldn't sleep and came up to see if there might be some coffee here on the porch."

Anabelle smiled, reminding Jake of warm honey and tinkling bells. He pushed away the foolish thought, hoping his cheeks weren't as bright red as he imagined.

"Well, you're in luck," Anabelle said. "I just made a pot and was about to clean off a place there on the table for it. How about if I get the space ready, and you go on inside to the kitchen and bring that big heavy pot out for me? I'd surely appreciate it."

Jake did his best to calm his throbbing heart, reminding himself that Anabelle was as good as promised to Clint Jordan. "Yes, ma'am, Miss Anabelle. I'd be glad to." Nearly tripping over his own boots, he hightailed it into the kitchen and brought the coffeepot out in record time.

They had it set up, along with a stack of cups, in a matter of minutes.

"Well," Anabelle said, as she stood back with her hands on her hips, inspecting their handiwork, "I do believe we make quite a team. We got that up and ready in no time."

Jake's mouth went dry, and all he could do was nod. Pulling his eyes from her gaze, he grabbed a cup, nearly dropping it before he could fill it with the dark, steamy liquid.

Anabelle laughed and took the cup from him. "Here, let me get that." Effortlessly, she filled the cup and placed it in his outstretched hand. He just hoped she didn't notice it trembling.

"Enjoy," Anabelle said, pouring herself a cup and then turning back toward the house. "I need to go finish getting ready for church." She stopped at the door, speaking over her shoulder before grabbing the handle and stepping inside. "I do hope you plan to join us."

Jake stood, cup in hand, staring at the now closed door. Join her—correction, *them*—at church? That was just about the last thing on his mind.

————

Lively piano music greeted Jake as he neared the building, the choice and tone of the music surprising him. Somehow he'd expected somber organ music, and he had to admit he preferred the faster tempo of the piano.

What was that song? It sounded so familiar. As he tethered his horse to the hitching post out front, it came to him. Something about "when the roll is called up yonder." *Funny what your memory pulls up from childhood*

He made his way inside and chose a seat midway toward the front. With the exception of a few scattered worshipers, he was one of the first to arrive. *No sign of Mr. Floyd or Anabelle. I wonder what she'll think when she comes in and sees me here. She obviously knows I'm not in the habit of attendin'.*

He spotted two books at the far end of the pew and decided to check them out. One was a Bible and the other a hymn book. He laid the hymn book down beside him and flipped through the Bible, looking for familiar stories.

Before he got far, he heard more people entering the building. He looked up just in time to see Jasper Floyd and his beautiful daughter passing down the aisle. Anabelle spotted him and flashed a smile. His cheeks flamed again as he smiled and nodded in return.

Jake sat quietly as the room filled, trying not to stare at Anabelle, who sat toward the front with her father. And then he spotted Clint Jordan, making his way up the aisle to sit beside Anabelle. They greeted one another, and then Clint reached over Anabelle to shake hands with her father. If Jake hadn't already been boxed in with parishioners on each side, he would have beaten a hasty retreat out the back door.

Trapped, he resolved to sit through the service, then head for the ranch and never set foot in the church again. Meanwhile, the service had been called to order, and he did his best to pull himself together and do whatever was necessary to keep from drawing attention to himself.

When the singing started, he rose to his feet, trying to identify the songs and find them in the hymnal. The songs were nearly over by the time he located them, but he hummed along as best he could with any that were familiar.

After a few announcements, which he tuned out as he stared at the back of Anabelle's head, her gorgeous red hair done up and hidden beneath a frilly bonnet, the preacher began his sermon. Jake heard him ask everyone to turn in their Bibles to John 14. It took him awhile to find the right place, but he did and tried to focus on the words as the preacher read them.

His mind, however, wandered freely, as his eyes were drawn, time and again, to the woman who had so captured his heart and the tall blond cowboy sitting beside her. The only thing he remembered was the preacher pointing out verse six, which said, "Jesus saith unto him, I am the way, the truth, and the life: no man cometh unto the Father, but by me." Having been raised by Christian parents, Jake was well aware who Jesus was, and he was relatively certain he believed in him, but the verse made little sense to him. He imagined part of the problem was his lack of sleep the night before.

After what seemed to be the longest hour of his life, the service ended and Jake bolted out the door as quickly as he could without knocking anyone down. He wanted nothing more than to jump on his horse and race toward the ranch, where he would get out of his hot suit and back into his comfortable cowboy clothes as quickly as possible.

8

Jake spent the next week vacillating between going home to Juniper to help his parents and staying on at the Double Bar-J. So far, the lack of a clear answer either way was the only thing keeping him there.

On Friday, he and most of the other ranch hands—minus Clint, of course, who always landed some easy job up at the house—were busy branding cattle. Jake wondered if they'd get done before the heat melted them right into the hard, dusty Panhandle ground. At mid-morning he wiped the sweat from his forehead as he finished up with one cow and went on to the next. Mr. Floyd had purchased one hundred new head of cattle, and they needed to be branded before they could be turned out to pasture.

Must be nearly 100 degrees already. He cast a quick glance at each of the other cowboys. They looked like they were holding up, but that didn't mean they wouldn't appreciate a chance for a cool cup of water. That should hold them until they finished the branding, most likely just before lunchtime. He was glad they got an early start.

"Finish the one y'all are workin' on," he called out, "and then take a break. This heat is brutal."

Within a few minutes they were gathered together under the shade of a huge live oak tree, gulping cool water and trading branding stories. Jake smiled as he listened. He'd come to care for these guys, and he would miss them if he returned to Juniper. Still, he believed his parents needed him, regardless of his mother's reassurances to the contrary.

I think she was just tryin' to keep me from givin' up my life for theirs. What they don't know is I really don't have a life beyond workin' this ranch. It ain't like the rancher's daughter returns my affections.

The vision of Anabelle and Clint sitting beside one another at church on Sunday had nagged at him all week. When she'd encouraged Jake to come to church on Sunday, he'd dared to hope she might be at least somewhat interested. But that torturous hour, as he sat on the hard seat with a perfect view of the two of them in a pew up front, had dispelled any false hope he might have had. *She's not interested in you,* he told himself for perhaps the hundredth time. *When are you gonna get that through your thick head?*

And then she was standing beside them, a long white apron covering her green dress. Red tendrils framed her face, which shone with perspiration. When had she arrived, and what was she doing here?

"Hello, boys," she said, smiling as she took them all in before fixing her gaze on Jake. "I see y'all have stopped for a much-needed drink of cool water. That's good. This heat is terrible. Anyway, I just wanted to let all y'all know to head straight to the chow hall as soon as you're done, whatever time that might be. I've made several pitchers of lemonade, and they'll be waitin' when you get there, along with lots of cold sandwiches and salads."

Murmurs of thanks circulated among the men, Jake included. He watched as she smiled and excused herself to return to the ranch house. She'd said nothing to him personally, and yet it was enough to re-enforce his desire to stay rather than go back to Juniper. *You are some kinda glutton for punishment.* Then he plunked his hat back on his head and said, "All right, boys, let's get back to it. Those cows ain't gonna brand themselves."

————

Anabelle was glad to see Jake and the others finally wrap up their branding and come inside for a cool drink and some lunch. It was still hot inside the house, but not nearly as bad as working outside under the sweltering summer sun.

As she watched them wolfing down their sandwiches and reaching for more, she realized she had underestimated their food capacity—something she seldom did after cooking for ranch hands all these years. She had been about to go upstairs and check on her father, who hadn't been feeling well that morning, but instead she scooted into the kitchen and made more sandwiches. She hoped she wouldn't run out of bread before she got those boys filled up. This was hardly the day to bake bread. Anabelle made a mental note to fix the dough this evening, let it rise overnight, and then bake it long before the sun came up the next morning. Though a regular chore, this time it was a priority.

She was relieved when they pushed their plates away and leaned back in their chairs, moaning happily about how full they were. When she asked if she could get them anything else, they answered, almost in unison, "Couldn't eat another bite."

She chuckled, knowing that might last until suppertime, and then they'd be back for another meal. She was glad she'd made the pies early this morning. The boys would enjoy them this evening, along with a last cup of coffee for those who could sleep after drinking it.

As the ranch hands filed outside, Anabelle caught Jake's eye. "Bet you're glad to be done with that brandin'. That's some hard, hot work."

She noticed his face flush slightly before he answered. "Sure is. But it's gotta be done." He held his hat in front of him, loosely fingering the brim as he spoke. "I can't thank you enough for that delicious lunch, 'specially the lemonade." He shook his head. "Can't say I've had any that good since my mama made it for me back in Juniper, more than ten years ago."

Anabelle made a mental note to fix lemonade more often. "Juniper," she said. "I haven't been there in years. I have to say, though, it's just about the prettiest place I've ever seen. I can't imagine why you'd want to leave there and come here to our dry, dusty corner of the world." She gave in to the impulse and took a chance, offering her sweetest smile. "But I'm sure glad you did."

The man's flush deepened, and she wondered if he was going to ruin his hat, clutching it so tightly. Maybe she shouldn't have said anything. It was foolish, not to mention forward. Hadn't she tried to get his attention in the past, dropped hints, and even downright flirted with him? And what did she get in return? Nothing. Was he so slow he didn't get it? Worse yet, was he simply not interested? Of course, there was always the chance he was interested but was so painfully shy he simply didn't know how to respond. She wanted to believe the latter, but if so, how could she bring him past that shyness so they could explore the possibility of a relationship?

"I, uh …" He cleared his throat. "I'm right glad I did too." He scrunched his hat back on top of his head and beat a hasty exit before she could say another word.

———

I wonder what she meant by that. He headed toward the barn to saddle up Blaze. The latest additions to the Double Bar-J herd had all been branded. Now it was time to get back to those pesky fences, a never-ending job as far as Jake was concerned. He and his horse were exiting the barn and about ready to break into a trot when he heard someone call his name. Not just any someone, but Anabelle. Why did her voice pierce his heart with fear?

Turning toward the house, he saw her standing on the porch, waving her arms at him. "Jake! Jake, come quickly! It's Daddy!"

The fear that had pierced his heart now clutched it until it hurt. What had happened? Was something wrong with Mr. Floyd? And why wasn't Anabelle calling out to Clint, who almost always hung out around the ranch house? He remembered then that Anabelle had mentioned earlier that she'd sent him into town for supplies.

All these thoughts and more flooded Jake's mind as he jumped from his horse and raced for the porch. "What is it?" he asked as he took the three steps in one leap. "What happened?"

"It's Daddy," she cried. "It's his chest. He's in pain. He's on the couch in the parlor. We've got to get him in to see Doc right away."

All thoughts of fence-mending flew from Jake's mind as he ran into the house and into the parlor. There, sprawled out and pale as a sack of flour, lay the man Jake often thought of as invincible. His eyes were closed, and his hands clutched over his heart.

Jake dropped down to one knee beside the couch. "It's me, Mr. Floyd. Jake. I'm gonna get you in to see Doc. Don't worry, sir. You're gonna be fine."

Anabelle spoke up before her father could answer. "I sent one of the other men to get the spare wagon. I'll go spread out a blanket in back if you can get him loaded in."

"Sure. Of course. You take care of the blanket. I'll carry him out there."

Mr. Floyd moaned when Jake lifted him, but he didn't speak a word. Jake wasn't sure if the man was aware of what was going on or not, but he carried him as gently as he could. By the time he got to the wagon parked in front of the porch, Anabelle had already spread out a soft, thick quilt in the back.

"I'll ride back here with him," she said, climbing in. "You drive."

Thankfully the doctor's office, like the church they'd attended, was on the outskirts of town, less than a thirty-minute ride. Jake, driving as fast as possible without jostling his boss, thought the journey would never end.

At last they arrived. Jake tethered the horse and lifted Mr. Floyd from the back of the wagon. He had just started up the steps to the office when Doc Mayfield appeared in the doorway. His eyes went wide when he eyed who Jake was carrying. He stepped back to let them inside.

"Take him in there," he instructed, pointing to a nearby doorway. "Just lay him down there on the examining table."

As Jake laid him down, the doctor grabbed his stethoscope. "What happened?"

"He ... he ate breakfast this morning, and then said he didn't feel well," Anabelle said, her voice choking up. "So he went back to bed, something he never does."

Jake noticed then that Anabelle's green eyes were wet with tears. He swallowed, wishing he could comfort her somehow.

"I asked him then if I should send for you, but he refused. Said it was probably just something he ate. But he hardly ate a thing, not even close to his usual breakfast." She wiped away the tears. "I should have insisted, should have sent for you then. Why didn't I realize something was truly wrong? Oh, I'll never forgive myself if anything happens to him."

"Don't blame yourself. It's not your fault," the doctor said, catching Jake's eye. He motioned toward Anabelle with his head. "Why don't you take Miss Anabelle out to the waiting room so I can take a look at her daddy? I'll let y'all know what I find as soon as I've finished examining him."

Jake nodded and gently put his hand on the small of Anabelle's back. "Let's go sit down," he said, his voice soft but firm. "We need to let Doc Mayfield do his job."

Still swiping at her tears and looking back over her shoulder at her father's still form, she allowed Jake to escort her from the room and over to a couple of chairs in the small, empty waiting room.

"What am I gonna do if somethin' happens to him, Jake? I never knew my mama. Daddy's all I've got."

"I'm ... sure he's gonna be fine," Jake said, hoping he wasn't giving her false hope. "We got him here quick, and he's in good hands."

"Yes, I know he's in good hands," she agreed. "Doc's been takin' care of our family for years, and he's never let us down. But what if I ..." She leaned toward him slightly. "What if I could have saved him if I'd brought Daddy in first thing this mornin' instead of lettin' him go back to bed while I spent the day in the kitchen?" She shook her head. "If I'd just gone up and checked on him, he wouldn't have come down on his own. By the time I saw him, I barely got him as far as the couch before he collapsed." She sobbed. "Oh, Jake, I couldn't bear it if I lost Daddy!"

Without thinking, he reached out and pulled her to himself, where she cried on his shoulder while he awkwardly patted her on the back. He wished he could think of something to say to take away her fear and pain, but all he could do was wait with her until the doc came out with some news.

9

In less than thirty minutes, Doc Mayfield emerged from the examination room, a wary smile on his face. Jake watched him approach, praying he brought good news. This was the first time Jake had noticed the many lines on the elderly man's face. He looked weary.

Anabelle pulled away from Jake and leaped to her feet. "How is he?" she demanded. "Is he going to be all right? Can I see him now?"

The doctor held up his hand. "He's awake, and yes, you can see him, but only for a moment. He needs to rest." He cleared his throat and lowered his voice. "He's had an episode of angina, which can be quite serious. But—"

Anabelle gasped, interrupting before the doctor could finish. "Angina? It's his heart then. Oh no! I knew it was my fault. If only I'd gotten word to you sooner ..."

"Anabelle," the doctor said, a stern tone to his voice, "listen to me. I've known you your entire life, so I'm gonna pull rank here and tell you to stop that kind of talk. It's not good for you, and it's certainly not good for your daddy. He needs rest, lots of it, and no stress. Talkin' like that will just upset him. Do you understand?"

Anabelle paused before answering. "Yes. I understand. May I see him now?"

"Sure. But like I said, only briefly. I want him to stay here for a couple days so I can keep an eye on him. We'll reevaluate then."

Jake waited outside the room while Anabelle and the doctor went in. He heard soft voices but couldn't make out what they were saying. Still stunned by how quickly the situation had developed, he touched the shoulder of his shirt where Anabelle had drenched it with her tears. The material was still wet, assuring him the last couple of hours had really happened. Grateful his boss's situation wasn't worse, he still recognized the events of these last couple of hours were going to make it that much harder for him to leave the ranch behind and go back to Juniper.

Though he was convinced his parents needed him, he now believed Jasper Floyd and his daughter needed him as well. This was no time to run off and leave them without a foreman.

———

Jake was pleased when Anabelle climbed up beside him for the ride home. He didn't kid himself that it meant anything other than the seat was more comfortable than riding in back, but he still enjoyed having her near. He resisted the temptation to touch the shoulder of his shirt where she'd cried her tears.

Anabelle stared straight ahead. "It's going to be so different at home without Daddy in the middle of everything, barking directions and keeping us all in line."

Jake smiled, anxious to encourage her. "You're right about

that, but it won't be for long. Doc says he just needs plenty of rest. No doubt he'll be good as new after that."

She turned to look at him. "You think so? I hope that's true, but I also got the feelin' Doc thinks he'll have to slow down a bit. And knowin' Daddy, gettin' him to do that won't be easy."

They both chuckled. "That's for sure," Jake agreed. "He's used to goin' full-speed at everything he does. I noticed that from the first day I arrived at the Double Bar-J."

"I remember that day."

Jake raised his eyebrows, surprised her cheeks had flushed. "You do? I wouldn't have thought it was different than any other day."

She turned away and focused her eyes on the dirt road ahead. "Well, for the most part, it was. But when you rode in, I could tell you'd end up stayin'."

Jake was even more surprised. "Really? How?"

She shrugged, still looking forward. "Oh, I don't know. Just a woman's intuition, I suppose."

"Hmm. I've heard of that but never really understood it. My daddy used to say my mama had it."

"Really?" She turned back to him, her green eyes wide.

Jake swallowed. Wow. Could she be any more beautiful? "Um ... Yeah. He said my mama knew what was goin' on even before it happened."

Anabelle grinned. "I think I'd like your parents."

"I think they'd like you too."

A sadness returned to her face as she said, "I suppose you know about my mama."

Jake had heard she died years earlier, but no details. "Um, not much."

"She ... died giving birth to me." Her voice cracked as she finished her statement, and tears once again pooled in her eyes.

"Wow. I didn't know that. I'm so sorry."

Anabelle nodded. "I never even got to meet her. My daddy says I'm a lot like her, though."

"She must have been a wonderful lady then."

"So I've heard. Strong, beautiful, and hard-working. It's a lot to live up to."

Jake was surprised. "Really? Why would you feel the need to do that?"

She shrugged. "I don't know. Daddy always tells me I don't have to, and I know he's right. But I've always wanted to." She picked at her nails as her voice dropped. "I suppose it's because ... because I feel guilty about her dyin' while I was bein' born. I've told myself a million times that I shouldn't feel that way, but I just do. And now I can't help feelin' like it's my fault Daddy had that attack. If only I'd checked on him sooner!"

It was all Jake could do not to stop the wagon and pull her into his arms, but that would be out of line. It was one thing to hold her when she practically fell into his arms crying. It was another to think that gave him leave to hold her again, though he did feel they'd grown closer during the past couple of hours.

"Neither one was your fault," was all he said, as he shook the reins to hurry the horse along. When Anabelle didn't respond, they rode the rest of the way in silence.

———

She thought they'd never get there. After opening up to Jake about her mama's death, she had an emotional letdown. When he'd scarcely responded, she'd felt physically drained as well. She had to stop reading more into Jake's words and actions than were there. It was just wishful thinking on her part that he might care for her personally.

The first thing she saw as they pulled up in front of the

house was Clint, standing on the porch and looking anxious. As soon as they drew up, he hurried to the wagon.

Dear Clint. He's always right there for me anytime I need him. It was just a fluke he wasn't here when Daddy collapsed. Otherwise he would've been the one takin' us to the doctor.

"Are you okay?" Clint asked, reaching up to help her down from the wagon. "What happened? Where's your daddy? Is he all right?"

The barrage of questions exhausted her, but she understood and appreciated Clint's concern. "I'm fine," she said quietly, allowing Clint to help her down. "Just tired is all. Daddy's had an episode of angina, but Doc says he's gonna be all right. He just needs to rest."

She heard Clint gasp. "Angina? That's terrible! What can I do to help?"

Anabelle looked into his wide eyes. "You can do the same thing all of us will have to do once he comes home from Doc's —make sure Daddy rests and doesn't overdo." She shook her head. "You know that won't be easy."

"That's for sure." He took her arm and escorted her to the porch. "But I'll do anything else needs doin'. Just ask."

Anabelle nodded, too tired to elaborate. "I just need to go inside and lie down," she said.

She could sense his reluctance as he released her arm and excused himself. As he walked away, she glanced at the spot where the wagon had been a moment earlier. Apparently Jake had already taken it to put away. She imagined he'd then go to the barn to brush down the horse and put it away as well. If only she'd had a moment to thank him for all he'd done for her and her father, but her thanks would have to wait for later.

10

As hard as he tried, Jake couldn't erase the image of Clint Jordan helping Anabelle from the wagon and escorting her to the front door. How foolish he'd been to think he and Anabelle had grown closer during their shared experience with her father. All it took to dispel his wishful thinking was the tall, handsome, longtime Floyd-family friend stepping onto the scene. It was a clear reminder to Jake that he was the interloper, not Clint.

He finished brushing the horse then headed toward the bunkhouse. The afternoon was about over, but there were still some end-of-the-day tasks to finish up. If he found one of the hands standing around with nothing to do, he'd grab him to come and help. If not, he'd finish by himself.

Jake rounded the corner of the bunkhouse and came face to face with Clint Jordan, the one ranch hand he'd just as soon not take with him on his final rounds. He decided to nod a greeting and walk by.

Apparently Clint had other ideas. "Hey, Jake, glad I ran into you. Got a minute?"

Not for you. He scolded himself for his bad attitude, then stopped, irritated that he had to look up at him. It wasn't enough to be handsome and a family friend—the man had to be tall too. "Sure. What's up?"

"I understand you drove Anabelle and her daddy to Doc's place. I surely do appreciate it."

Jake's irritation level refused to be quieted. Who did this guy think he was, expressing gratitude for the Floyd family? It's not like he was part of that family ... yet. Jake nodded and waited to see where the conversation would go next. He didn't have long to wait.

"So how is he? I mean, *really*? Anabelle said it was an attack of angina and he's gonna be fine, but I'm wonderin' if she's just down-playin' it a bit."

Jake shrugged. "You'd have to ask Doc Mayfield."

"I suppose. I just ... well, I wondered if you might know a little more."

"'Fraid not." Jake grudgingly admitted to himself that the good-looking cowboy appeared sincerely concerned. "Sorry I can't help." He turned to leave.

Clint stopped him. "Wait a minute. Where you headed?"

Jake took a deep breath and counted to ten before answering. "Just gotta grab somethin' from the bunkhouse and then go finish my chores for the night."

"Great! I ain't got nothin' to do right now, 'specially since Anabelle went upstairs to lie down and hasn't come back. What can I do to help?"

Jake hadn't ground his teeth since he was a kid, but he was right on the edge. "Not necessary," he mumbled without looking up. "I can handle it on my own."

"Sure you can," Clint said. "But work always goes faster with two instead of one, know what I mean?"

Jake sighed and nodded. Yes, he knew what he meant.

"Fine. Just give me a minute." He entered the bunkhouse and closed the door behind him. There was no doubt in his mind the irritating cowboy would be waiting for him when he came back out.

———————

Anabelle awoke with a start. Something wasn't right. The angle of light in the room told her it was late afternoon, almost evening. What was she doing in bed?

The day's memories flooded her mind then, and she winced at the pain they brought. *Daddy! Oh, please, Lord, let him be okay!*

Doc Mayfield had assured her it was a minor attack and with plenty of rest, he would recover just fine. And yet the doctor had insisted on keeping her father there with him for a few days so he could keep a close eye on him. That told her the only parent she'd ever known wasn't out of danger yet.

And it's my fault. He told me this mornin' he wasn't feelin' well and was going back to bed to lie down for a while. That should have been enough to tip me off that somethin' was seriously wrong. I can't remember the last time Daddy stayed in bed during the day.

It hit her then that she hadn't fixed supper for the crew, nor had she made arrangements for anyone else to do so. She shot out of bed and patted her hair into place before racing down the stairs toward the kitchen. The last person she'd expected to see standing at the sink was Cranky, but there he was, washing dishes.

The old cowboy turned when she entered the room. "Miss Anabelle," he said in greeting. "I hope you got some rest."

"I did," she assured him, "and I'm so sorry I wasn't here to feed the men."

Cranky grinned, revealing the gap in his upper front teeth.

"Not a problem," he said. "I ain't much good for a lot of things these days, but I can still throw together a buckskin barbecue at the last minute. Everybody's been fed, and I set some aside for you."

Tears of gratitude pricked her eyes. "Oh, Cranky, I can't thank you enough. Whatever would we do without you around here?"

"You'd probably do just fine, but I'm glad you don't know that." His hands still in the soapy water, he nodded toward the kitchen table. "That's your dinner over there, underneath the tea towel."

Gratitude washed over her, and though she wasn't hungry in the least, she wasn't about to hurt his feelings. She sat at the table and pulled back the muslin towel that covered the plate full of delicious smelling barbecued chicken and cornbread. Suddenly she thought she just might be hungry after all.

Cranky busied himself cleaning up while she ate, but when she finished, he came and sat down across from her. "So what's goin' on with your daddy, Miss Anabelle? Rumor in the bunkhouse is he had heart pains. That true?"

She sighed. "I'm afraid so. Doc says it was a mild angina, but he wants Daddy to stay there for a few days so he can keep a close eye on him. He says he should be fine if he takes it easy for a while. I surely do hope he's right."

The old man reached over and patted her hand. "I'm sure he is. Old Doc's been around for years, and he's seen his share of all sorts of things, includin' angina. Trust him." He paused. "And trust the good Lord. He knows what He's doin'. I know you've been talkin' to Him since this happened."

"I have," she admitted. "Almost non-stop."

Cranky smiled. "Me too. And if He'll listen to an old coot like me, He'll listen to most anybody."

She chuckled. Cranky had lived and worked on the Double Bar-J as long as she could remember, and she hoped he'd be around for many years to come. He didn't talk much about his life before the ranch, but many speculated it included a broken heart.

"You're a good man, cowboy," she said.

His face flushed, he cleared his throat, then got up and excused himself to go back to the bunkhouse.

————

Jake was up early the following morning. He'd no sooner stepped outside than he spotted Anabelle sitting on the porch, sipping coffee.

"Mornin'," he said, tipping his hat as he approached. "Any news about your daddy?"

She shook her head. "Nope. I plan to ride in later to check on him and see what I can find out."

He nodded. "Good plan." Should he offer to drive her in the wagon?

Before he could ask, she indicated the large pot and extra cups beside her. "Coffee's ready. Help yourself."

He poured a cup, hot and black, then hesitated until she invited him to sit down.

"What have y'all got planned today?" she asked. "Anything special?"

Surprised, he said, "No, just the usual." Was she hinting she wanted him to offer her a ride to go see her father? He would be more than happy to oblige, as there was nothing needed doing at the ranch that couldn't be done without him for a few hours. He took another sip of coffee and was about to open his mouth and plunge in when Clint showed up, spurs jangling.

"Mornin', Anabelle," he said, tipping his hat as he went straight to the coffee. "Jake."

Jake nodded a greeting, irritated once again. Clint's arrival threw his plan to drive Anabelle to town right out the window.

Clint didn't wait for an invitation to sit, instead plunking down in the seat nearest Anabelle. It was the seat Jake had considered taking a few moments earlier but thought it would be too forward. Instead, he had taken a chair a few feet away.

"What did you hear about your daddy?" Clint asked. "Anything?"

"Not a word. I'm prayin' no news is good news, but I'm plannin' to ride in later to see for myself."

"No need to ride in on your own," Clint said. "I'll gladly take you in the wagon. You don't need to go through this alone, know what I mean?"

Jake imagined Anabelle knew very well what Clint meant, as did he. He wondered if the man's constant use of the phrase irritated her half as much as it did him. He doubted it.

Jake sat still and quiet until Anabelle thanked Clint for his "kind offer" and agreed to let him take her to Doc Mayfield's place. That settled it, as far as Jake was concerned—not just about the ride today but about the entire situation as it related to Miss Anabelle Floyd. Quite obviously she and Clint were on their way to a serious relationship, one that left no place for Jake. Any decision he made now about staying on to help Mr. Jasper or going home to help his parents had to be made without consideration of Anabelle. She had made her choice, and he would respect it.

11

Jake was surprised to see Jasper Floyd return to the ranch on Sunday afternoon. He was not surprised to see it was Clint and Anabelle who brought him home in the wagon. The relationship lines had been drawn, and he was on the wrong side.

Still, he was pleased to see his boss walking on his own—albeit a bit slower than usual—from the wagon, up the porch steps, and into the house. Once Jasper was inside, Jake turned away. It was obvious he wasn't needed.

"Jake, wait!"

He stopped, surprised and a bit wary that Clint had called his name. He turned to find Clint approaching him.

"Mr. Floyd asked me to bring you to the house."

Jake raised his eyebrows. "Did he say why?"

Clint shook his head. "No. Just said he wanted to talk."

Jake followed the tall cowboy back to the house and into the parlor, where his boss lay on the couch, propped up with several pillows. Anabelle hovered nearby.

"You wanted to see me, sir?" Jake asked when their eyes met.

"Yes. We need to talk. Please, sit down." He indicated a nearby chair.

Jake perched on the edge, wondering what was going on. A jumble of thoughts raced through his mind, including the possibility that Mr. Floyd was demoting Jake and giving the foreman job to Clint, who would no doubt soon be his son-in-law.

"Anabelle," Mr. Floyd said, looking up at his daughter, "why don't you take Clint and go outside for a little while? I need to speak with Jake privately for a few minutes."

Anabelle's eyes darted to Jake, and a smile flickered across her face. Jake offered a brief nod but remained solemn, then turned his head, refusing to watch her walk away with Clint.

Jasper cleared his throat. "So, Jake, how's everything been goin' in my absence? Anything I should know about?"

Jake noticed the man's usual booming voice was a bit subdued and his face slightly gray. Otherwise, he looked the same, though it would take some gettin' used to seeing him in a prone position. "Not really," Jake answered. He gave a quick summary of the work he and the ranch hands had accomplished over the last few days, assured his boss there had been no real problems, then waited.

Mr. Floyd hesitated before answering. "Good," he said. "I'm glad to hear it. I can't tell you how hard it was to be layin' around at Doc's these past few days, doin' nothin' when there was so much needin' to be done here. The only way I got through it was remindin' myself I had a responsible foreman takin' care of things for me. And believe me, I appreciate it."

Jake's eyes widened. He hadn't expected a compliment, but it surely was good to receive one, especially from someone he so respected. There were times he still couldn't believe the man had made him foreman of his ranch. *Don't forget*, he reminded himself, *it was only after those two other guys turned him down.*

"Thank you, sir," he answered, wondering if this was just the build-up before the let-down.

"Welcome. And because of that, I've decided it's time for a change ..."

A slight cough interrupted the man's words, and Jake held his breath. *Here it comes.*

"Excuse me," said Mr. Floyd. "Now, where were we? Ah yes, a change. Now that I'm not going to be as active or involved as I have in the past—at least, that's what the doc tells me—that means you're gonna have to pick up some of the slack. So far, you've have done a great job as foreman, and I'm completely comfortable turnin' over more responsibility to you. But first I need to know you're okay with that."

Jake was stunned. This was not what he'd expected to hear, but it was obvious his boss was waiting for an answer. "Um ... well, yes, sure. That's fine with me."

Mr. Floyd beamed. "Excellent. I'll rest easier knowin' I have someone dependable overseein' things. I'll go over some of those new responsibilities with you in a minute, but first I want to say I'm givin' you a well-deserved raise, startin' today."

Jake caught his breath. "I ... I don't know what to say, sir. It's really not necessary. You've been so generous with me from the beginnin' ..."

Jasper waved away his words. "Now, let's talk about what'll be added to your responsibilities, shall we?"

———

Anabelle sat outside on the porch with Clint, waiting for the two men inside to finish their discussion. She assumed this was about Jake, as foreman, filling her daddy in on what went on in his absence. It would be no easy chore to keep him from jumping back into work before he was ready. She hoped Jake would be a help to her on that front.

Jake. He had been so supportive and understanding the day they took her daddy to see Doc Mayfield. But since then, he'd seemed distant. Of course, he'd always been a man of few words, but she thought they'd made some progress—until now, when he acted farther away than ever.

"A penny for your thoughts."

Clint's voice interrupted her musings. She looked over at him, almost surprised he was still there. "Sorry," she said. "I'm afraid I was ... daydreamin'. What did you say?"

His smile was warm, as were his eyes when he gazed at her. She really had to find the right time to tell him they would always be friends—like brother and sister, actually—but never anything more. It was the thought of hurting him that had stopped her so far.

"It wasn't important," he said. "I was just wonderin' what you were thinkin' about. Your daddy, of course."

She tried to swallow the lump that had suddenly popped into her throat. "Yes, of course. Daddy. I was thinkin' how hard it'll be to keep him restin', especially as he starts feelin' better and wantin' to get back to work." She shook her head. "I honestly can't imagine him not workin'. He's always been so strong, so ..."

Tears burned her eyes before spilling over onto her cheeks. The last thing she'd wanted was to go on another crying jag. First in front of Jake and now Clint. And yet, the image of her father, lying pale and helpless, had haunted her for the past three days. *Please, Lord,* she prayed, even as Clint scooted his chair closer and gathered her into his arms, *please heal my daddy. I love him so much, and I can't bear the thought of losing him.*

She allowed herself to cry on Clint's shoulder for a moment, then gently pushed him away. "I'm ... fine," she assured him. "Thank you, Clint. You're so very kind and thoughtful."

"I'm here for you, Anabelle, and for your daddy, too, of course. Anytime."

She nodded. She didn't doubt it, but his words only reinforced her need to set things straight with him regarding their relationship and its boundaries. But now, sitting on the porch with tears staining her face, was hardly the time.

———

Jake wrestled between surprise and guilt—surprise at Mr. Floyd's compliments toward him, not to mention a raise in pay, and guilt at accepting before he'd made a decision about staying on at the ranch or going home to help his parents.

He plopped his hat back on his head as he stepped out onto the porch, only to come to a complete standstill at the sight of Clint with his arms around Anabelle, comforting her as she cried on his shoulder. *Just like she did with me on Friday. I can't believe what a fool I was to think we were growin' closer. She belongs to Clint now, and I'd best accept that once and for all.*

He headed for the bunkhouse, needing some time alone to think. If Mr. Floyd hadn't just added to his responsibilities and his wages, he'd be packing up and heading for Juniper. But how could he leave his boss in the lurch after all the man had done for him?

The bunkhouse was hot, but empty, and he breathed a sigh of relief. He wasn't up to yakking with Cranky right now, or anyone else for that matter. And yet there it was, a letter sitting on his pillow. Even before examining it, he knew it was from his mama. And he had a pretty good idea what the letter contained.

Kicking off his boots, he nearly fell onto his bed, determined to make his decision soon. He'd spoken to Mr. Floyd. Now he needed to hear what his mama had to say.

My dearest son,

I am writing today because the Lord has laid it on my heart to tell you once again that you shouldn't come home. We miss you and would love to have you here with us, but not for the wrong reasons. Your daddy and I are doing just fine. Everyone has pitched in and helped so much, and so many are praying for his sight to be restored. Whether that happens or not, we know God is taking care of us. So do what God wants you to do, not what I want or your daddy wants or even what you want. If you don't know what that is, ask Him. And keep asking until He answers. Until then, sit tight and listen.

She went on to fill him in on other news from Juniper, but the words didn't settle in Jake's mind. All he could think about was his mother's letter, confirming he should stay at the ranch, at least for now.

But ask God what He wanted him to do? Jake shook his head. How was he to do that? He'd long since grown out of his childhood habit of praying and expecting God to answer. It sounded like a pointless pursuit as far as he was concerned, but his mama had asked him to do it, so he figured he really had no say in the matter.

He closed his eyes. "Are You there, God? Are You listenin'? Because my mama wants me to ask what You want me to do about staying here or goin' home. So I guess I'm askin'. Could You show me somehow? I'd surely appreciate it, Lord." He added a quick amen before drifting off to sleep.

12

Annabelle's heart ached each time she saw her daddy propped up on the couch or lying in bed. She missed his strong image striding around the ranch, confident and sure.

Still, I suppose I should be glad he's followin' doctor's orders and restin'—at least for now. She cleaned up the last of the supper dishes then made her way out to the porch.

The evening breeze welcomed her as she settled into one of the rockers set out for just such a moment. She closed her eyes and leaned her head back, allowing the slightly cooler air to drive the tension from her shoulders and neck. She wasn't sure if that tension came from the extra work she and the others had absorbed since her father's attack, or from worrying that he might have another one. *Most likely both. But the extra work is the easy part. It's tryin' not to worry about Daddy that wears me out. Still, I know there's nothin' I can do to keep him safe.*

Only You. She switched from talking to herself to talking to God. *Only You can heal him and keep him safe. I know my worryin' doesn't help one bit. So please remind me, Lord, each time I start frettin' over Daddy's health, to stop worryin' and pray instead.*

She sighed. *Easier said than done. Worryin' seems to be an inherited gift of sorts. Everyone tells me my mama was the same way. Worryin' about everyone and wanting to fix them, even though she was well aware she couldn't.* But those same people had also said her mama was a strong woman of faith and would eventually turn her worries over to God. *If she could do it, so can I. Help me, Lord!*

"A penny for your thoughts."

The familiar voice and phrase interrupted her reverie, and she opened her eyes to see Clint Jordan standing in front of her.

"Mind if I sit down?" he asked, broad-brimmed hat in hand.

She nodded toward the nearest seat, surprised he'd asked permission. "Be my guest." She waited as he settled in, then asked, "What brings you out tonight?"

"You," he answered without hesitation. "And your daddy, too, of course. How's he doin'?"

"Not much change," she answered. "But Doc says he seems to be regainin' his strength. I do know he's eatin' better, so that's a good sign."

Clint nodded. "I reckon so. My mama always used to tell me you could gauge a person's strength by how he ate."

Anabelle wasn't sure if she totally agreed with that statement, so she didn't answer.

"Sure has been hot lately," Clint observed, and Anabelle realized he was working hard at making small talk. Did that mean he had something bigger to bring up eventually? She hoped it had nothing to do with her.

A gust of wind ruffled her hair, and she sighed contentedly. "Hot, yes," she said, "but this evenin' breeze is wonderful."

"That's for sure," Clint answered. "Evenin's have always been my favorite time of day."

"Mine too," she said, then grinned. "Except for mornin's.

Evenin's are a good time for reflection and relaxation, but mornin's hold such promise. Don't you agree?"

"I s'pose."

When he didn't say anything else, Anabelle dared to hope she'd been wrong and he wasn't going to bring up something more serious after all. Her hope died quickly with his next words.

"Miss Anabelle," he began, his voice slightly gruff, no doubt due to his nervousness over what he was about to say. "I've been thinkin'—'bout us."

He paused, and she scarcely restrained herself from telling him there was no "us," so please change the subject. But she cared enough about him to hold her peace and let him speak.

"I, um ... I believe you know how I feel about you. I ... I think I've been in love with you since we were kids."

Anabelle shuddered, then hoped he hadn't notice. She desperately wanted to avoid this conversation, but it had been coming for a long time. Apparently it was time to deal with it, once and for all. She just hoped she could do so without causing her longtime friend anymore pain than necessary.

"The first time I saw you," Clint continued, "with the sun shinin' on your red curls, I told myself I would marry you one day." He cleared his throat again. "I can't help but wonder if ... if this might be that day. I know I have no right to assume it, and maybe I don't even have the right to ask, but ..."

Anabelle held her breath as he paused. Was he about to propose to her? *Oh, please, God, no! What will I tell him if he does?*

The answer came silent but clear: *Tell him the truth.*

She sat up straighter. There wasn't a doubt in her mind she had heard from God Himself. She swallowed. *Help me, Lord,* she prayed. *Help me speak that truth without breaking his heart.* Even as she prayed those silent words, she sensed God was telling her that at times, there simply was no way to speak the truth without breaking a heart. *But I mend broken hearts. You do your part and tell him the truth. I'll do my part and heal his heart.*

He was right, of course, but ...

Trust Me, daughter.

Anabelle nearly jumped from her seat when Clint laid his hand on her arm. She looked into his eyes and steeled herself for what must be done.

He took her hand in his, and she saw him swallow before he spoke. "Will you marry me, Anabelle?" he asked. "Will you make me the happiest man on earth and be my wife?"

Panic teased her as she tried to remain calm. *Help me, Lord,* she prayed again. *Please.* A sense of peace flowed over and through her then, and she knew God would give her the right words.

"I'm ... I'm so sorry, Clint," she said, holding his gaze. "You know I think the world of you. You've always been like a brother to me, and I will always love you in that way." She saw the pain take hold in his eyes, but she plunged ahead. "I wish I felt differently, truly I do. There's nothin' I'd like better than to say yes. You're one of the finest men I've ever met or ever hope to meet. But I can't, Clint. I just ... can't."

Tears shone in the man's steel-blue eyes, even as they pricked her own. There simply was no easy way to do this, but she'd done the best she could. And she believed the good Lord had helped her through it and would now help Clint as well.

The tall, tough cowboy nodded once and dropped her hand. "I understand," he said, standing to his feet. "And I'm sorry. I should've known ..." He took a deep breath. "Deep inside, maybe I did. But I just kept hopin'."

———

Jake was on his way back from the barn that evening when he rounded the corner toward the bunkhouse and caught sight of Clint and Anabelle, sitting together on the front porch. Clint was holding her hand, gazing into her eyes, and speaking softly. Jake couldn't hear what the man was saying, but from the look of things, he suspected Clint was asking her to be his wife. Jake wasn't about to stick around and watch her accept.

He stormed into the bunkhouse, slammed the door behind him, and jammed his hat onto an empty peg. Why hadn't he told his boss he was leaving and heading back to Juniper to help take care of his daddy? It was a reasonable excuse. Besides, it would give Jasper Floyd the perfect opening to offer the foreman position to his future son-in-law, Clint Jordan.

"Bad day?"

The question caught Jake off-guard. He glanced up to see Cranky sitting on the edge of his bunk, polishing his belt buckle. Jake had been so preoccupied with what he'd seen going on between Clint and Anabelle, he hadn't even noticed the old man sitting there.

"Not really," Jake lied, not wanting to let anyone in on his personal pain. No sense making a bad situation worse by trying to explain it.

Cranky shrugged and continued his task. "Glad to hear it," he said. "Just thought maybe your bad mood had somethin' to do with Clint and Miss Anabelle."

Jake straightened his shoulders and frowned. What was Cranky talking about? What did he know about Clint and Anabelle that he didn't? Disgusted, he stalked over to his bunk and plunked down.

"Any news on Mr. Floyd?" Cranky asked.

Jake had been about to lie down and hope the old man would leave him alone if he ignored him, but he'd waited too long. Now he had to say something, like it or not.

"Not much I know about," he said, forcing his gaze from the floor to the weather-beaten man across the room. "I talked to him a while ago, and he seemed somewhat better."

Cranky nodded. "That's good. He's a tough old coot. I 'magine he'll come 'round."

Jake nodded, thinking now it might be better to head outside if he was looking for solitude. Once again, he waited too long to make his move.

"I thought you might've heard about Clint askin' Miss Anabelle to marry him," Cranky said matter-of-factly, staring down at his shinier-than-ever buckle. "He told me not more than an hour ago he was gonna pop the question first chance he got. Hope I'm not talkin' out of turn, but he didn't say nothin' 'bout it bein' a secret. Course, who knows if she'll say yes?"

Slowly and silently, Jake counted to ten, then stood up and snagged his hat from the peg. Without another word, he paced himself to the door and was about to head back toward the barn, when Cranky spoke up one more time.

"Don't know 'bout you," he said, "but if it was me in your boots and feelin' sweet on Miss Anabelle like I know you do, I'd have to take a chance and say somethin' to her 'fore it's too late. But then, that's just me ...."

"It's already too late," Jake growled and strode out the door.

13

Jake had tossed and turned most of the night, but finally took a chance and headed for the main house to see if the coffee was ready. It was, but Anabelle was nowhere in sight. He breathed a sigh of relief. He was in no mood to hear her happy news.

Now, several miles from the house with his work crew, Jake watched closely as the clouds darkened and grew thicker throughout the morning hours. By noon, lightning flashed in the distance, but the thunder took its sweet time getting to them and could scarcely be heard. *Nothin' to worry about*, he thought as he and the men took a quick lunch break. *It's nearly the end of tornado season, and the Panhandle gets storms like this all the time.*

By the time they finished eating, Jake decided to press ahead with their chores. Though the storm appeared to be heading in their direction, it didn't seem as ominous as others they'd weathered in the past few months.

He and the other hands had scarcely gotten back to work when the first raindrops fell on his face. He looked up and felt his eyes widen when he realized how much closer the storm was than an hour earlier. Should he tell the boys to pack it in and head for home, or try to finish up before the storm broke in earnest?

Sorely tempted to finish the day's work before heading back, he was about to announce that decision to his men. After all, it was a lot easier not to think about Clint and Anabelle when there was a good distance between him and the ranch and plenty to keep him busy. The crew would follow his lead, whatever it might be, but that only added to his sense of responsibility in making the right call. Then he noticed the restlessness of the horses, and his decision was made.

"Let's head back, boys. I'd like to stay and finish up, but that storm looks to be gatherin' strength and headin' our way fast. Even the horses are nervous."

The crew loaded their tools into the sacks already hanging on the horses, then swung their legs over their steeds and turned toward the ranch just as the clouds, now swollen and black, unleashed their fury on anyone unfortunate enough to still be outside.

Jake's eyes darted from side to side, but the driving rain made it impossible to find a temporary shelter. Besides, in such flat and barren terrain, the best they could hope for was a stray tumbleweed or two. And so they pressed on.

They were within sight of the ranch when Jake spotted a funnel cloud coming down out of the sky, headed straight for the Double Bar-J and anyone who might be there. That included Anabelle and her father. His heart raced as he spurred his mount to go faster. It couldn't, since it was already galloping at full speed. Jake, nearing the familiar buildings in what seemed to him slow motion, watched helplessly as the twister raced toward the ranch, sucking up everything in its path.

He was nearly there and could see no one outside. For that he was grateful. But would they be safe inside the bunkhouse or even the ranch house itself? He pictured Mr. Floyd propped up on his pillows on the couch downstairs, with Anabelle sitting faithfully at his side, no doubt praying for God's protection.

Somethin' I should be doin' too. If only I had my mama and daddy's faith.

The answer was immediate and grabbed his attention. *You don't need their faith. Your need your own, and I will gladly give it to you if you will just ask.*

His heart skipped a beat at the strength he heard in those silent words. Was God truly speaking to him? If so, what should he do?

Just ask ...

He responded without further thought. "Give me the faith You know I need to get through this," he whispered. "And show me what You want me to do."

The wind was stronger now, nearly knocking Jake off his horse as he reined in as close as he could get to the house. He didn't even try to give directions to his men because he realized they couldn't hear him over the roar of the tornado that was now almost directly above them. Pushing against the wind's formidable strength, he managed to get within a few feet of the porch when the tornado got there ahead of him and sucked the porch right up, rocking chairs and all, knocking him to the ground.

The house is next, he realized, nearly blind now and clawing his way forward on hands and knees. Were his men safe? *Please let them be all right,* he prayed silently, knowing he could do nothing to help them at that point. If only he'd paid more attention to his initial misgivings about the storm and headed in sooner. He recalled having recently made a similar decision about a dust storm and regretting that decision later, even though everyone had survived.

But what then? What if I had paid attention and headed for the ranch sooner? Would we all be inside the house now, waiting to be sucked up into the storm and thrown out at its whim?

Taking advantage of a slight lull in the wind force, he nearly launched himself into whatever might be left of the house, calling out in vain for his employer and Anabelle. Where were they? Even now that he was inside the house where they, too, no doubt awaited their fates, what could he possibly do to help them?

"Anabelle! Where are you?" He could scarcely hear his own words, and no one else could hear them either. Frantic, he refused to give up and inched his way closer to what he hoped was the living room where he would find Jasper and Anabelle. "God, if You're there," he spoke into the storm, "help me. Show me where to go. Help me find Anabelle and her father."

A loud crash interrupted his progress and his prayers, and an unimaginable weight crushed in on him. Then everything faded into oblivion.

———

"Daddy? Daddy, where are you?" Anabelle had called to her father for what seemed forever, but with no answer. When she tried to crawl toward where she had last seen him, a sharp pain shot up her leg. She tried to ignore the pain and press forward, but she quickly realized she was pinned down and couldn't move.

"Help us, Lord," she whispered. "Help us all, and please help Daddy. He needs You, Father. We all do."

Peace like warm honey flowed down upon her, and she sighed, sensing God's presence and love in the midst of the storm that still raged around her, though not as strongly as it had moments before. "You're here, Father. I know it. Thank You, Lord. And please help someone find Daddy. You know where he is, Father, and You know I can't move to find him myself. Please send someone else. Please, Lord!"

"Anabelle?"

The sound of her name being called was so faint she thought perhaps it was God Himself speaking to her. But then she heard it again, slightly closer this time, and the voice sounded familiar. "Jake? Jake, is that you?"

The voice carried a hopeful note when she heard it yet again. "Anabelle? Yes, it's me, Jake. Where are you?"

"I think I'm in the parlor," she called, relief washing over. "At least, that's where I was when everything collapsed. But I can't move, and I can't find Daddy!"

"It's going to be all right, Anabelle. I'm coming. Keep talking, and I'll move toward your voice."

"Yes, yes, I will," Anabelle promised. "I'll keep talkin'. Please keep comin'! You know, just before I heard your voice, I was prayin' and askin' God to send someone to find Daddy because I couldn't move. And there you were, callin' my name! It's a miracle, you know."

She paused, waiting for an answer. When it didn't come, she was about to resume talking so he could find her, but she stopped when once again she heard his voice.

"Well, I don't know if it's a miracle or not," Jake said, "but I will admit that somethin' brought me around after I got hit on the head. The next thing I knew, I was prayin', too, askin' God to help me find you. Anabelle, can you still hear me?"

Anabelle's heart swelled with gratitude. "Thank You, Lord," she said, "and thank you, Jake. Yes, I can still hear you. I think you're gettin' closer."

They continued to call back and forth until, moments later, even as the storm waned, Jake broke through the rubble, and Anabelle cried out with joy. "Thank You, Father," she said. "Thank You, thank You, thank You!"

14

J ake hoisted the beam that had fallen on Anabelle's leg, and though she said her shin bone was sore, nothing appeared to be broken. She was soon on her feet and helping Jake look for her father, but it was slow going as they inched their way through the rubble in the direction of the sofa where Anabelle had last seen him.

"Daddy! Daddy, where are you? Please answer me," Anabelle cried, over and over again.

"Mr. Floyd," Jake called out. "Where are you?"

They had moved only a couple of feet when they heard a faint moan just ahead of them. Jacob heard Anabelle gasp. Encouraged to know Mr. Floyd was still alive and it appeared they were headed in the right direction, he doubled his efforts, pulling away anything in front of them so they could get to the sound.

Anabelle dug right alongside him, continually calling out, "Daddy! Daddy, it's me, Anabelle! We're coming, Daddy. Hold on!"

Another moan, this time a bit louder. Then a weak, muffled

voice. "I'm right ... here," he said. "On the floor next to the couch. I don't ... I don't think I can get up."

"Don't even try," Jake said. "Just be still. We're almost there."

In moments, Jake broke through a pile of splintered wood —furniture moments earlier. Mr. Floyd's still form lay on the floor beside the couch, exactly as he'd said.

"Anabelle," Jake called, "here he is! Right here."

In less than a moment, Anabelle was sitting beside her father, cradling his head in her lap and assuring him he was going to be all right.

"What ... what about you?" Jasper asked, straining to catch his breath as he spoke.

"I'm fine, Daddy. Don't worry about me. We'll have you out of here and to the doc's place in no time."

Jake doubted getting Mr. Floyd to Doc Mayfield's would happen as quickly as Anabelle thought, but there was no need to tell her that now. And of course, when they did get there, the doc would undoubtedly have other patients to attend to as well. They'd cross that bridge when they got there.

"Can you move your arms and legs?" he asked. "Try slowly, just an inch or two. There you go. That's it. Any pain?"

Mr. Floyd shook his head. "No. No pain. Just a little in my chest."

Jake and Anabelle exchanged glances, and Jake found himself praying they could get his employer to the doctor in time. As the realization he was praying again hit him, he filed the thought away for future reference.

———

By the end of the day, Jake felt a lot better about the situation. He and Anabelle had succeeded in getting Mr.

Floyd in to see Doc Mayfield, who had given him a clean bill of health—at least so far as the tornado's effects were concerned.

"I still want you restin' up for several more days," the doctor told his patient and longtime friend. "I know you're itchin' to dig in and help clean up the place, but you have plenty of help at the ranch to take care of that."

Anabelle nodded. "That's true, Daddy. We'll all pitch in. You don't have to worry about a thing."

Mr. Floyd smiled. "I know that, honey, and I appreciate it. But it's tough for an old cowpoke like me to sit by while everybody else does all the work."

Jake laid a hand on his boss's shoulder. "That's what we're here for, sir. Like your daughter said, you don't have to worry about a thing except gettin' better."

With the doctor's blessing, they brought Mr. Floyd home and settled him into bed. "What a miracle our entire house wasn't destroyed in that tornado," he said.

Anabelle nodded. "It sure is. The porch and parlor are gone, but everything else is nearly untouched. What a blessing!"

"Except for the bunkhouse." Jake's boss looked from him to Anabelle and back again. "I saw it when we came back from Doc's place. It looks nearly flat." Jake, the rim of his white hat clutched in his hands, watched him swallow and take a breath before asking, "Was anyone ... hurt?"

Before Jake could figure out how best to answer that question, Anabelle spoke up. "Don't worry about that, Daddy." She patted his shoulder and leaned down to kiss him on the forehead. "Get some sleep, and we'll talk about this in the morning."

Jasper frowned. "I may have had an attack of angina, sweetheart, but my brain is workin' just fine. Your answer to my question is no answer at all. Unless you want me to lie awake all night, wonderin' what's really goin' on, you'd best tell me the truth—all of it—right now."

Anabelle sighed, then turned to look at Jake. He could see the hesitancy in her green eyes, and he nodded to let her know he would handle the situation, though the lump in his throat wouldn't make it easy.

"Actually, sir, according to the doc, we did have a few injuries out in the bunkhouse. Most are minor, but ..." He cleared his throat, but the lump persisted. "Only one serious injury. Seems a beam fell right on Cranky. Doc says he probably has several broken bones and possibly some internal bleedin'. He's keepin' Cranky in town to watch him for a few days."

Mr. Floyd raised his eyebrows. "You mean ... it's possible he ...?" He swallowed and took a deep breath. "Does Doc think Cranky might ... might die?"

Jake ran his fingers around his hat's brim as he turned it slowly in his hands. He had to tell his boss the truth, but he wished there were another way. "I'm ... afraid so, Mr. Floyd. There's still a chance he might pull through, of course, but the doc is worried about the bleedin'. He said we just have to wait ... and pray."

Tears glistened in the older man's eyes, but he nodded. "Yes, we will definitely pray. Cranky might be ... well, cranky ... and cantankerous and even ornery at times, but he's been with us so long he's like family." He shifted his eyes from Jake to Anabelle. "Please tell Doc to do whatever he needs to for Cranky. Money is no object."

Anabelle took her father's hand. "I will, Daddy. Now you rest, and we'll talk more tomorrow."

Mr. Floyd's smile was weak. "Thank you, sweetheart. I will ... so long as I know both of y'all are prayin' for Cranky—and anyone else who might have been hurt by that tornado."

Jake held his tongue. He wanted to explain to his employer

that he really wasn't a praying man. But lately, he was sure headed in that direction.

————

Anabelle was about ready to turn in after the long, exhausting day, when she realized she had no idea how Clint had fared during the tornado. She assumed he wasn't injured seriously because Jake had said only Cranky had been hurt badly. Still, she felt guilty at not having at least checked on him. Jake had told her the ranch hands had fixed up part of the barn to use until the bunkhouse was rebuilt, so she assumed that's where she would find Clint.

She peeked in on her father, who was sleeping soundly, then threw on a shawl before heading down to the barn. *Should've brought a lantern*, she thought as she carefully picked her way, one wary footstep at a time, through the rubble and debris that littered the ranch. *The ground is a mud pit right now, and it surely would be nice to be able to see where I'm walkin'.* When she finally reached her destination, she knocked before walking in. Who knew what state of undress the men might be in as they prepared for bed?

After a brief pause, someone shouted out, "Who's there?"

"It's Anabelle Floyd. I wanted to see how y'all are doin'."

Another pause. She wondered if some of them might be making themselves presentable. At last the door swung open, and she was invited inside by none other than Jake. Why did she feel surprised to see him there? After all, he might be the foreman, but he couldn't very well sleep at the main house where she was. With the bunkhouse gone, where else would he go but to the barn with his men?

Jake escorted her to the back of the barn where makeshift

beds had been laid out for the hands. "Got one up in the loft too," Jake explained.

Anabelle nodded. "Forgive me, gentlemen," she said, her eyes scanning the dozen or so men that now occupied the animals' haven. "I didn't mean to intrude, but I wanted to check and make sure everyone is all right." The fact she hadn't yet seen Clint disturbed her.

"We're all fine," Jake said. "A few bumps and bruises, but overall, nothin' serious." He grinned. "Like your dad said, no doubt a miracle."

She let her shoulders relax, though she still wondered where Clint might be. She had initially felt badly about turning down Clint's proposal, but somehow those feelings had gotten lost in the chaos of today's events. Still, he was a family friend and she needed to know he was all right.

"And ... Clint?" she asked, directing the question to anyone in the room but not surprised that Jake was the one to answer.

"Clint's fine," he said, and Anabelle noticed his jaw muscles twitch. Had she hit a nerve? "Like the rest of us, a little beat up but nothing we can't deal with and get on with our work."

"I'm glad to hear it," she said, though she had yet to lay eyes on him since their uncomfortable discussion on the front porch. *The front porch that no longer exists,* she reminded herself.

Once again, a familiar voice interrupted her thoughts. "Anabelle?"

She turned to find Clint Jordan standing behind her. She let out a breath she didn't realize she'd been holding. "I'm so glad to see you weren't hurt."

"Kind of you to check on me." He offered a wan smile but didn't move.

"I ... guess I missed you on the way in."

Clint shook his head. "No, I was up in the loft." He glanced at the men behind Anabelle. "I figured it was either sleep down here with all these guys and listen to 'em snore all night, or climb the ladder and sleep in the loft alone."

Anabelle smiled at his attempt at humor. Clint could be a bit arrogant at times. Perhaps he thought himself above the other ranch hands and wanted to make a symbolic gesture to that effect.

"Well, I'm glad you're well," she said. "I'll let Daddy know in the mornin'. He asked about you, and I told him I'd check."

Clint nodded. "Thank you. And how's he doin'? Home safe and sound, I see."

"Yes. Thank the good Lord, Doc Mayfield says he should be fine. Just needs to continue restin' for a while."

"Good. Please let him know I'll come see him when he's ready for company."

Anabelle assured Clint she would do so, then excused herself from the group. "I need to get back and check on Daddy, as I'm sure y'all understand."

She turned to head back to the still open barn door, pleasantly surprised when Jake escorted her outside. She was even more pleased when she realized he had brought a lantern and offered to walk her back to the house.

"I'd like that," she said, her heart racing at the possibilities. Would she and Jake finally have a breakthrough in their relationship? She certainly hoped so, but she still had her doubts.

15

J ake almost felt guilty over the pleasure he experienced walking Anabelle back to the house. It didn't help assuage his guilt to know Cranky could be hanging between life and death, even while Jake could do nothing but think of the old man's recent words about taking a chance with Anabelle before it was too late.

Before it's too late. Was it already too late? Did he even have a chance? Or had she accepted Clint Jordan's proposal and agreed to become his wife? He thought then about how stand-offish Anabelle and Clint had been toward one another back at the barn a few moments earlier, and he decided to take that chance.

He cleared his throat. "I, um ..." Why did his mind go blank when he needed it most? The last thing he wanted to do in front of Anabelle was to appear not only naïve but stupid as well. But Cranky's words still echoed in his brain.

I'd sooner take on a wild grizzly than have this conversation, he told himself, then took a deep breath. *It's now or never* ....

"Miss Anabelle, I ..." Another deep breath. *Here I go!* "I don't know how serious your relationship is with Clint Jordan, so maybe I have no business even bringing this up, but ..."

Anabelle stopped, turned to Jake, and peered up into his face, her green eyes shining in the light of Jake's lantern. It was obvious she was waiting for him to complete his thought. There was no backing out now.

"I ... I guess what I'm tryin' to say—and not doin' a very good job—is I think you're the most beautiful woman I've ever laid eyes on—inside and out—and I surely would like a chance to court you if you and your daddy are willin.' Course, I'll ask his permission first, but I need to know if it's all right with you. If not, I'll understand, and I'll never bring it up again. I ..."

Before he could continue, Anabelle reached up and laid a finger on his lips. "Enough," she said. "You don't need to say another word, not to me anyway. But yes, go talk to Daddy right away. I'm sure he'll agree."

Jake felt his eyes go wide. Had he heard her right? Did she just accept his offer to court her? His heart raced at the implications. "Are you sure ...?"

She increased the pressure on his lips. "More sure than you can imagine. In fact, if you hadn't said somethin' right now, I was fixin' to bring it up myself. Now stop wastin' time, Cowboy."

———

Anabelle spent another sleepless night tossing and turning, but this time it was joy and excitement that kept her awake. At last, Jake had taken the step she feared he'd never take. Although she imagined her father would be a bit surprised that it was Jake who would be courting her and not Clint, she knew he'd be pleased. He'd often said what a good man

Jake was and what a fine husband he'd be for some special lady.

I guess that special lady will be me. She smiled into the darkness. *I can't wait to start spendin' time with him and gettin' to know more about him and his family back in Juniper. I hope I get to meet them soon. Not only his parents, but those two cousins of his. It sounds like they were a trio to be reckoned with when they were kids.*

Kids. The thought ricocheted in her mind. Could she finally start planning to be a mother someday? It was something she'd always wanted but never met the right man to bring that about—until now.

But did she have the right? The Bible was clear about a believer not marrying an unbeliever. And though Jake had said enough to assure her he was raised in a Christian home and had godly parents, he hadn't said anything to make her believe he had received Jesus as his Savior.

Oh, Father, I should have acknowledged this problem and talked with You about it before this. Should I bring it up now, try to lead him to You? I can't marry him if he doesn't have a relationship with You.

The answer was clear and comforting. *Trust Me. I have this under control, and I will work it all out as it should be.*

Anabelle relaxed, comforted by her heavenly Father's words. And yet she found herself wishing her mother were with her so they could walk through this time together, sharing it all along the way.

————

A few days later, Jake found himself wanting to turn in early and catch some much-needed shuteye, but when he heard the first notes of a familiar hymn drifting into the barn, he was drawn to join Jasper Floyd's campfire worship.

Maybe I should, he thought. *After all, Mr. Floyd gave me permission to start courtin' his daughter, but he reserved permission for anything further until—as he put it—he learned more about my relationship with the Lord.*

Jake frowned. *Not sure I know exactly what he meant by that. Do I have a relationship with the Lord? I think my mama and daddy do, and Mr. Floyd and Anabelle, and others I've met through the years—including my two aunts back home. But somehow I don't think I do.*

He shrugged and grabbed his hat from the peg and plunked it on his head. *I'm sure not gonna learn much about a relationship with God if I hang back here alone. Might as well go join the group. After all, it's Mr. Floyd's first time gettin' one of these campfire meetin's started since his angina attack. I should be there to give my support.*

Jake grinned as he stepped outside into the evening air. *Besides, Anabelle will be disappointed if I don't come.*

He hadn't gone far when he spotted her, standing slightly off to the side, the campfire illuminating her enough that he could see she was peering into the darkness. Was she looking for him? He hoped so.

And then he was there, standing almost directly in front of her, as a welcoming smile broke out on her face. He wanted to take her hand and hold it throughout the meeting, but he didn't. *Might seem forward so early in our relationship. After all, I just got permission to court Anabelle a few days ago.*

Instead he stood beside her, enjoying her presence and marveling at how well Jasper Floyd was doing. Though the older man was seated on a chair on the podium rather than standing as he usually did, he was obviously improving and regaining more strength every day.

A slight movement caught his eye off to the right, nearer the fire. He turned his head to find Clint Jordan eyeing him.

Jake hoped they weren't headed for a confrontation, but Clint's expression wasn't one of anger or jealousy. Instead, Jake detected a hint of sadness on his face. Then Clint offered him a weak smile and nodded his head, a sign the man was letting him know he understood and had accepted the way things were with Anabelle.

His attention turned then to Mr. Floyd who asked for ongoing prayer for Cranky. "He's doin' better," he announced, "but we need to keep prayin' he continues to improve. Doc says he can come home soon, but he's got some healin' to do. Since the bunkhouse is gone and I don't think he's up to sleepin' in the barn, my daughter and I have decided to offer him a room at the house—at least until he's fully recovered and the bunkhouse is rebuilt."

Jake smiled down at Anabelle, who readily returned the gesture before looking back toward her father. Offering Cranky a room in their own home was just like something Jake would imagine Mr. Floyd and Anabelle to do. Did that have anything to do with their "relationship with the Lord" status? *Most likely.*

As his boss led a group prayer for Cranky's continued healing, Jake found himself praying for his father as well. His most recent letter from his mama said his daddy might be getting his sight back. Though the healing wasn't yet complete, the doctor was hopeful.

He pulled himself back to the present. Jasper Floyd was about to read from the Bible, and Jake didn't want to be disrespectful.

"I'll be reading from the fifteenth chapter of Luke," Mr. Floyd said, "verses 11-32, commonly known as the parable of the prodigal son." As Jake listened, he thought God was speaking directly to him.

"And he said, A certain man had two sons: and the younger

of them said to *his* father, Father, give me the portion of goods that falleth *to me*. And he divided unto them his living. And not many days after the younger son gathered all together, and took his journey into a far country, and there wasted his substance with riotous living."

Can't say I've done much riotous living, Lord, Jake prayed silently, *but I've certainly journeyed into a far country, at least so far as leaving my family behind.*

Mr. Floyd continued. "And when he had spent all, there arose a mighty famine in that land; and he began to be in want. And he went and joined himself to a citizen of that country; and he sent him into his fields to feed swine. And he would fain have filled his belly with the husks that the swine did eat: and no man gave unto him. And when he came to himself, he said, How many hired servants of my father's have bread enough and to spare, and I perish with hunger! I will arise and go to my father, and will say unto him, Father, I have sinned against heaven, and before thee, and am no more worthy to be called thy son: make me as one of thy hired servants."

I'm not exactly goin' hungry either, God, but I got the feelin' I should pay attention to this, so I will.

"And he arose, and came to his father. But when he was yet a great way off, his father saw him, and had compassion, and ran, and fell on his neck, and kissed him. And the son said unto him, Father, I have sinned against heaven, and in thy sight, and am no more worthy to be called thy son. But the father said to his servants, Bring forth the best robe, and put *it* on him; and put a ring on his hand, and shoes on *his* feet: and bring hither the fatted calf, and kill *it;* and let us eat, and be merry: for this my son was dead, and is alive again; he was lost, and is found. And they began to be merry."

A sense of longing took root in Jake's heart as he listened. The more Mr. Floyd read, the stronger the longing became.

"Now his elder son was in the field: and as he came and drew nigh to the house, he heard music and dancing. And he called one of the servants, and asked what these things meant. And he said unto him, Thy brother is come; and thy father hath killed the fatted calf, because he hath received him safe and sound. And he was angry, and would not go in: therefore came his father out, and intreated him. And he answering said to *his* father, Lo, these many years do I serve thee, neither transgressed I at any time thy commandment: and yet thou never gavest me a kid, that I might make merry with my friends: but as soon as this thy son was come, which hath devoured thy living with harlots, thou hast killed for him the fatted calf. And he said unto him, Son, thou art ever with me, and all that I have is thine. It was meet that we should make merry, and be glad: for this thy brother was dead, and is alive again; and was lost, and is found."

Jake was confused. He didn't have an older brother, and he hadn't spent his money on harlots. And yet he knew God was speaking to him. *Is it me, Lord?* Jake prayed silently. *Am I the prodigal son?*

God's answer was clear. *You are one of My many prodigal sons and daughters, but right now it's you I'm calling. Come home, Jacob. Let Me forgive your sins. Do you want to be My beloved child and live with Me forever?*

Tears stung Jake's eyes as he whispered, "Yes, Lord. Yes, that's what I want."

Walk forward toward Mr. Floyd. He'll understand.

Jake scarcely remembered taking those few steps or falling to his knees in front of his employer's chair. The next thing he knew, Mr. Floyd had reached out his hands and laid them on Jake's shoulders as he prayed for him.

Joy like he'd never experienced washed over and through him, and he was confident God had heard his prayer. He realized at that moment that yes, he did indeed have a relationship with Jesus.

A gentle hand rested on his arm. It was Anabelle, rejoicing with him. Jake knew his parents and cousins would rejoice with him as well, and he couldn't wait to write to them before the night was over.

EPILOGUE

Jake and Anabelle stood together that next morning, leaning on the top rail of the corral and watching the sun come up. Rays, soft at first but gaining in brilliance, spread across the prairie, pouring out warmth as a gentle blessing.

"I never realized sunrises were so beautiful, especially here in the Panhandle where we can see forever," Jake said without turning his head. "Each one is a gift from God, a promise of a new day to spend with Him."

Anabelle took his hand, though she too kept her eyes on the horizon. "Yes, it is. And I'm so very glad to share this one with you."

Jake squeezed her hand. "May we spend all our sunrises together—you, me, and the Lord."

He paused, then said, "And by the way, feel free to call me Jacob. It's what our Father calls me."

The End

ABOUT THE AUTHOR

Kathi Macias is a bestselling author of more than fifty books, including *Red Ink*, winner of the 2011 Golden Scroll Novel of the Year. She served for a time as acquisitions editor for Elk Lake Publishing and wrote/edited for several other publishers over the years, including New Hope Publishers, Regal Books/Gospel Light, Thomas Nelson, Harvest House, Broadman & Holman, and Abingdon Press. She also edited Molly Noble Bull's award-winning novel *When the Cowboy Rides Away*. A wife, mother, grandmother, and great-grandmother, Kathi is a popular speaker at writers' conferences and women's events, as well as a freelance editor and collaborative writer. She lives in Southern California with her husband, Al.

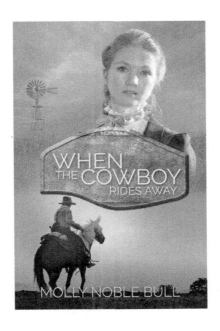

land. Kind-hearted and a Christian, Maggie nurses him back to health despite all her other chores.

How could she know that Alex has a secret that could break her heart?

———

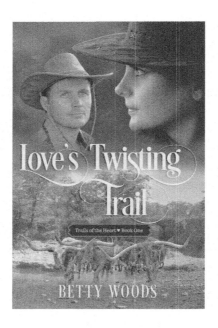

Love's Twisting Trail

by Betty Woods

Stampedes, wild animals, and renegade Comanches make a cattle drive dangerous for any man. The risks multiply when Charlotte Grimes goes up the trail disguised as Charlie, a fourteen year-old boy. She promised her dying father she'd save their ranch after her brother, Tobias, mismanages their money. To keep her vow, she rides the trail with the brother she can't trust.

David Shepherd needs one more successful drive to finish buying the ranch he's prayed for. He partners with Tobias to travel safely through Indian Territory. David detests the hateful way Tobias treats his younger brother, Charlie. He could easily love the boy like the brother he's always wanted. But what does he do when he discovers Charlie's secret? What kind of woman would do what she's done?

The trail takes an unexpected twist when Charlotte falls in love with David. She's afraid to tell him of her deception. Such a God-fearing, honest gentleman is bound to despise the kind of woman who dares to wear a man's trousers and venture on a cattle drive. Since her father left her half the ranch, she intends to continue working the land like any other man after she returns to Texas. David would never accept her as she is.

Choosing between keeping her promise to her father or being with the man she loves may put Charlotte's heart in more danger than any of the hazards on the trail can.

———

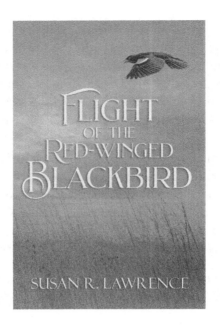

Flight of the Red-winged Blackbird

by Susan Lawrence

In 1932, Ruth Russo flees the farm where she arrived as an orphaned teenager and seeks refuge at Sisters of Mercy Home for unwed mothers. When the haven she hopes for becomes a place of tragedy, she flees again, and attempts to support herself in a culture of discrimination and a country burdened by the Great Depression.

Her days brighten when she reconnects with Jack, a friend from high school. But Jack is a budding lawyer, and she is a maid in his cousin's house. Will Ruth be able to lay down her burden of shame and accept love, not only from Jack, but also from God?

————

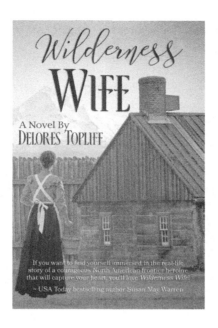

Wilderness Wife

by Delores Topliff

Marguerite Wadin MacKay believes her 17-year marriage to explorer Alex MacKay is strong-until his sudden fame destroys it. When he returns from a cross-Canada expedition, he announces their frontier marriage is void in Montréal where he plans to find a society wife-not one with native blood. Taking their son, MacKay sends Marguerite and their three daughters to a trading post where she lived as a child. Deeply shamed, she arrives in time to assist young Doctor John McLoughlin with a medical emergency.

Marguerite now lives only for her girls. When Fort William on Lake Superior opens a school, Marguerite moves there for her daughters' sake and rekindles her friendship with Doctor McLoughlin. When he declares his love, she dissuades him from a match harmful to his career. She's mixed blood and nine years older. But he will have no one else.

After abandonment, can a woman love again and fulfill a key role in North American History?

———

Stay up-to-date on your favorite books and authors with our free e-newsletters.

ScriveningsPress.com

Made in the USA
Coppell, TX
27 March 2022

75622039R00208